HOUSE (

Broadway: bright lights, big stars, sheer evil . . .

The highly anticipated premier of *Coward's Fare* is derailed in the third act when the play's star, Bertrand Woodford, is struck dead on stage . . . *Murdered!* Before the police can effectively investigate the crime, the actor's body disappears into thin air. The murder goes unsolved but one thing is certain: it is the death knell for the play and theatre. Woodford's Theatre is darkened, shuttered and chained. *Coward's Fare* is tossed in the dustbin and is only faintly remembered as that "cursed play."

Years later, the original cast return to Woodford's Theater to launch a revival of the cursed play. But Woodford's ghost now haunts the stage and murder is in the wings. First rehearsals reawaken the primal horror that stalks the players once more: the play must not be shown! Get out! . . . This time, though, the cast and stagehands band together for the fight of their lives.

Wadsworth Camp's *House of Fear* (1916) predates the dawn of the Golden Age of Mystery by a mere four years, but it contains many of the elements that would become the staple of the golden era. Camp's writing is fresh and invigorating, his story compelling. As with much of his fiction (a half dozen novels and numerous stories) Camp weaves the plot with elements of the Supernatural. Bruin Crimeworks is proud to make this extremely rare novel of mystery and suspense available again.

Wadsworth Camp, a highly successful writer in his day, was also the father of Madeleine L'Engle, author of *A Wrinkle in Time*. *House of Fear* was filmed in 1929 as *The Last Warning* by the great Paul Leni. It was to be his final film and is now available for the first time in a 4K restoration.

HOUSE of FEAR

WADSWORTH CAMP

Illustrated by ARTHUR I. KELLER
Introduced by BILL ECTRIC

BRUIN BOOKS

HOUSE OF FEAR by Wadsworth Camp
First published in 1916 by Doubleday, Page & Company, Country Life Press

Edited by Jonathan Eeds

Cover design by Michelle Policicchio

Original cover art provided by the Viet Hung Gallery,
Ho Chi Minh City, Vietnam

The Mystery Of Wadsworth Camp © Bill Ectric

Back cover art originally appeared on the cover of the Collier's March 4, 1916 issue, depicting the Wadsworth Camp short story *The House With The Hidden Door*

Special thanks to Bill Ectric, who provides the introduction to this book. Introduction © Bill Ectric. Bill's website can be found at www.billectric.com, along with his blog, reviews and interviews

The photograph of Wadsworth Camp that appears with the introduction is derived from his passport photo, date unknown

This book was crafted in the USA but is printed globally

Printed in the USA
ISBN 978-0-9987065-7-3
Published August, 2019
Bruin Books, LLC
Eugene, Oregon, USA

For inquiries: bruinbooks@comcast.net

Introduction
The Wadsworth Camp Mystery

CHARLES WADSWORTH CAMP wrote at least six mystery novels, but the man is himself something of a mystery. Camp was born on Oct. 18, 1879 in Philadelphia, and died on Oct. 30, 1936 in Jacksonville. In the last years of his life, Camp lived in a cottage on First Street in Jacksonville Beach.

There are almost no photos of him on the Internet, save a recently discovered passport photo and some old home movies of Camp and his family, which have surfaced on YouTube. Biographical information about him is scarce. The "mystery" is this: Is Charles Wadsworth Camp's minimal Internet presence due to lack of interest in his work, or is a lack of interest due to his minimal Internet presence?

Almost all references to Camp appear in the numerous biographies of his famous daughter, Madeleine L'Engle Camp, who won a Newbery Medal award for her classic children's book, *A Wrinkle in Time* (1963). L'Engle, who, like her father, dropped one of her names from her byline, simply going by Madeleine L'Engle, probably learned to love the written word from her father, a well-known author in his own right who usually wrote under the shortened named Wadsworth Camp. There are movies based on his work and his books.

Camp's *The Abandoned Room* (1917) is a little gem of a murder mystery with supernatural overtones. The story moves briskly and the denouement is no less satisfying than many of the Sherlock Holmes adventures. *The Gray Mask* (1920) is a fun crime serial, part Dick Tracy and part Green Hornet. Camp was also a drama critic, a war correspondent, and the author of a non-fiction book about his time in 305th field artillery during World War I, when his lungs were damaged by mustard gas on the battlefield. Some of Camp's novels were serialized in magazines like *Colliers* and *Metropolitan* before being published in book form. This was true for many famous writers in Camp's day, including F. Scott Fitzgerald, Edna Ferber, Jack London, and even Theodore Roosevelt.

The Gray Mask* first appeared in Collier's Magazine in 1915. The film version came out the same year. The book version of *Gray Mask* was published in 1920.

The movie *Love Without Question* (1920) was based on Camp's mystery novel *The Abandoned Room* (1917).

In 1922, actor/playwright Thomas F. Fallon wrote a play called *The Last Warning*, a murder mystery based on Wadsworth Camp's novel, *The House of Fear*. A silent film version by Universal Pictures, also called *The Last Warning*, followed in 1929. *The Last Warning* was the last picture directed by the gifted German filmmaker Paul Leni, known by film buffs for directing the classic old-dark-house movie, *The Cat and the Canary* (1927, Universal). A remake of the movie, titled *The House of Fear* (not to be confused with the 1945 movie, *Sherlock Holmes and the House of Fear*, came out in 1939. To make matters even more convoluted, some sources call the original story *Backstage Phantom*, but all currently available versions of the book are called *The House of Fear*. It is, of course, possible that the story was reprinted at some point under the name *Backstage Phantom*.

The UCLA Film & Television Archives has a print of *The Signal Tower*, based on Camp's story of the same name, which first appeared in the May 1920 issue of *Metropolitan*

Magazine. That particular issue is notable for also including an article called "Spiritualism – Truth or Imposture?" in which George Bernard Shaw, H. G. Wells, Arthur Conan Doyle, Sir Oliver Lodge, G.K. Chesterton and Sir William Barrett debate the reality of the spirit world. It calls up a line from Camp's mystery novel *The Abandoned Room*, where he wrote, "'No one,' the doctor answered, 'can say what psychic force is capable of doing. Some scientists have started to explore, but it is still uncharted country.'" *The Signal Tower* featured acclaimed actor Wallace Beery, who later won an Academy Award for his role as a boxer in *The Champ* and portrayed Professor Challenger in the 1925 film version of Arthur Conan Doyle's dinosaur adventure, *The Lost World.*

L'Engle's obituary in The New York Times states that her mother "came from Jacksonville, Florida and was a fine pianist; her father was a World War I veteran who worked as a foreign correspondent and later as a drama and music critic for *The New York Sun.* He also knocked out potboiler novels."

Though L'Engle passed away in 2007, it seemed plausible that her website's managers could point us in the direction of more information about Camp. Sadly, an email to the Madeleine L'Engle official website was also a disappointingly fruitless quest to find out more about her mysterious mystery novelist father.

The reply from L'Engle's website came back the next day: "We are not aware of any resources online about Mr. Camp. Sorry. Thanks for your interest."

L'Engle's granddaughter, Léna Roy, who is also a writer, was also unable to provide any additional details.

There is some Jacksonville-related information in a 2004 *New Yorker* profile of L'Engle by Cynthia Zarin, which details the spectacle of an alligator climbing up the steps of L'Engle's Florida home (she later moved back to

New York). Zarin wrote, "Madeleine L'Engle Camp was born in 1918 in New York City, the only child of Madeleine Hall Barnett, of Jacksonville, Florida, and Charles Wadsworth Camp, a Princeton man and First World War veteran, whose family had a big country place in New Jersey, called Crosswicks. In Jacksonville society, the Barnett family was legendary: Madeleine's grandfather, Bion Barnett, the chairman of the board of Jacksonville's Barnett Bank, had run off with a woman to the South of France, leaving behind a note on the mantel." Zarin continued, "Madeleine found Florida stultifying and surreal. One afternoon, she watched an alligator pick its way up the porch steps."

Another bit of Wadsworth Camp trivia involves singer/musician Rudy Vallee. In a 1932 interview with Sidney Skolsky, Valle said his favorite book was *The Guarded Heights* by Wadsworth Camp. This nugget of information may be related to the cinema. Sidney Skolsky is widely credited as the first person to use the term "Oscar" for the Academy of Motion Picture Arts & Sciences Award.

Other films based on Camp's work are *A Daughter of the Law* (1921) and *Hate* (1922).

The Office of Vital Statistics in the Arlington section of Jacksonville provided Folio Weekly with a copy of the official death certificate of Charles Wadsworth Camp. The trade/profession section contains one word: Writer.

According to this document, a Dr. E.C. Swift attended the ailing author from Oct. 29, 1936 until his death at 1:40 p.m. on Oct. 31. This differs from information available on sites like IMDb, which always lists his last day of life as Oct. 30. It is, of course, possible that someone, likely a member of his family, wanted to avoid any mention of Halloween.

Though the cause of death is blocked out to all but

family members, it's relatively easy to discover that Camp died from pneumonia at age 57. The most common story goes like this: Because Camp's lungs were already weakened by mustard gas he inhaled in WWI, he was especially vulnerable to respiratory disease. But in the previously mentioned New Yorker profile, Zarin quotes a member of Camp's family as saying, "He used to smoke Rameses cigarettes . . . he used to drink a lot. Uncle Charles was not ailing in his life. He was a big, handsome man in a white linen suit, smoking cigarettes on the porch and drinking whiskey. He was a favorite of my mother's, and she was a talker, and she never mentioned anything about him being gassed in the war." So perhaps Camp's medical problems were related to something other than mustard gas. On the other hand, many people choose not to talk much about war experiences, and millions who smoke and drink live to a ripe old age. The truth is left behind in the sands of time.

The death certificate lists Camp's residence as "Red Gables" in Jacksonville Beach, and says he'd lived in this area for three years before his death, which means he probably didn't write any mystery books here. He was also a critic and an editor, however, so it's quite possible he did some work in Jacksonville.

Some biographical material can be found in one of L'Engle's non-fiction books, *The Summer of the Great-Grandmother*. L'Engle tells us that her mother, Madeleine Hall Barnett and her father, Charles Wadsworth Camp, were married in Jacksonville and went to nearby St. Augustine for a brief honeymoon, where they spent at the Ponce de Leon hotel. They then moved to New York, where Camp worked as a newspaper critic, writing reviews of plays, operas and concerts; consequently, many of their friends were musicians. Camp dressed elegantly every evening, whether he was dining at home or taking a horse-drawn trolley to a theater or concert hall.

In the book, L'Engle tells this story:

One hot summer evening, long before I was born, my mother walked through the hall and glanced at the etching of Castle Conway and said, 'Oh, Charles, it's so hot. I wish we could go to Castle Conway,' 'Come on!' he cried, and swept her out of the house without toothbrush or change of clothes, and into a taxi, and by midnight, they were on a ship sailing across the Atlantic. In those days, a trip could be as spontaneous as that. My parents were not poor, but neither were they, by today's standards, affluent. Father was a playwright and journalist, and their pocketbook waned and swelled like the moon; this must have been one of the full-moon cycles.

Though there are occasional glimpses of the man in the pages of history, Charles Wadsworth Camp remains as enigmatic as ever. For now, in honor of Jacksonville Beach, his last home, here is another quotation from his only daughter:

If I frequently use the analogy of the underwater area of our minds, it may be because the ocean is so strong a part of my childhood memories, and of my own personal mythology. If I am away from the ocean for long, I get a visceral longing for it. It was at the ocean that I first went outdoors at night and saw the stars. I must have been very little, but I will never forget being held in someone's arms — Mother's, Father's, Dearma's, someone I loved and trusted enough so that all I remember is being held, and seeing the glory of the night sky over the ocean. – Excerpt from *The Summer of the Great-Grandmother* (1974, Farrar, Straus & Giroux), Chapter 8, by Madeleine L'Engle.

Bill Ectric
August 2019
Jacksonville, Florida

HOUSE OF FEAR

CHAPTER I

UNDER the circumstances McHugh would probably have been wiser never to have attempted such a revival. Had he cared to open his ears he might have heard warnings in plenty, for Woodford's Theatre had become a tradition in the profession, an evil one, a menace, in short, for the superstitious.

It is difficult to trace such beliefs to a reasonable source. Few along Broadway attempted it. The stock company, which five years ago had opened the house for a winter's campaign, offered sufficient testimony. If there was nothing more than rumor behind the theatre's reputation, why, people asked, had that company within a week abandoned its lease and forfeited its guaranty? Why had its leading man on the final night rushed from the stage, his eyes fixed, shaken throughout as if by some experience beyond human comprehension?

Such questions remained unanswered, while other stories persisted, gathering about a black cat which had mysteriously made itself felt and heard, frightening the timid, puzzling the better-controlled, fitting disturbingly into the somber history of the place.

So Broadway accepted as fact Woodford's unhealthy atmosphere, avoiding it discreetly. Arthur McHugh was the logical exception. An aggressive, ambitious Irishman, he had fought his way from the headquarters detective force to a managerial throne from which he wielded a supreme power over many actors and actresses and plays. He went his stubborn and successful way, untrammeled by the gossip of the profession. Therefore, when he conceived the idea of reopening Woodford's with a revival of "Coward's Fare," he remembered only that half a century ago the play had placed the crown of dollars on the theatre and had made its old director, Bertrand Woodford, famous. He did not bother to recall that in the end it had caused Woodford's death, or that, during the forty years since, prosperity had strangely neglected the house.

Richard Quaile, chosen by McHugh to make a modem version of the play, paused opposite the theatre one fall afternoon and appraised it curiously. His script was completed. Nothing remained but the arranging of the lease. He was on his way to McHugh's office now, and that, he understood, was the purpose of his summons.

Quaile was not of a credulous disposition. Successful as a playwright and with a plentiful income, he was too completely interested in the world about him to bother with abstractions. But he had heard the gossip concerning Woodford's, and, as he stared across the street, he wondered at McHugh's courage.

Woodford's blind exterior appeared to repel the thought of intrusion. It had an air of asking to be left alone in its decay. The anxious northward march of theatrical prosperity had long deserted it. On one side it was flanked by a towering loft building. A motion-picture house nestled impudently close on the other. From such surroundings, although it was no more than sixty years old, the structure projected an atmosphere of antiquity as arresting as that which reaches one from a mediaeval castle in some foreign countryside. From the beginning, indeed, it furnished a plausible setting for the tragedy which, during so long within its dingy walls, was to challenge reason with a serene and provocative assurance.

Quaile could not foresee that, but he could and did look back. It was as if the crumbling facade of the theatre had forced the past palpably into his mind. Passersby jostled him, but he continued to gaze thoughtfully across the street, reconstructing the building into the most famous playhouse in America, fancying its tired eyes sparkling with light, seeing its slender columns divide eager crowds of men and women in the dress of another period. Then the end of all that and the commencement of Woodford's evil reputation came back to him—the extraordinary death forty years ago of its director, Bertrand Woodford.

His imagination of an author contrived an active picture. He could see the packed auditorium and the curtain rising on "Coward's Fare," revived to show Woodford in his greatest, his favorite rôle. He saw the actor limp on, ill, but too jealous and vindictive to resign his part to an understudy. He watched the man struggle along with the genius of which his disability could not entirely strip him. But it was on that last destructive moment that Quailed mind lingered uncomfortably. He experienced almost with the tensity of an actual spectator the clamorous excitement which had filled the house when Woodford, at the height of his most impassioned scene, had toppled to the stage, had lain still, had failed for the first time to respond to the emotions of his audience.

Details scarcely heard, dimly remembered from the mass of gossip, obtruded themselves. The black cat, he recalled, Woodford's constant companion off stage, had rushed from the wings and curled itself on the motionless body. It had fought and scratched tigerishly when anxious hands had tried to snatch it off. It had remained close to its master until his burial.

Quaile shook his head, turned, and went on to his appointment. His brief view of Woodford's desolation had reduced his enthusiasm for the plan. The place, even from the outside, was gloomier than he had imagined, probably gloomy enough to account for such stories. But if it had driven into his brain these unpalatable memories, it would almost certainly breed trouble should McHugh select for his cast men or women of a particularly nervous or sensational temperament.

He found the atmosphere of the manager's office restorative.

He stepped from the elevator into a hallway crowded with the prosperous and the unfortunate, many young and a fraction old: leads, ingenues, character people, comedians—all seekers and all forewarned that in this office success would welcome only a few.

He nodded at those he recognized and passed into the reception room, whose broader spaces were similarly taxed. He marveled that McHugh could be the lodestone of this expectant multitude. He knew it was only ten years since the man had left the detective bureau for minute beginnings on the Rialto. That had been through the influence of a manager for whom he had ferreted an important case to a successful and profitable conclusion. Since then, because of a natural, if incoherent, instinct for the dramatic, he had discounted his lack of education and had taken his rank with the handful of large producers. Now he sat, czar-like, in a secluded office, forbidden to the many, a privilege for the elect.

Quaile noticed a man who elbowed his way through the crowd toward the door. He was slender and tall, so that above the bobbing heads Quaile could see his face, striking, nearly handsome, yet a trifle too pallid. Moreover, it recorded at this moment a vague dissatisfaction, an uncertainty of purpose.

Quaile nodded pleasantly in that direction and the man altered his course and approached. Quaile stretched out his hand.

"Hello, Carlton," he said. "You're in a hurry."

"I came up to see McHugh," Carlton answered. "Can't find out whether he's in, and I've another appointment. He's offered me a contract for Woodford's part in this revival of 'Coward's Fare' you're putting on in the old barn."

"You'll do it well," Quaile said. "Looks like a long winter. Sentiment will draw big audiences."

He watched the uncertainty in the other's face increase. Reluctantly he admitted its cause. He guessed that Carlton's mind harbored the unhealthy gossip which centered about the ancient house. He gathered that to an extent it overshadowed his satisfaction at the prospect of a profitable engagement.

"You don't look overjoyed," he added dryly.

"I'm glad of the job," Carlton answered. "I'm no fool, but it's curious, Quaile. I ran into a girl only last night who played with that stock company at Woodford's five or six years ago. Actually, she tried to argue me out of accepting the contract. Talked about Woodford's influence persisting and resenting the presence of the living in his theatre. Uncomfortable feeling about the dressing-rooms and all that. A lot of rot, too, about Woodford's black cat. She said Bertrand Woodford had worked himself to death rather than let any man play his part, and a lot of people felt he never would let any man play it now that he was dead. You know, she seemed to believe the nonsense. Funny how such stories cling. I suppose it's because he made such a bad reputation for jealousy and temper. Give you my word, I thought no manager would take another chance with the place."

Quaile grinned.

"I'd back Arthur McHugh against the meanest dispositioned spook that ever walked."

Carlton's laugh irritated Quaile. It lacked conviction. It was prophetic. It transferred to him some of the other's uncertainty.

"I'm off," the actor said. "I'll see McHugh in the morning. Good luck to the sentimental engagement."

Quaile turned away, facing the reception room again. He glanced about. Then his perfunctory interest swayed toward a girl who sat near the inner door. Her back was turned, so that he could see little more than the glow of light hair beneath a hat of pronounced simplicity here. She appeared unaware of those moving nearby. She was bent forward, as if eager to pass the door, which remained closed, a stubborn and provoking barrier.

Quaile watched her for some time while his memory stirred. Her withdrawal sharpened his interest. Surely he had seen the graceful figure before. He must pass that door. If he turned there her face would no longer be hidden.

He stepped forward. He placed his hand on the knob. He opened the door a little and turned. And now he knew that he had seen her, more than once on the stage, and from time to time casually at dinners or in offices like this.

He held out his hand. Recognition drove the lassitude from her eyes.

"You've not forgotten me, Miss Morgan?"

Her smile was charming.

"I never forget a friend at court. Mr. McHugh sent for me. He said it had something to do with you."

The announcement reached Quaile pleasantly. He had congenial recollections of her ability. Moreover, her quiet gray eyes indicated a serviceable lack of temperament.

"It's the lead, then, in rather a unique revival. I'm glad you'll be with us. How long have you waited?"

"Since four o'clock. It's inexcusable. Do you think he's ever coming?"

"Probably here now," Quaile laughed. "He has as many entrances and exits as a criminal. If he's inside I'll tell him how you've suffered."

With his hand on the knob he turned back. He glanced at her quizzically.

"By the way, you're not afraid of ghosts?"

"It isn't 'Hamlet!'" she cried gayly.

Still smiling, he shook his head and went through into the presence of a small, neat young woman who attended to McHugh's correspondence, and, simultaneously, did her best for the chewing-gum manufacturers.

"Hello, Ethel. Boss here yet? He sent for me."

Her jaw rested momentarily, permitting her mouth to expand in a grin of fellowship, of perfect understanding. She nodded at the door through which Quaile had just entered.

"That's what they all say, the poor nuts. And I have to fib until I'm ashamed to go to church on Sundays. Yep. Came in ten minutes ago."

"Busy?"

"Yep. Just took him the evening paper."

"Did you tell him how many were waiting?"

"Yep. Said let 'em wait and turn 'em over to Morley when he comes in."

"Does he know Miss Morgan's outside?"

"Nope. Didn't know myself. Say, he's expecting her."

"Bring her in here," Quaile said, "and I'll tell him. You feel I dare beard the lion?"

"Oh, you go on, Mr. Quaile. He thinks you're great."

Quaile crossed the room and knocked at a mahogany door. Always on approaching this presence he experienced an amused humility. The voice that reached him through the heavy panels was querulous, expressive of an outraged solitude.

"What the devil you want, Ethel?"

"Not Ethel," Quaile answered mildly.

The door was flung open. McHugh stood on the threshold. An unlighted and bitterly used cigar depended from his thin lips. As he motioned him in, his shrewd, narrow eyes fixed Quaile with resentment.

"See here, Quaile. You're five minutes late."

"Indulgence," Quaile begged. "By the way, I've just seen Miss Morgan. She tells me you're an hour late. According to her, you're not here at all yet."

"Too bad. Would rather not see her till tomorrow anyway."

McHugh raised his voice.

"Ethel! Step out and tell Miss Morgan to come back tomorrow."

Barbara Morgan appeared in the doorway. Her manner was unruffled. Her eyes showed no unusual light. There was a firmness about her manner which pleased Quaile.

"I am not coming back tomorrow," she said. "An hour already out there! You might at least give us things to read. Even doctors do that."

"Doctors get your money, young woman, while I give you the money to pay 'em. Never mind, now you're here. Script will be read day after tomorrow, provided we arrange a lease. Quaile and I are going to see about that now. If we don't, nothing doing. Met Mr. Quaile, Miss Morgan? He fixed the play up. Thought after you looked her over, Quaile, you'd agree she'll do."

"I've met Miss Morgan," Quaile said.

He smiled at her.

"And I agree she'll do."

McHugh waved the girl away.

"Rushed now. I know your terms. Contract will be ready if the lease goes through. Looks like all winter unless this pen-pusher's hypnotized me into throwing my money down a well. So long, Miss Morgan. Go out this way if you like."

She crossed the room, laughing.

"And I've waited an hour for this minute!"

"Say, young lady, you're engaged. What more do you want?"

"Clothes in the contract," she said seriously, and went out.

McHugh glanced at his haggard cigar.

"Clever girl, that!"

He thrust the cigar again between his teeth.

"I've seen the agents."

"There's no hitch?" Quaile asked anxiously.

"We're up against a queer proposition," McHugh answered. "We've got to deal with that old scoundrel, Josiah Bunce."

From his contempt and misgiving he might have been speaking of Nero on one of his less restrained days, but Quaile caught a different menace. The name was eloquent. Bunce's eccentricities were notorious. He was rich in real estate to which he clung tenaciously. Report credited him with the disposition of a miser, yet he lived in an old house just off Fifth Avenue, and kept next door an empty lot, probably worth half a million, in order, his neighbors said, that he might take convenient strolls, undisturbed by traffic and the populace.

"Owns Woodford's," McHugh explained, "jointly with his brother, Robert. You can't tell what quirks an old fossil like him will have. They say he hasn't been off his place for fifteen years. Wish we had Robert to dicker with."

Quaile nodded. The slightly younger brother, who shared the house with Bunce, was less terrifying to his memory. He offered, in fact, a pleasant contrast. He was a successful broker who had added radically to his share of the estate. Moreover, he had never displayed Josiah's reluctance to amiable spending. For many years he had been a familiar figure in the world and a scourge to ambitious mothers. Like Josiah, he had persisted in the grave indiscretion of celibacy.

"I've made an appointment," McHugh said with disapproval. "We're to go over there right away."

"Not often you're a seeker," Quaile ventured.

McHugh grunted.

"Never do as well with people by going to them. Can't be helped."

He raised his voice.

"Ethel! Tell 'em outside I've been called to the country."

He noticed, lying on his desk, the evening newspaper, which he had barely opened. He flung up his hands.

"My God! I never even get a chance to read the noos. Wish I was an author like you. Then I wouldn't have anything to do except draw royalties."

He led the way down a rear staircase, avoiding the suppliants without. Stealthily they reached his limousine, drawn up in a side street.

When they had alighted before the Bunce house the manager's attitude borrowed something of the applicant's timidity. With Quaile at his side he climbed the steps of the rusty brownstone dwelling and rang the bell. Quaile, himself, felt none too confident of the outcome.

A gray-haired manservant opened the door. Over his shoulder Quaile saw a star of gas light toward the ceiling. It had been reduced with an exceptional skill. It served to show him only the servant's bent figure, clothed in a livery of remote beginnings.

McHugh pushed past.

"Mr. Bunce is expecting me. I am Arthur McHugh."

The servant relaxed his attitude of repelling an assault. He conducted them the length of the hall and opened a door. McHugh entered. Quaile paused on the threshold, examining the interior with a pronounced curiosity. One or two bookcases gave the apartment an academic touch. Chairs, a desk, and a sofa—not antique, but melancholy survivals of a bad period—were scattered at haphazard. The light here, too, suggested a sparing disposition. A single oil lamp burned on the desk, radiating a subdued glow on the master of this economical and uncommon establishment.

Bunce sat hunched forward in an elliptical pose. A shawl was draped across his rounded shoulders. His knees were covered with a rug from beneath which his feet, in carpet slippers, protruded. But Quaile's attention was held chiefly by the face, unkempt, hairy, intricately wrinkled, out of which infused eyes gleamed with a suspicion equal to the servant's. His voice rose on a whining, nasal note. It carried a perpetual complaint.

"You're not somebody else?"

McHugh advanced fearlessly.

"Often as I've wanted to," he answered, "I've never been able to make a change. Suppose you're in much the same fix. Mr. Josiah Bunce, I gather."

He took a fresh cigar from his pocket and tendered it.

"Put some fire to this torch, and we'll get to cases."

Bunce, with a gesture of disgust, repelled the gift.

"No smoking here. I have to keep reminding Robert of that."

His voice sharpened.

"Think he'd learn in the course of fifty years."

He drew the shawl tighter about his shoulders. He coughed.

"You made a draught coming in. So you're McHugh, the show man? People try to get to me on all sorts of pretexts. Agents say you want to rent Woodford's. If it's something else, understand I haven't any money to throw away in your cheap leg shows and plays about fallen women—that's all I see in the papers nowadays. Sit down."

Quaile and McHugh obeyed the explosive command. McHugh turned and winked broadly, then faced Bunce again. Bunce leaned forward.

"Watson!" he called.

The serving-man opened the door.

"If my brother hasn't left," Bunce directed, "tell him to come down."

When the serving-man had closed the door, he permitted a little curiosity to slip into his voice.

"What you want Woodford's for! Robert and I been talking it over. We'd decided there was no income there. Nobody's made money in the house since Woodford died."

Suddenly an angry flush swept across his face.

"Look here! You wasting my time to talk about moving pictures?"

McHugh's jaw protruded, giving his face a belligerent strength of which one would scarcely have thought it capable.

"Naw! How much time you think I got to throw away! Quaile here's brought 'Coward's Fare' up to date. Maybe you remember that play of Woodford's. I'm getting an expensive cast together—all the old people I can. Dolly Timken, who played with Woodford, and old Mike Brody, his property man forty years ago—all the sentimental slush I can think of. I'm going to make the old barn what it was, and with its own play, but I got to get good terms. You understand? Fair terms."

He placed the cigar he had proffered Bunce in his own mouth and bit at it savagely.

Quaile had seen memory stir in the old man's eyes at the mention of "Coward's Fare."

"That's different," Bunce said. "That was a first-class play. I used to have a chair at Woodford's two or three times

"Seems promising," Robert answered, buttoning his coat. "If I remember, wasn't there rather too much atmosphere the last time they had it open?"

a week forty years ago."

This crouched and slovenly figure in a theatre was an anomaly before which Quailed imagination halted; yet, as he watched a real enthusiasm increase in Bunce's manner, he became confident that the threatened difficulties would not materialize. McHugh must have caught the same symptoms, for he let Bunce ramble on while it became evident that his remembrance of Woodford's was one of his choicest inheritances from youth. He had been proud to own a share of the theatre in its brilliant period. He had regretted its decline, commencing with Woodford's death. He had always hoped it might return to its own. He appreciated that McHugh offered fulfilment.

"Might take a seat myself," he grinned.

The rental he mentioned was voluble proof of his complacence.

"What about your brother?" McHugh asked.

"He leaves such things to me. I told you I'd been talking to him. The boy'll do what I say."

The door opened. A new atmosphere, pretentious and incompatible, disturbed the tawdry room. Quaile smiled. The "boy" who stood in the doorway was, at a hazard, sixty-five years old. He wore evening clothes. His handsome face, with a grizzled moustache, was distinguished. That the same family should have produced two such divergent specimens was nearly unbelievable.

"There's no point," the newcomer said dryly, "in my intruding. Children should be seen and not heard."

The elder Bunce's shawl fell, neglected, to the chair arms.

"You come in, Robert. Your parties can wait a minute. These gentlemen have brought a surprise. They're going to take 'Coward's Fare' back to Woodford's."

"Sounds familiar," Robert mused. "Oh, yes. To be sure.

Doubtless I should rejoice. Sorry I must limit my enthusiasm. I have an appointment with some other bald-headed boys. Here, Watson, help me with my overcoat."

"It's going to be a fine thing," McHugh put in. "Full of atmosphere. That pulls everybody if you play it up right."

"Seems promising," Robert answered, buttoning his coat. "If I remember, wasn't there rather too much atmosphere the last time they had it open?"

"What you mean?" McHugh asked.

The general gossip and Carlton's talk flashed back to Quaile's mind. He saw the elder Bunce stir uncomfortably. He was surprised at the gravity which entered the nasal voice.

"You mind your own business, Robert. He will have his joke, Mr. McHugh. Don't you fret about that. It was just some talk among the players about Woodford's being a little jealous."

McHugh stared.

"Jealous! He's been dead forty years."

Robert laughed.

"Isn't that atmosphere? No old building complete without it. See that we get our price for that, Josiah."

He turned on McHugh with a whimsical smile.

"I'm renting a theatre," McHugh grinned. "The air inside comes free."

"Arrange it with elder brother," Robert said. "I'm off."

He nodded and hurried out briskly. The front door slammed.

"Don't you worry," Josiah complained. "Lease will be ready in the morning. You can fix details with the agents."

He displayed an eagerness to discuss McHugh's plans. He showed real regret at their departure. Once Quaile dreamed he was on the point of asking them to remain for dinner, but probably calculation frowned on such a generous impulse.

Quaile stopped McHugh as he was entering his limousine. He did not like this reinforcement of the gossip. It impelled him to put the manager on his guard.

"Bunce seemed actually frightened at that nonsense," he said. "You've heard superstitious talk about Woodford's?"

"I daresay. Natural enough—any old place. Nothing to remember."

"I saw Harvey Carlton this afternoon," Quaile said, a little abashed at the necessity of repeating such a conversation. "He spread himself on rumors that Woodford's influence survived down there. Seemed to take it seriously on the whole. It's worth thinking about. I mean, there's no use getting troublemakers in the cast. I fancy it will seem pretty desolate at first. There's a lot of talk about that stock company forfeiting its lease five years ago."

McHugh placed his hand on Quaile's arm. He spoke impressively.

"Don't fool yourself, my boy. Carlton's right. The old bird with the shawl's right. A ghost was responsible for that failure. The company did go to smash on account of it. It was terrible. The ghost didn't walk at all."

CHAPTER II

McHUGH sprang into the limousine and slammed the door. As he drove off he turned back to Quaile his grinning face, which marvelously retained a pendulous cigar.

The next day, nevertheless, the unexpected intruded once or twice, and failed to retreat before it had startled even the matter-of-fact manager.

Quaile spent most of the afternoon in the office, completing with McHugh the casting of the piece. Mike Brody had reported and gone down to Woodford's with a squad of electricians. He had already sent word that there was little to be done, since the wiring had been modernized five years ago. The manager had promised Quaile they would visit the theatre and inspect it for themselves as soon as their task was completed.

It was late when Quaile saw Mike enter and go through to the private office.

More than sentiment had urged McHugh to engage the old man. He had worked for him off and on during many years. He understood and fitted easily into his system. Quaile had frequently heard the manager boast that Mike, in spite of his years, was the most reliable property man in New York. Without initiative, he possessed a useful memory. It was said that he had never forgotten a property or its correct placing.

Within five minutes McHugh was roaring for Ethel. She went in, returned, and nodded to Quaile.

"Boss wants you."

Quaile opened the door and stepped into a room crowded with discontent, even timidity.

The manager sat back, facing Mike. The square jaw, signal of opposition to be overthrown, was well forward.

The property man leaned against the wall, unwilling to meet McHugh's tempestuous glance. He looked instead in the direction of his cap, at which he picked with purpose-less fingers. The lights had not been turned on, so that it was difficult for Quaile to gather details. The posing itself, however, was declamatory. He was not unprepared for McHugh's scornful announcement.

"What do you think, Quaile? The old numbskull wants to quit on me. Aren't you ashamed of yourself? Haven't you got a blush left? 'Cause I'm going to give you away to Mr. Quaile."

Mike made an embarrassed appeal.

"I only told him, sir, that I thought maybe I'd better not take on the job."

"I understood," Quaile answered, "that you were pleased at the prospect of going back."

"Yes, sir, I was. I had some of the best times of my life when I was a kid at Woodford's, but that's been forty years, and—and—"

He broke off and returned to the restless fingering of his cap. Quaile hesitated to prompt the man. He guessed that McHugh had had a purpose in summoning him. Through him, unquestionably, McHugh expected to mold Mike to his wishes. No ordinary situation would have urged such a course. He shrank from the possibility that the antiquated and lonesome theatre might already have imposed on Mike's uneducated mind a sense of fear. If that was so,

McHugh had assumed a promising attitude. Mike was uncomfortable, perhaps, ashamed. He shifted his weight from one foot to the other. He cleared his throat, but no defense followed.

"First time anybody ever wanted to resign on me," McHugh said in a hurt tone. "Fall down on your job once, Mike, and you won't have to wait to resign. What do you think's biting him, Quaile?"

"Somebody's offered him more money."

McHugh shook his head. He burst into unrestrained laughter.

"No. I'm the best pickings in the business. Old fool's afraid of Bertrand Woodford."

Quaile joined in the mirth.

"Do you know how long he's been dead, Mike?"

"Hold on," McHugh gasped. "Not of Woodford. When he's got me—a real live one—to be scared of, he's afraid of Woodford's spook."

The manager's antidote was powerful. A reluctant grin appeared on Mike's face.

"I didn't say that, Mr. McHugh. Maybe you're right, though. If you want me, I'll stay."

"Go on, Mike," the manager said good-naturedly. "Wait for us downstairs. Mr. Quaile and I will go to Woodford's with you in a minute. We want to see what's been done."

But when the man had left McHugh turned a puzzled face to Quaile. With a thoughtful air he drew on his un-lighted cigar.

"Guess you had the right dope last night after all," he admitted. "Got to keep our eyes open and make it cheerful at Woodford's."

"Surely," Quaile said, "Mike isn't such a fool as to think he saw anything?"

"No. But Mike's pretty old. I guess it took him back to go into that barn after forty years. He didn't say anything you could put your finger on. Was just frightened. Said it was dark and cold, and he couldn't help thinking of his old boss. Seemed like he stood by him all the time. Say, I never realized what a disagreeable devil Woodford was. Mike says he used to limp around—seems he had rheumatism a lot toward the last—being as nasty to people as he could. Going there today certainly put him on Mike's mind. Got to talking about the night he died. Mike says Woodford worked himself to death because he was too jealous to let anybody play his part."

"That's about what I hear," Quaile said. "Did Mike mention anything about a cat—the way he acted the night of Woodford's death?"

McHugh looked up.

"Mean to say Carlton gave you that, too?"

"Yes—mentioned it. As he said, it's funny the way these foolish stories cling."

McHugh arose.

"I've laughed Mike out of it, anyway. I may take a shot at Carlton. You know, Mike was honestly afraid something might happen to him down there. Come on. Let's go."

They joined Mike on the sidewalk, entered McHugh's automobile, and drove to Woodford's.

Quaile had looked forward with something approximating a thrill to his first invasion of the property. The prospect, however, was shadowed by the rumors he had heard, and, particularly, by Mike's apprehension, which, he noticed, had, to an extent, survived McHugh's laughter.

The night had descended by the time they arrived at the theatre, but the glitter of the streetlights was deceptive. It softened the scars of the old building. It penetrated beyond the iron railing which guarded the lobby, long undisturbed. It exposed the display boards at either side, cracked and colored by the weather, to which paper shreds and the stains of paste still adhered.

"Where's Tommy Ball?" McHugh said. "I told Tommy Ball to meet me here."

A young man, too sedulously clothed, deserted his contemplation of a shop window and stepped forward. Quaile recognized McHugh's assistant stage manager—a youth who always amused him with his fervent efforts to copy his employer's eccentricities.

"Been in yet, Tommy?" McHugh asked.

"Not since noon. But I don't guess you'll find a whole lot to do."

Mike thrust his hand in his pocket, producing a heavy, old-fashioned key.

"Stage entrance is this way, Mr. McHugh."

He led them, not very eagerly, into a narrow alley which penetrated the block between the theatre and the loft building. Within this meagre space the thoroughness of the night became apparent. The dingy side of the theatre and the towering wall of the loft building gave Quaile an illusion of leaning toward each other perilously. The end of the alley was blocked by a high board fence. Mike turned there and inserted his key in the lock of an iron door.

The thrill Quaile had expected was not lacking, yet its quality scarcely conformed to his fancy.

Because of the unrelieved night he knew that the door was open only through its own voice. The hinges, abandoned until today for so long to the weather, complained shrilly; and, as if from an unexplored and adventurous cavern, arose an echo. The black, empty stage of Woodford's flung back into the alley the dismay of its opened door.

Quaile sniffed. He breathed with distaste, for the alley had filled with a dank, insufferable odor which he could not describe. The air, imprisoned at the last closing of the door, rushed out of Woodford's with the eagerness of escape.

A match scraped. Its flame flickered on Mike's wrinkled face, which wore for Quaile an expression of disapproval, of positive disinclination. The property man stooped, fumbled within the doorway, and found a candle to which he applied the match.

"Better not let the fire department catch you at that," McHugh warned.

Quaile wondered if the manager took in the shaking of the candle in the knotted hand.

"Get in there," McHugh directed, "and switch on your kitchen border, so we won't break our necks. Place smells like a one-night stand in the great and glorious provinces."

Mike's face set. It was evident that he subordinated his own judgment to a sense of pride. He had the appearance of one who invades a place notorious for some unexplained danger. His candle moved slowly into the cavern and turned to the right.

Quaile's eyes became a little accustomed to the darkness. He could see that a nebulous reflection from the street entered the alley. It reached him with a sense of companionship. Then light flashed in the cavern, illuminating vast spaces, and Mike's voice came.

"All right, Mr. McHugh."

And they entered those spaces, and, oppressed by their emptiness, stood for some time, ill at ease, attentive.

Quaile resented his discomfort. After all, there could be nothing here beyond age, disuse, loneliness—at the most, unpalatable memories. Yet he was honest. With Mike's misgivings still lively in his mind, he would not deny that weakness, nearly universal, which hesitates, a little over-awed, on the threshold of the past whose dead activities often impress one with the imminence of a revival.

He acknowledged, as he glanced around, a stimulus here for the imaginative. The single row of lights, depending from the flies, gave scarcely more than a suggestion of form to the auditorium and the two galleries sloping upward. But he could see that the seats were shrouded with gray cloths. They forced on him a fancy of standing in a huge, improvised mortuary after some intolerable catastrophe.

The stage itself offered more definition. He saw the vast expanse of the brick curtain wall, the circular staircases at either side leading to dressing-rooms and fly galleries. To the right there was a small door which almost certainly opened on a passage connecting with the auditorium.

He caught in McHugh's manner no response to the factors which had depressed him.

"Don't build stages like this nowadays," the manager said with admiration. "Could give a three-ring circus here. Tommy, you've got the lists. You and Mike run over to the storehouse in the morning and chase that furniture in. Company's called for four o'clock. Mr. Quaile's going to read the script to 'em right on the stage just like old Woodford done. This engagement's going to be all-fired artistic."

His sudden blatant laugh set Quailed nerves on edge. It jeered at the empty spaces, the shrouded seats. It did not belong here, nor did McHugh persist in it. He found another cigar and inserted it between his lips. His keen glance took in everything.

"Come through here, Quaile. Let's have a peep at the auditorium."

He walked to the little door which Quaile had noticed, and opened it. Quaile saw Mike and Tommy start toward the stage entrance. He understood, but McHugh pretended not to.

"Where you and Mike going, Tommy?"

"By the stage door, sir. It's pretty damp in here."

"All right," McHugh said, "but I want you within call."

Quaile followed the manager into the passage. A certain amount of light entered with them, and a little more, diffused from the auditorium, showed at the other end. The passage was surprisingly constricted. It was necessary to go in single file. He gathered from its length—probably seven or eight paces—that it ran behind the boxes.

"Wouldn't be much use," he commented, "as an exit by way of the stage in case of fire."

His voice was magnified in the meagre space.

"Building meets the fire laws," McHugh, always practical, answered.

They reached the auditorium whose boundaries appeared to recede before them, demanding an impracticable pursuit. After a glance at the farther shadows, in fact, McHugh contented himself with, a casual inspection of the woodwork and the draperies near at hand.

"Agents didn't lie," he said with satisfaction, "and my own men gave me the right dope."

He walked down the aisle, thrust aside one of the gray cloths, and sat in the front row. He looked around.

"Not bad," he grunted.

Quaile joined him.

"Funny," McHugh went on, "how a little gold dust thrown in people's eyes will make them see millions. The place was fixed up five years ago. Now a few new hangings and a little tinsel on the box fronts—it's a cinch. Why you so talkative, Quaile?"

Quaile had not realized the thoroughness of his silence since entering the theatre. He glanced at the manager, questioning if his volubility wasn't a different response to the same impulse. He saw nothing to be gained by denying that impulse. It was the emptiness and the pervading desolation of Woodford's. He had never seen a theatre in this condition before, its machinery hidden or removed. He had a feeling of having invaded the shell of a thing long dead, quite beyond resurrection. The sepulchral dampness gave the final impetus to his bad humor.

"Frankly, McHugh," he said, "I begin to understand how these unwholesome stories start. Such an atmosphere as this has things to say to the ignorant and the superstitious. I hope I'm neither, but it does get on my nerves more or less. I mean, I quite understand why Tommy and Mike prefer the alley entrance."

"They'll have to get over it. Place feels all right to me."

McHugh's voice rose in a gigantic sneer.

"Woodford's ghost! A fine chance for a ghost around my theatre."

To Quaile it was almost as if a challenge had been accepted. The shadows might suddenly have gathered strength to smother the row of gleaming lights. Without warning they expired. He could feel the pit-like blackness rush upon him.

McHugh's hand touched his arm, then was snatched back. The manager's voice rose angrily.

"What the devil? Mike! Mike! Get into the switchboard. Switch something on. Don't bother about your candle."

As if the darkness had opposed a palpable barrier Tommy's exclamation and Mike's response reached them faintly. They heard the old man start on the stage. What followed seemed to Quaile at the moment inevitable, never to have been avoided. Through the black and heavy air Mike's cry arose, hoarse, difficult, half strangled by an irrational fear. It gathered itself into four words, almost unintelligible:

"My God! Mr. Woodford!"

Quaile shrank back. More than Mike's terror-drawn cry challenged his reason. Just across the blind footlights, almost within hand's reach, he heard dragging footsteps and a curious, stealthy padding.

He bent forward, staring impotently at the solid wall of blackness. The talk he had heard, the misgivings he had witnessed, threw upon that wall, as upon a screen for his imagination, an unthinkable picture. For the dragging footsteps continued to stray across the stage—the footsteps of one who limped, and in the intervals of their painful progress came that furtive pattering like the noiseless pursuit of a cat.

Quaile remained rigid. He was aware of McHugh's breathless tensity beside him. Then, as abruptly as they had commenced, the footsteps ceased, and from the wings, where Mike had cried out his impossible fear, came a low sob, choked and formless.

CHAPTER III

THE CAT

QUAILE waited, shrinkingly expectant of a return through the darkness of the limping footsteps, and the padding which had suggested the furtive tread of a cat. At last he relaxed. With uncertain fingers he fumbled in his pocket, found a match, and struck it.

The light was a little reassuring. It gave him courage to resent the readiness with which he had accepted Mike's cry and the testimony of his own senses. The ghost of Bertrand Woodford, who had been dead forty years! He sneered. He told himself that his nerves had played him tricks, that he could have heard nothing beyond Mike's senile abandonment to fear.

Then, as he swung on McHugh, there came again from the dark wings that incoherent sobbing. He saw McHugh's white face and his hand, trembling a little, as it grasped the side of his chair, and he knew that his imagination had not wholly deceived him. The match expired.

McHugh sprang up, grasped Quaile's elbow, and drew him to his feet.

"Another match," he whispered.

Quaile took another from his pocket and struck it. The matter-of-fact manager waited for no more. He sprang to the orchestra rail, vaulted the footlights, and hurried to the stage door. Quaile, carefully preserving the tiny flame, followed him.

The clearer air of the alley and the narrow, remote ribbon of the sky were, to an extent, curative. He resented his brief surrender.

Mike, however, was still vanquished. The old property man stood crouched against the wall of the loft building, his face hidden by his hands. Tommy was a dark shadow at his side. Quaile heard the little fellow say:

"Geest, Mike! What'd you see?"

Then, at his chief's presence, Tommy tried to carry it off.

"Mike's seeing things, boss. But say, those electricians must 'a' done a bum job."

McHugh walked straight to Mike and placed a heavy hand on his shoulder. His voice was savage.

"What did you think you saw?"

"I didn't see anything," Mike answered, his voice on the edge of another sob, "but I felt and I heard. Didn't you hear anything, Mr. McHugh?"

His voice gathered strength.

"Mr. Quaile! Didn't you hear anything?"

McHugh gave Quaile no opportunity to answer. He shook Mike's shoulder.

"What d'ye mean about feeling and hearing? Open up now. What scared you?"

Mike straightened. It was not to be doubted that he recognized the need of justification. It was also clear that he was satisfied with his excuse. He steadied his voice with a painful effort.

"I heard you speak, Mr. McHugh. You said something about Mr. Woodford, and then the border went out. Everything was dark and you called me to get to the switchboard. I didn't want to go, because it wasn't natural the border flashing out that way. Why should it go out, Mr. McHugh?"

"I'm no wire hanger," McHugh grumbled. "Go on. Go

on."

"I started for the board," Mike continued. "I was facing away from the door so I couldn't see anything. Nothing felt right. I had to stop. Then I heard him. I mean, I heard somebody walking with a limp, and I heard the cat. I thought it rubbed against my leg. I couldn't stand it, Mr. McHugh. I guess I gave a holler, and then I ran out. It was just like he had come out of his dressing-room when you spoke his name."

McHugh turned with a formless exclamation and stalked down the alley. The others filed at his heels through the narrow opening to the sidewalk. The light dazzled. The electric sign of the motion-picture house performed elaborately. The pavement failed to contain a hurrying, voluble crowd which overflowed to the street, hindering traffic. Automobiles signaled a raucous impatience. Street cars, overloaded and suffocating, jerked forward a few yards at a time. From the loft building men and girls poured, turning their foreign and unintelligent faces homeward. Woodford's alone presented a somber fissure in this wall of brightness and animation.

Quaile reacted quickly to the city's familiar spirit. He watched McHugh swing on Mike.

"Look around," the manager cried. "Got the nerve to tell me out here that they ever come back?"

But Mike, although the street had brought a look of uncertainty to his face, was not so easily released from his fear.

"I heard him," he persisted sullenly.

McHugh burst into unaffected laughter. He lied glibly while Quaile listened, acknowledging that the stratagem was legitimate.

"Now I see what's biting you. You had me so worked up I didn't get you at first. Lights went out. All right. That's up to Tommy and you for letting those electricians get away with a rotten job. Then you heard somebody limping around."

He laughed again. Mike's eyes widened.

"Limping around!" McHugh guffawed. "That was me, Mike—nobody but little me. Haven't you known me long enough? Think I sit still when things go wrong? I felt my way across the front of the orchestra—ran my hand along the velvet rail. Of course I went lopsided—sounded as if I was limping. Maybe my fingers made a noise like a cat. And you thought I was old Woodford!"

The shame in Mike's face had kept pace with McHugh's jocular explanation. Still doubt lingered.

"I thought it was closer to me than that, Mr. McHugh."

"You were ready to imagine anything," McHugh scoffed.

Mike's voice thickened.

"You don't think I want to believe the other? That's why I talked about quitting this afternoon. I didn't want to have it put up to me. I'm getting old. I don't want to go away believing anything like that."

McHugh spoke with an unaccustomed gentleness.

"You stick to me, Mike, and when you do leave, it will be with a peaceful mind."

"Thanks, Mr. McHugh. You must be right. I'm sorry I was so easy scared."

"Are we going back?" Quaile asked with a casual air.

McHugh turned away.

"I've seen all I want for tonight. Besides, the switchboard's out of business. Tommy, you go lock the stage door."

Tommy's resplendent figure moved none too quickly toward the alley. Curiosity urged Quaile after him. Tommy's glance was grateful. Quaile disclosed his purpose as soon as they were in the obscurity between the walls.

"You got a little start yourself, Tommy, didn't you? I've been watching. Mr. McHugh's explanation didn't go down whole. Why not?"

Tommy turned surly.

"I ain't giving the boss away."

That settled it for Quaile. Each one of the four, then, had experienced testimony of an incomprehensible presence in the theatre. He knew from his previous visit that when his eyes grew accustomed to the alley there would be a wan light here.

"Tommy," he said, "you were by the door, looking in. Did you see anything? Own up now."

"Nothing I'd have thought of," Tommy answered unwillingly, "if it hadn't been for Mike's hot air about a cat."

"Let's have it," Quaile persisted. "It might help."

Tommy reduced his pace.

"I could see Mike like a black splotch for a minute, he said, scarcely audibly. "Say, Mr. Quaile, you won't think I fall for any of this back from Woodlawn stuff?"

"I know you've good sense, Tommy."

The youth continued on an even lower key.

"Did seem once as if I saw a little black thing crawling along. It was too dark to be sure. Mike's getting scared at a cat made me think, but there's nothing funny about a cat on a stage."

"Except here," Quaile said thoughtfully. "This place has been closed."

"Might have sneaked in when the electricians were at work," Tommy offered.

"Of course, of course," Quaile agreed.

Tommy reached the iron door, slammed it shut, and locked it.

"Have to hand it to Woodford's," he said with an attempt at bravado. "Ain't it cold and damp? Might be a relief to some of these guys that had to go to the other place."

When they returned to the sidewalk Quaile gathered that McHugh had quite convinced Mike. The manager stepped into his automobile and beckoned Quaile to follow.

As the car started McHugh placed his feet on one of the delicately upholstered chairs. He drew at his unlighted cigar.

"Then you heard the footsteps, too, Quaile?"

Quaile nodded.

"I'm still at a loss. I'm uncomfortable from the feeling of the place. That isn't unnatural, and, McHugh, there must be a rational explanation of the sounds we heard."

"Must be," McHugh replied, "though I don't see how anybody could have played tricks on us."

Quaile chose to put himself on record.

"Understand," he said, "I don't think this revival would amount to much outside of Woodford's."

His belligerent expression returned to McHugh's face.

"Think I can be beaten by shadows?" he muttered. "Things'll look different in there by daylight. Probably find all the explanations we want tomorrow. But if anything is wrong, don't forget I made my bread and butter as a detective for twelve years, and people used to say I was a good one at that. I liked the job, too. Wouldn't be surprised if I liked it better than directing bum shows. If we get any more funny business at Woodford's I'll be able to say for sure."

CHAPTER IV

THE INFLUENCE AT WOODFORD'S

DURING the dark hours it was useful to recall McHugh's disposition. By day, however, last evening's curious interruption lost a good deal of its force.

Quaile spent the morning looking over his revision of Bertrand Woodford's famous play. He was contented with what he had done. While the piece was melodramatic and old-fashioned, it contained values of characterization and suspense that were still profitable. He had found it necessary to alter the dialogue of the biggest scenes very little. His deftness had expressed itself chiefly in the elimination of bombastic phrasing and the modelling of the fortuitous into a semblance of reality.

As he walked down to the theatre in the pleasant fall sunlight he agreed with McHugh's prophecy that Woodford's would look different by day.

It was four o'clock when he turned in at the alley. Mike, sitting in the stage doorway, gave him his first doubt. Clearly the property man had not forgotten last night's fright. Over his shoulder Quaile could see figures moving about a nearly brilliant stage.

Quaile assumed a humorous tone.

"Not going to let the lights go out today, Mike?"

Mike's glance wavered.

"Ask Mr. McHugh," he said, "about the switchboard."

"What do you mean?"

But before Mike could answer McHugh shouted from the stage:

"Here's the author! Come on in, author."

Quaile stepped through and glanced around.

While the only daylight entered through the alley entrance, more than one border burned today, so that the stage at first presented an appearance almost cheerful. The storehouse had yielded a Jacobean table, a red plush sofa, and a number of chairs, relics of former and lamented productions. Moreover, the men and women lounging about gave the place an air of habitation it had lacked last evening.

He saw Barbara Morgan sitting on the sofa. Her youthful beauty gained something from the white-haired woman beside her who looked about with a pensive air.

Quaile could understand and sympathize. To that old woman, if to anyone, Woodford's must have furnished a multitude of memories. This stage on which she sat had been her school. More than forty years ago she had played ingénue rôles and occasional leads with Bertrand Woodford. McHugh had engaged her ostensibly to act the mother in "Coward's Fare." He wanted her really because of her knowledge of the details of Woodford's production. Her proximity to Barbara, who was to have her old part, imposed on Quaile a real pity. He might have spared his emotion, for when he went over and spoke to the two women the white-haired one smiled up at him without regret.

"I've never met you, Miss Timken," he began.

"Everybody calls me Dolly," she answered. "They began that when I was Barbara's age—a mere child, and they've never let it die. Isn't it ridiculous?"

Behind her mask of wrinkles the spirit of youth was still

abundant.

"I've been telling Barbara if she does as well as I did back in the dark ages, she'll run away with the play. You're just as pretty as I was, dear."

Barbara, too, failed quite to hide her understanding of what this revival meant to the other.

"You're good," she said. "Too good. I'm glad you're to play my mother."

Dolly shook her head.

"But I'm a bad one. It's only your own virtue that gets you a happy curtain. You know, I wouldn't be surprised if they liked the piece. Some of the lines used to bring the gallery down."

She sighed. She glanced, retrospection in her eyes, across the shrouded auditorium.

"The same gallery," she said, "but where are the young people who used to sit in it and applaud me?"

She tapped the stage with her foot.

"Same old boards, but where's Bertrand Woodford who used to rule us with an iron hand?"

Quaile suspected moisture in her eyes, but she laughed.

"What a devil of a temper that man had! I never thought I should miss him."

Quaile crossed to the table and spoke to the others. There were Smith and Thomas, capable but ordinary actors, and Helen Hendon, a dark-haired girl who already displayed resentment at Barbara's superiority in the cast.

Of the principals the leading man alone was missing. Quaile wondered what detained Carlton. He walked over to McHugh.

"A little more cheerful today with the heat going," he said.

"Yes," McHugh replied, "but it looks damp. I've told Tommy to get some flats in by tomorrow. We'll set up an interior for the third act. Not a bad scheme to rehearse the big stuff right, from the beginning, and everything else'll go as well in that as on an empty stage. Besides, as I say, it'll make the place look more homelike."

Quaile drew him toward the rear.

"Find out anything?" he asked.

McHugh glanced around.

"Not what you'd think of."

"No signs of a cat?"

"No."

"Mike said something about the switchboard," Quaile prompted.

"Quaile," McHugh asked, "you'd take your oath you saw Tommy shut and lock that door last night?"

"There's no question," Quaile answered. Why?"

"There *is* something queer going on here," McHugh said under his breath. "I got to find out. Suppose it was dangerous? I came down with Tommy and Mike and a couple electricians this morning. As far as we could tell nobody had been in the house since Tommy locked up—no ordinary way to get in. The keys are on the inside of all the other doors. Of course, we went to the switchboard the first thing. Nothing to be done. Every connection worked. Lights were O. K. Then how did that border go out?"

"Unless somebody tampered with the switchboard at the time," Quaile suggested.

"And Tommy and Mike at the stage door!" McHugh said, "and you and me where we could see anybody cross the stage. It seems absolutely impossible those connections were touched last night. We got to believe they were, though. Well, I'm looking around. I got my eyes open. We'll see if anything goes wrong today."

"There's your company," Quaile said. It wouldn't do to start them with a scare."

"Where's the leading man?" McHugh asked.

He glanced at his watch. He raised his voice.

"Mike! See any signs of Mr. Carlton out there?"

"No, Mr. McHugh," Mike called.

"Give him a minute," McHugh said. "Where's your script, Quaile?"

Quaile took the manuscript from his portfolio, walked down, and tossed it on the table. McHugh followed. He struck a pose. He waved his cold cigar.

"Ladies and gentlemen," he began, "Mr. Quaile and I are offering you a unique and valuable opportunity, which I hope—"

He thrust the cigar between his teeth.

"Hang all that!" he went on fiercely. "I can't be a regular manager like this fellow Woodford seems to have been. Point is, Mr. Quaile's going to read the script, and we start rehearsals tomorrow afternoon. I tell you, boys and girls, you got a steady job for the winter unless all the signs fail, and, of course, if you make good. That's up to you, not me. Where the devil's Carlton? Go ahead and read those pretty words, Quaile. Hey, Mike! Bring a standing light."

Quaile arranged the sheets of paper while Mike crossed the stage with a piece of iron piping from which an electric globe and a green shade depended. Wire trailed after it.

"All set!" McHugh cried. "We're off!"

Quaile commenced to read. The others arranged themselves comfortably. Miss Hendon yawned.

Carlton arrived before the close of the first act. Quaile glanced up at him, certain that something unforeseen had delayed the actor, for Carlton's handsome face showed less color than usual, and his eyes could not conceal an unaccustomed agitation.

"Where you been, Carlton?" McHugh asked darkly. "Beginning with the rehearsals I'm going to post fines."

Carlton sat down, leaning his elbow on the table. When he spoke his mouth seemed dry.

"Sorry. Something unexpected came up."

He hesitated.

"At first I didn't think I could come at all."

"No more said," McHugh answered. "Shoot ahead, Quaile."

Quaile raised the manuscript and went on, but now, not infrequently, his glance shifted from the typewritten pages to Carlton's face, and his mind, from the dialogue to speculation as to the actor's extraordinary attitude. Recalling Carlton's gossip of the other day, Quaile was by no means certain that Woodford's wasn't vaguely responsible. "Bertrand Woodford," Carlton had said to him, "had worked himself to death rather than let any man play his part, and a lot of people felt that he never would let any man play it now that he was dead." No matter how lightly he had tried to carry it off, the thing had troubled the actor. Quaile wondered if Carlton's tardiness and his present lack of ease couldn't be traced to misgivings sprung from such stories. He wondered if Carlton had already heard of what had happened on this stage yesterday: of the footsteps that had dragged like Woodford's through a darkness, sudden and unaccountable, of the furtive pattering, reminiscent of a cat.

McHugh also seemed slyly interested by the new arrival.

At the end of the second act Quaile looked from the stage door to find it quite dark in the alley. When he resumed he noticed that a restlessness had invaded the little company. He saw that all of them—even McHugh occasionally—glanced about the vast stage and the auditorium with its army of shadows, as if expectant of something as yet too remote for definition. Quaile taxed his own fancy with the uncomfortable idea and hurried ahead. He approached the big scene of the third act, the one during which Woodford had been stricken a few feet from where they sat.

The situation at that point was theatric but strong. Marjorie's mother, not over-scrupulous, has forced a crisis. She has let herself be duped by Marshall. She believes that he is wealthy, that only an unsubstantial obstacle removes him from a title. Marjorie's revolt against such a marriage, however, must be overcome. Therefore, since the girl has refused to receive Marshall, the old lady gets her to his rooms by subterfuge, convinced by his boast that through an interview he can overcome her reluctance. During the previous act the girl has learned who Marshall really is, a brilliant London forger, a trafficker in shady transactions, a criminal whose success has been founded on an apparent gentility. The girl goes, but she is suspicious. As a safeguard she has used her knowledge. When Marshall springs his trap and the mother realizes the scandal she has brought upon her daughter, Marjorie takes the whip in her own hands. She lashes Marshall with his past. She laughs at the incredulous man who will not believe that she can prove her threats. She runs to the window and gives a prearranged signal. There is a disturbance downstairs. She tells the man that the police have entered the house. Marshall surrenders himself to reasonless passion. He answers only to the necessity of punishing this girl who has mocked his desire and placed him on the threshold of disaster. He springs to the mantel and snatches up a heavy candlestick.

"Marjorie! Look out!" the mother screams.

Marjorie shrinks against the wall, wide-eyed, her hands raised defensively.

"Be careful!" she gasps. "What are you going to do to me?"

Marshall turns and is about to start murderously forward, crying out:

"Pay what debts I can. Kill you, if the strength is in me."

But the police have burst in. The candlestick falls. He flings up his hands before he has finished his speech, and hides his face.

At this point, as they all knew, Woodford, in the middle of his line, had dropped to the stage.

Although it had happened forty years ago, Quaile mused, two had now returned to the theatre who had witnessed that tragedy. He could understand that it must occupy their minds with an exclusive compulsion.

Dolly Timken, who sat directly in front of him, confessed by her attitude, indeed, the course of her reflections. She was bent a little forward, as if absorbed by something more peremptory than the reading. Her glance had found and now rested on a portion of the stage beyond Quaile's shoulder.

He hurried. He wanted to get past that scene, if only to watch Dolly relax. Carlton's exclamation, just before the close of it, therefore, came with an abrupt surprise. It startled everyone. A murmur of halting curiosity began. The actor had arisen. He stood, braced against the table. His hand jerked unevenly in a gesture toward McHugh. He spoke with a labored and unfamiliar intonation.

"I'm sorry, Mr. McHugh. Not feeling well. Perhaps I shouldn't have come. You're nearly through. Might I go? You could send my part to me."

McHugh's eyes were puzzled.

"Sure," he said.

Perhaps seeking an anchorage, he turned to Quaile.

"Say, young man, you read well."

"I'm sorry to interrupt," Carlton said hoarsely.

"Go on home," McHugh ordered. "I'll send the part, and you might let me know in the morning what your sawbones advises."

He called:

"Tommy! Tommy Ball! Go with Mr. Carlton and see that he gets a taxicab. Fire ahead, Quaile, it's getting late. Bad enough to have to hear plays on a full stomach."

Carlton walked, lurching a little, from the stage. Quaile watched him go, curiously convinced that fright rather than illness had urged him. As he took up the manuscript again he sought blindly for some connection between what had just happened and last evening's unhealthy puzzle. Could the fact that Carlton had broken down and retreated at such a point suggest more than coincidence?

He went on. All at once he realized how familiar these words were to the dingy walls, the empty seats. Yet how different was his voice from the ones they remembered!

There wasn't much more. At the close he looked up, expecting the usual chorus of gratitude or disappointment, but the company accepted the play in silence.

"Well?" McHugh prompted.

"I think I can do well enough with Marjorie," Barbara said.

"Of course you can," McHugh snapped. "What do you think I hired you for?"

The others made equally formal comments.

While he gathered up his manuscript Quaile noticed that Dolly and Barbara stood apart at that portion of the stage toward which the old woman had glanced so often during the reading. She whispered, and Barbara appeared to listen with a sort of fascination.

The picture worried Quaile. It prompted him to meet Barbara, as if by accident, when she stepped from the stage door. They spoke aimlessly for a few moments.

"Miss Timken," he said at the first opportunity, "seemed a little reminiscent today. I daresay she was telling you just now how Woodford died. Wasn't it over there where you stood?"

Barbara nodded.

"Yes. She told me all about his pride and jealousy, and the way he struggled to go on playing when he was too ill, and how the black cat ran out—"

She drew her coat closer about her.

"She gave me the shivers. Said she had a feeling there was a cat near her all the time this afternoon."

Quaile was uncomfortable. Such a fancy fitted too neatly with last night's scare.

"I'm sorry," he said.

"Why?"

He reached out and touched her hand. The contact, cold, in itself a verification, was, curiously, to him stimulating.

"I thought so," he said. "She's played on your nerves."

"Now, please!" she laughed. "For an actress I've always prided myself on having none. You can't blame her. I admired the restraint with which she took it all this afternoon. She ought to hate me."

"Her disposition is too fine," Quaile answered. "Besides, old people love and hate less readily than young."

"At least, Mr. Quaile," Barbara said, "if I have the blues don't blame them all on Dolly. It made me sad to go in that empty, tawdry place. I've been thinking of nothing but departed glories, and the tragedy of having to give up. You've had no feelings like that? But then you're not an actor."

He smiled, indicating the alley entrance.

"Your blues won't last long out there. Shall we go on?"

He walked to the street with her. He placed her in a cab. He experienced a special welcome for himself in the lights and the activity.

CHAPTER V

THE TRAGIC REPETITION

CARLTON did not appear for rehearsal the next day, but McHugh had talked with him over the telephone. His doctor had prescribed a few days' rest, so McHugh had sent the part up to him.

"That's a relief," he said, "because Carlton's a good actor."

"Why this sudden attack of nerves?" Quaile asked.

McHugh grunted.

"Cut that out, Quaile. No more nerve business here. I got my eyes open, but nothing else has happened, and nothing will."

Quaile found, however, that the manager had taken an unprecedented step. Instead of turning the early rehearsals over to one of his men, he announced that he would direct the production from the beginning himself. It fixed Quaile's belief that McHugh, in spite of his attitude of a scoffer, was still apprehensive.

Quaile spoke pleasantly to the players, examining each one for signals of discontent. Dolly alone preserved the scars of last evening's uneasiness. Barbara, he was glad to find, had regained her good spirits. She greeted him with an unstudied smile.

McHugh beckoned him to the auditorium, then clapped

his hands.

"Company down stage!" he roared.

When they had gathered at the footlights he thrust his thumbs in the armholes of his waistcoat.

"The leading man," he announced, "is under the weather for a few days. Until he comes back Tommy Ball will feed you his sides. So, play up to him as if he was Carlton."

Tommy, gorgeous for the occasion in tan shoes, check suit, and a lavender necktie, blushed engagingly, and, to hide his embarrassment, fingered the pages of the part.

McHugh, without further preliminary, dashed into the rehearsal. Quaile always found it difficult to take his work seriously until the results commanded his admiration. The manager, with a fatherly familiarity, customarily preferred Christian names, and it never seemed to occur to anyone to resent it. While the others read their dialogue he gave them the first suggestions of action.

"Say, Barbara," he would shout, "paint the horror a little thicker there. Look as if somebody had told you didn't know how to buy a fall hat. No! No! Ain't you more pride about buying hats than that? Remember your mother's a regular old demon—used you like a busted penny all your life. How would you look if somebody really put it up to you strong that you had to marry a yap you knew was such a crook the sheep would run at the sight of him? Bet you'd want to slap her face, but she's your mother, and you've too much respect for your Sunday-school teaching. All you can do is look. Then look hard. And, Dolly, maybe you heard Woodford tell 'em different, but my idea is the old skirt you're playing's cold as a fish when the skating sign's up. Freeze her out. Now you got it. Make her want to wear furs in August."

Meantime Tommy's voice went on, reading Carlton's lines with harsh, uncultured power. Quaile had to hide his mirth. He was convinced he would never be able to purge

Marshall's rôle of Tommy's voice. The worst of it was the youth had an instinct for the stresses, but he exaggerated them insufferably. He would cap Barbara's or Dolly's pleasing modulations with the roar of a lion.

Quaile sat back, enjoying it, aware, too, that the interest and industry had for once given him a sense of placidity in Woodford's. It was Dolly who routed it. Her angry gesture, her quick advance to the footlights, even before she had spoken, reminded him that the past had not been conquered.

McHugh looked up, surprised.

"What's frettn' you, Dolly?"

Dolly's answer came on an unexpected wave of ill-humor.

"I can't stand it, Mr. McHugh."

Nothing in the script about sitting down here. Get it off your mind."

"You ought to guess, Mr. McHugh. It's Tommy—the way he's reading."

Tommy's blush returned. McHugh grinned.

"Tommy's mother didn't raise her boy to be an actor. Jealous of his style? What's the matter with Tommy?"

"I tell you it puts my nerves on edge," the woman persisted. "Maybe I'm an old fool, but it seems like sacrilege. It's enough to make Woodford turn in his grave."

Quaile sprang up and went to McHugh's side. Tommy slammed his book shut.

"Ah! I never claimed to be a Henry Irving or Charlie Chaplin. Mr. McHugh tells me to read the part and I reads it. Never knew I was bad enough to frighten women and children."

Dolly turned away, her sullenness replaced by a remorse wholly feminine.

"I'm sorry if I've hurt your feelings, Tommy," she said softly. "Don't hate me. I can't think why I burst out that way."

She put her handkerchief to her eyes.

"I'm old and fanciful. It seemed if I had to. Don't forget this house is full of ghosts for me."

Barbara went to her and whispered. Quaile, anxious only to have the disturbing interruption concluded, suggested to McHugh that he read the part until Carlton's return, but the manager's jaw was thrust well forward.

"I'll step on these nerves at the start," he muttered. "Tommy! Cheer up! Nobody's going to make you stand in the corner. Go ahead! Only don't read like you was telephonin' 'Frisco. Gentle, gentle! Coney Island boat stuff— talkin' to your best girl."

Tommy took the book again, but he had borrowed Dolly's moroseness. He read now in a voice, unstressed, sullen, barely audible.

At the close of the rehearsal Dolly apologized to Quaile.

"I get the queerest feelings in here," she defended herself. "Remember it takes me back forty years. These new faces don't belong. They make me miss my old friends."

She glanced over her shoulder. She spoke sharply.

"There's a cat around here!"

Quaile started.

"Not unusual on any stage," he answered.

"But I haven't seen one," she said, looking from side to side with a perplexed manner.

"Then why are you so sure?"

"I'm one of those unfortunates," she replied. "Cats give me the creeps. I can feel them before I've seen or heard them. They make me want to scream. They make me think of death."

Quaile tried to laugh incredulously, but he had frequently heard of people to whom cats are repugnant, who answer to their simple presence with a nervous reaction. Therefore, to credit Dolly, impression was more reasonable than to accept Mike's story of the other evening, than to believe in what McHugh and he had fancied on this stage.

Dolly's assurance at least offered a clue. He spoke of it to the manager who directed Tommy to make an exhaustive search of the place. The next morning Tommy reported his perfect confidence that there was no cat in the building.

For several days, nevertheless, the rehearsals progressed with smooth haste. McHugh had set up the flats so that the stage presented a comfortable interior, approximating the actual setting of the third act. Yet Quaile still responded to the depression of the theatre. It housed always for him a wistful air which seemed to gather and brood in the shadows. He breathed reluctantly its musty atmosphere which from the start had offered an odor he could not name.

McHugh, with a blunter imagination, had recaptured his confidence. He ventured to poke fun at Mike for his recent fright. Even the property man had assumed a less expectant attitude.

But Carlton, who returned after a week, brought back restlessness and dismay to the building. By chance Quaile met him on the sidewalk at the alley entrance. The man did not look very ill, but his eyes were unsteady. His movements lacked smoothness.

Quaile shook hands.

"I'm glad to see you back, Carlton, but you don't like your part," he said baldly.

Carlton was frank.

"You've guessed it, Quaile."

"Going to throw it over?" Quaile asked. "It seems scarcely fair after stringing McHugh along."

Carlton moistened his lips.

"I shan't throw it over."

Quaile took the other's arm and led him to a restaurant across the street.

"I want to talk to you," he said shortly.

He found a quiet corner and ordered a bottle of mineral water.

"Now, for heaven's sake, Carlton, tell me what's up. Don't think I've forgotten the gossip you gave me the other day. You almost make me believe you're seriously afraid of Woodford's."

Carlton looked up.

"Suppose I was?"

"Then," Quaile answered impatiently, "you'd better throw the part over. It's childish. We've worked there for a week. It's all right."

Carlton raised his glass. His voice groped.

"Maybe waiting for me."

"Of course we've been."

"Not you," Carlton said slowly.

Quaile gasped.

"Who, then? You're off your head, Carlton. Should I say, what, then?"

"Probably that," Carlton answered.

It was impossible to read derision in his voice, or to suspect a hoax in his haggard appearance. Either the man had been drinking, or else he was, for the moment, unbalanced. Those alternatives must have been in his own mind, for he burst forth defensively.

"I'm not off my head, though I'd rather think what you do."

"Good Lord, Carlton! You haven't been brooding over that old woman's talk! Or have you heard something?"

"I've heard something," Carlton said.

He drained his glass and set it down.

"I believe you're friendly, Quaile. I'm glad to tell somebody this. I want somebody to know if anything goes wrong in there with me this afternoon it won't be an—accident."

"What are you driving at?" Quaile asked.

"I mean," Carlton answered, "that I've forced myself to come down today to find out if there is actually a force in that theatre capable of preventing me playing Woodford's part."

It annoyed Quaile that his scorn rang artificially in his own ears.

"What am I to think of you? I realize now that the day of the reading you were not sick. You were afraid."

"You're right. Principally the latter," Carlton admitted. "I'd had my first warning that afternoon. The second came the next night."

His face twitched. He looked up appealingly. The word, however, stimulated Quaile.

"Warnings!"

"Yes. There have been several."

Quaile's interest grew. Warnings were tangible factors whose source could be traced.

"How did they come?" he asked eagerly. "Letters?"

"Out of the air," Carlton answered. "That's as near as one can put it. Out of the air. Don't think I'm mad, Quaile. They seemed to be from Woodford."

Quaile sat back.

"Have you been fooling with spiritualists? That's absurd. Tell me definitely about these warnings."

As Carlton was about to answer Tommy rushed in from the street on the wings of duty.

"Better hustle," he cried. "I've been looking everywheres for you two. Mr. McHugh's getting hotter by the minute."

He snickered, pointing at the bottle.

"Funny habit! I wouldn't face what you have to for a glass of water."

The worst of it was Tommy clung. Carlton had no opportunity to speak privately, nor Quaile to urge him before they were in the presence of the irate manager.

"Too bad you're only a week late, Mr. Carlton," he snarled.

Quaile clambered across the footlights, walked to McHugh, and whispered:

"Let it go. Another queer angle! We'll get it out of Carlton after rehearsal."

"All right," McHugh called. "Mr. Quaile takes the blame. You ought to be ashamed, Quaile, to make a little fellow like him late for school.

He clapped his hands.

"All your first act props on, Mike?"

"Yes, Mr. McHugh."

"Then chase your shadow off the stage. Get set, everybody. Mr. Carlton ought to know his part. No books today. Tommy, you hold the script, but don't prompt until you're sure they've nothing on their minds but their hair. Dolly! Smith! Ready for your entrances. Orchestra!"

He whistled a few bars, off key, from a popular song.

"Curtain!"

He hauled at thin air with his hands.

"Empty stage. Enter Dolly. Came on, Dolly. Don't look as if you were pleased to see me out here. Remember the sheriff'll close you out if you don't get away with this marriage. Now for the dirty work! Ha, ha!"

They stumbled through the first two acts to an accompaniment of valuable sarcasm.

Carlton held Quaile's attention. The mechanics of a good actor survived, but that was all. His work showed no animation. His voice was uneven, his gestures futile. Quaile, as the third act started, watched the man grasped closer and closer by a vigilant morbidity. The meaning of such surrender became clear to him. It was logic that Carlton, considering his state of mind, faced with, reluctance the big scene during which Woodford had died. It was at that point that he had left the day of the reading. It was there, doubtless, that the warnings of which he had spoken had centered. Yet what could conceivably happen? That the lights should expire again was unthinkable. But Quaile confessed his doubt by strolling down to the footlights and leaning over so that he could see the switchboard.

Dolly's sharp exclamation altered his thoughts. He turned to the old woman. The color had left her face. Her eyes sought every corner of the stage, even explored the shadowed auditorium.

"What's this?" McHugh roared. "Jump on the chairs, girls. Dolly sees a mouse."

But Quaile knew, and he guessed that McHugh knew, what had startled the woman. He tried to caution her with a glance, but her eyes were still vainly seeking. She spoke from a tight throat.

"No. But I tell you there *is* a cat on this stage."

Carlton swayed against the table. He clutched the edge, staring at Dolly with the ardor of one who has seen a prophecy fulfilled.

"I didn't see any cat," McHugh said.

"I feel it. I know it's here," Dolly answered.

She shuddered.

"It frightens me. What does it want?"

Barbara tried to quiet her.

"It's all right. There isn't any cat."

McHugh chose a different method.

"Where's Dolly's cat?" he scoffed. "Somebody find it. Dolly won't be happy till she gets it."

The twisting of the manager's fingers behind his back betrayed to Quaile the fact that he was acting.

"Tell me one thing," McHugh said. "Can we go on with the rehearsal, or will I have to send out to a fur store for a pussy?"

Dolly shrugged her shoulders.

"I'm sorry," she said, "but I was certain."

"Then fire ahead," McHugh directed. "Barbara! Carlton! Put some life in this. It's the big scene, but it would draw more spoiled eggs than roses the way you're playing it."

Carlton took a long breath. He straightened. He resumed his interrupted speech. His voice lacked body. Barbara's manner, too, was without assurance. Her denunciation failed to ring with conviction. When she defied Carlton, telling him the police were in the house, the words scarcely carried to Quaile at the footlights.

Carlton followed the business with an automatic precision. He walked to the mantel and snatched up the heavy candlestick. He had the bearing of a somnambulist, the appearance of one who paces in that gray borderland with a fatalistic and unalterable purpose.

Quaile wished the rehearsal was at an end.

Dolly, according to the directions, screamed her line.

"Marjorie! Look out!"

Barbara shrank against the wall, her hands raised, gasping:

"Be careful! What are you going to do to me?"

Abruptly, while Quaile started back, another sequence intervened with an ease and a rapidity not to be borne.

Carlton turned, lifting the candlestick, about to start forward. His lips moved. The words came huskily.

"Pay what debts I can. Kill you, if the strength—"

The candlestick slipped from his hand. His voice died away. He toppled, crashed to the stage, lay motionless, his pallid face upturned to the shadows beyond the lights.

The rest held their poses of the moment statuesquely. The very point, the very line at which Woodford forty years ago had died! It was Dolly's scream that released them.

Quaile, as he vaulted the footlights, saw the old woman spring back as though something in passing had frightened her.

He ran to Carlton's side and knelt. McHugh came up, breathing hard.

"He's fainted," the manager said. "Tommy! Get some water here! Quick!"

Quaile stretched out his hand and fumbled beneath Carlton's coat. He snatched his hand back. It was as if he had touched a forbidden thing and shrank from some unavoidable and erratic punishment.

"Good God, McHugh! Not fainted! There's no use. He's gone."

CHAPTER VI

McHUGH DECIDES TO STICK

MUTE horror bound the little group. They all stared, unbelieving, at Carlton's body. Quaile reproached himself for not accepting the actor's fears more seriously. Why had they let him go on to the point where Woodford had died, the point from which, justly or unjustly, he had clearly shrunk? Certainly there had been sufficient warning. He remembered how the first night steps like Woodford's and his cat's had startled them through the darkness, and the next day Carlton had received his first warning—out of the air, he had described it. He recalled, too, how Carlton had repeated that rumor, which then had seemed the height of absurdity, that Woodford dead, as jealously as Woodford alive, would permit no man to play his part.

The thing was past credence, yet there Carlton lay, stricken. The immaterial and inexplicable puzzle had become a tragic fact. As such it had to be met.

He guessed what the scene must mean to Dolly and Mike, who, forty years ago in the same spot, had witnessed the precisely similar death of a tempestuous and jealous man.

It was a glimpse of Mike's twitching, wrinkled face in the doorway that returned him to a saner mind. It was clear that the property man had surrendered himself abjectly to terror. Quaile arose and grasped McHugh's elbow. Dolly stumbled forward.

"I saw Woodford go like that," the old actress breathed. "I was afraid when I felt the cat—so close."

McHugh shook off Quaile's hand.

"Shut up, Dolly. Mike! What are you staring at?"

For the first time in Quaile's memory the manager's voice was without authority.

"There's been an accident. You better get a cop, Mike. And, Tommy, find a doctor. Get Mr. Carlton's if you can."

The dapper assistant and Mike went. McHugh waited until he had controlled his agitation, then he beckoned the company forward.

"You can go," he said, "and don't talk. Call's for ten o'clock in the morning. I'll have something to say to you."

Barbara, the last to leave, forced upon Quaile's turbulent mind a picture of grief and uncertainty that drew him after her toward the stage door. The fresh air there restored him.

He spoke without calculation.

"I hate to see you go this way."

"Why?" she asked. "Why?"

He stammered a little, seeking excuses for his intrusion.

"Because—because you are shocked—frightened. You look ill."

The manner of her turning on him was unexpected. The beauty of her face was distorted by an unreasonable resentment.

"Why do you single me out?" she demanded on a suppressed note. "Dolly has more need of your sympathy."

He stepped back, waving his hand aimlessly.

"I'm sorry. I—"

She was gone. He did not attempt to follow her.

At a loss, he returned to McHugh. For a brief period they were alone in the theatre with that pitiful and terrible reminder of life's inescapable climax. Constantly Carlton's body impressed him with the fact that the unbelievable had happened, that he was not in the midst of some feverish nightmare from which he must soon awaken.

McHugh had sought the solace of his unlighted cigar. He stared. He had the appearance of one who ponders deeply.

"What about it now?" Quaile said. "Are you still a good detective? Do you think that would help here?"

At last McHugh altered his position.

"I'm Irish," he said, "and proud of it. Maybe we're all a little superstitious, but we're also stubborn, my boy. I'm like old Mike. I don't want to go away believing. Tell me one thing honestly: ain't I in any way to blame for this?"

"Certainly not," Quaile answered.

"Then I'm going to try to be a better detective than a manager. I was doubtful for a few minutes, but, by gad, the supernatural's got to convince me before I give in. This is the place to hand it a chance. If there are human devils at work, this is the only place to show them up. So we stick, Quaile. We go ahead."

Quaile pointed at the silent form.

"You're right," he said. "If Carlton wasn't murdered, deliberately, brutally, the supernatural did for him. The fact that he died at the same point of the play, in the same way as Woodford, is no mere coincidence."

"Not unless I've lost my mind," McHugh agreed.

"What is one to think?" Quaile went on. "As a matter of fact, there was no chance for a human hand. Listen here, McHugh. Carlton told me just before the rehearsal that he had forced himself to come here today to find out if there was actually a force in this theatre capable of preventing his playing Woodford's part. That's what made us late. He started to tell me about warnings he had had—out of the air. He believed they were from Woodford, or Woodford's spirit. I tried to laugh him out of it. Tommy interrupted us before I could make Carlton explain. Anyway, there was and Carlton knew it. He said if anything happened to him it wouldn't be an accident. It makes you doubt your sanity."

"Warnings!" McHugh mused. "Might have made something of those, although he'd probably been fooling with fortune-tellers."

Steps rang with an empty sound beyond the flats. Mike led a policeman on. McHugh directed the property man to go home.

"Don't talk to me now," he said impatiently in response to the other's white-faced reluctance. "Be here in the morning at ten o'clock."

The policeman expressed a brisk unintelligence. While the manager told him how Carlton had fallen he made out his report.

Sometime later the coroner and Carlton's doctor, led by Tommy, arrived. Their proceedings partook of a formality abhorrent to Quaile. After the examination they nodded at each other.

"Strange, but a clear case," the coroner said.

"I wouldn't have expected it of Carlton," the doctor agreed, "but these sudden lesions are beyond forecast."

"What are you trying to say?" McHugh demanded.

"His heart simply stopped without any apparent reason," the physician answered. "I gather it was an emotional part. At the moment he was probably very much in it, was worked up to a high pitch of excitement."

McHugh's reply was indifferent, but Quaile knew it was not the emotional nature of the part that had placed a strain on Carlton. He felt something should be said of that. He waited for McHugh to speak of the warnings. He knew how difficult it was to bring up such a matter in the presence of these practical and contented men. He forced himself to do it, however, when he saw nothing was to be hoped for from McHugh. The coroner and the doctor smiled at each other.

"Don't fret," the coroner answered. "The usual precautions will satisfy you. There will be a more thorough examination. If there's anything wrong we will find it. I'm afraid, young man, this has been a great deal of a shock to you."

Quaile loathed the good-natured pity in the other's voice. He walked out of the theatre.

A nearly sleepless night made him doubt the wisdom of McHugh's obstinacy. What if something like that should happen again? He tried to imagine a subtle material trickery, for men, free from pronounced organic disturbance, don't die that way. No theory offered itself. The autopsy, to which his last hope had clung, verified the coroner's superficial examination. Carlton's heart had stopped without reason. There was no trace of an exterior cause.

McHugh told him that when he entered the theatre the next day. He was early. He felt oppressed again by the musty odor which, in spite of the constant draught of fresh air, never left the building. He forced himself to take a deep breath. He fancied again that he was about to define the odor, to give it a name. But as usual he failed.

He found the manager alone, pacing back and forth with a calculated insolence. After he had spoken to Quaile he stared moodily for some time at the spot where Carlton had fallen. Suddenly Quaile saw temper flash across his face. His mouth distorted by an ugly sneer, McHugh swung around, and, stretching his arms to the shrouded auditorium, raised his voice in a puerile defiance. It was as though he believed there was something there with ears and a soul capable of panic and retreat.

"Why don't you try to take a fall out of me, Woodford—"

The somber place flung back the echoes of his passion. He turned sheepishly.

"I meant it."

Quaile could not jeer. He was glad when the others commenced to arrive. McHugh ordered Mike to switch on more
light. The old man obeyed with a stealthy air of eluding a
presence.

"I've fixed him," McHugh said to Quaile. "I've got him so
he's more afraid to leave than to stay. I don't mind, because
I doubt if there's anything after him, or you, or me. I've an
idea it's the man who plays Woodford's part that we've got
to watch."

His grin was sickly.

"If Woodford's ghost is here it's after him."

"Have you any one in sight?" Quaile asked.

"Yes. Tyler Wilkins."

The name was a relief to Quaile, for he knew that Wilkins, in addition to uncommon ability, possessed a sturdy
physique and a notorious lack of imagination.

"Is it quite fair?" he asked.

McHugh was offended.

"I've always played on the level, Quaile. Wilkins knows
all that you or I know. He jumped at the chance."

"But Wilkins has never been here," Quaile said dryly.

The company, he noticed, was well supplied with the
morning papers. He himself had read the brief paragraph,
recording Carlton's unexpected death from heart failure
during rehearsal, followed by a formal account of his
career.

He awaited Barbara's coming anxiously. He was still
puzzled by her ungracious attitude last night. She walked
in among the last. Except for the subdued note of her clothing and a lack of spirit in her face, she retained no traces
of last evening's tragedy.

He tried to catch her eye. Whether his failure was due to
her purpose or to chance he could not tell. Her nod was
general. It might have been intended to include him.

Miss Hendon went to her immediately, discarding her

former jealousy with the air of one who craves companionship.

McHugh rapped on the table.

"Attention now!" he began. "We're all upset and hurt by the death of a fine boy and a good actor. I've heard the result of the examination. There's nothing queer about Carlton's death. As sometimes happens, his heart just gave out. He'd not been well. He wasn't fit to rehearse, but he had too much spunk. He would go on."

Quaile, standing nearby, heard Dolly whisper to Miss Hendon.

"That's what they said of Woodford."

"Keep quiet," McHugh snapped. "Maybe you're wondering why I'm saying all this. I'll tell you. I don't need an oculist. I see what you're all thinking, so I got to talk to you like a lot of children or ignorant savages. You're remembering he died like Woodford."

He glared from one to the other.

"Nothing in that," he went on. "Just happened so, but any nervous people can vamoose right now. It's sad, but the world can't stop. This revival's going on. I'll make that auditorium look like the Metropolitan Opera House when all the old dames have got their hardware and glass and warpaint on. Say, what's the matter with you, anyway? Didn't you have an education? Haven't you read the papers? But if anybody wants to quit, do it now and no more said, but if you decide to stay, cut out the nervous stuff. If you give me your word now and throw me down later, I'll blacklist you in every manager's office in the country. That's strong talk, but got to be. What say, Dolly? You've earned the head of the class."

"I don't like it here," Dolly said frankly. "I don't like what happened last night, but at my age good parts talk louder than fancies. I can't afford to throw this away. I'll stay, and I'll try not to disappoint you."

"Say, what's the matter with you anyway? If anybody wants to quit, do it now and no more said; but if you decide to stay, cut out the nervous stuff."

McHugh brightened.

"Tommy! Go buy Dolly a box of peppermints on me. Up to you, Barbara."

She seemed surprised.

"I'm all right. Of course. I'm neither a child nor a savage."

Miss Hendon, Quaile appreciated, was of a temperament which would shape its course by the popular trend. Such unanimity was bound to have weight with Smith and Thomas. Moreover, there was a bustling, sunlit world outside.

"Then rehearsal at two o'clock," McHugh said. "Run along and play this morning—all but you, Dolly. You wait a minute."

Quaile gave Barbara every opportunity, but she walked off without once glancing in his direction. He could not understand her attitude, sprung solely, as far as he could tell, from his blundering attempt to reassure her. It irritated him that he should attach importance to the incident.

CHAPTER VII

THE SHADOW OF A PERFUME

QUAILE joined the manager and one old actress.

"I'm glad you'll see it through, Dolly," McHugh was saying. "Maybe you can help me, but I want you to quit these tantrums in front of the others, but don't hesitate to come to yours truly with anything you hear or see or think. Now that talk of yours about a cat yesterday. That got 'em all worked up. Say, you haven't felt anything like that this morning?"

"Yes, I have," she answered, "but not so close. After the way you took me yesterday I knew there was no use speaking of it."

McHugh bobbed his head approvingly.

"That's right. That's right, but come to me and ease your mind whenever you feel like it."

Resolution strengthened her face.

"All right then, Mr. McHugh. It's on your own head. When Mr. Carlton fell I had a distinct feeling that a cat rushed past me just as Woodford's cat did the night he died."

"*Hm-m*" McHugh mused. "That one sat there and fought and scratched, I hear. You're full of fancies, Dolly. Keep 'em from the rest of the company, but don't mind me. You come to me with 'em all."

Dolly was about to speak when involuntarily Quaile sniffed again. Once more he felt himself on the point of giving that elusive, musty odor a name. He chanced to see Dolly's handkerchief on the table. It was suggestive. With a sense of discovery he walked over, picked it up, and raised it to his face.

"Caught cold, Quaile?" McHugh asked. "That ain't yours."

But Dolly had run across and was pulling at his arm.

"What are you doing that for?" she cried.

He drew away, amazed at her anxiety.

"Tell me why you do that?" she repeated.

"I scarcely know."

He turned to McHugh.

"Hasn't the smell of this place ever bothered you?"

McHugh shook his head.

"About what you get in most of the holes on the road."

"Tell me what you mean?" Dolly urged.

"I've never been able to describe it," Quaile answered. "Just now when I saw the handkerchief it occurred to me that it had a hint of perfume. Then I realized that might have been brought in by one of the company. I wondered if it was on your handkerchief."

Dolly breathed hard.

"Was it?" she asked.

He handed her the square of linen.

"Not the least like it. It was more like the shadow of an odor—what you might get from a glove or a handkerchief, closed from the air for many years in an old box. That sounds quite absurd, I know, but perhaps you understand what I mean."

Dolly's lips trembled.

"I understand."

"Then you've noticed it yourself?"

"Yes—last night, for instance, and I would know it

sooner than you, for to me it is like a shadow—the shadow of the perfume he used."

Quaile stared.

"You're sure?"

"Quite."

"What's this?" McHugh asked, sniffing laboriously. "I don't smell any perfume."

"At least," Quaile suggested, "you might take that cold cigar from your mouth,"

McHugh accepted the advice meekly.

"That's so," he said.

But he failed to sense the odor that troubled them.

"Funny I don't get it," he murmured, replacing his cigar. "You say, Dolly, it reminds you of the perfume Woodford used?"

"Yes," she whispered.

"That's curious," he said. "None of this foolishness in front of the company, but you come to me with all your cats and perfumes. I like to talk to you. Coming uptown, Quaile? Wilkins will be at the office to sign his contract."

In the alley McHugh beckoned Mike.

"Say, Mike, I know it's forty years ago, and you probably wouldn't have noticed such a thing anyway, but do you remember by any chance if your old boss used cologne?"

Mike's tired eyes turned with an appeal toward Quaile. It was evident he suspected the manager of crude and distasteful humor. Quaile read into the question nothing of the sort. He disliked, in fact, the very seriousness with which McHugh had accepted Dolly's explanation of the odor.

"Talk up," McHugh said. "If you don't recollect, say so."

"I recollect," Mike answered slowly. "He did."

McHugh turned to Quaile.

"Pretty habit for a man! I suppose, Mike, you couldn't tell me what it smelled like? Don't look at me as if I was trying to borrow money."

Mike shook his head.

"Why do you ask, Mr. McHugh? Once or twice about the stage I've thought—I've thought—"

"You think too much, Mike. It's bad when you're not used to it. I was just wondering what kind of a card the man was. Now that you tell me he smelled himself up with cologne, I know. Come on, Quaile."

Quaile's curiosity was aroused. His questions made it seem possible that McHugh already had a definite line of thought. If he had, he kept it to himself.

"I just talked to Dolly and Mike," he answered Quaile. "Got to start somewheres. Got to pretend to be at work on deep ideas. Don't you know that's the first necessity for a good detective? You seem to think I'm pretty good."

Wilkins was waiting in the outer office. Quaile shook hands with him, more than before convinced of the wisdom of McHugh's choice. The lively eyes, the complexion, ruddy and clean, the shoulders which spread powerfully, all advertised an intolerance of the morbid and unhealthy.

McHugh's secretary thrust her head out the inner room and beckoned the manager mysteriously.

"From what he told me," Wilkins said when McHugh had disappeared, "you must have a neurasthenic lot down at Woodford's. Of course, Carlton's going the way he did must have been an awful shock. I'm glad I never knew him well. I'd have hated to step in his shoes under the circumstances."

"Probably you'll cheer us up," Quaile answered.

The secretary ran out with an air of flight.

"For heaving's sake, Mr. Quaile, the boss wants to bite somebody's head off, and he's asked for you."

Quaile hurried through. Within the sanctum he realized that the girl had not much exaggerated. McHugh's face was purple. His fists beat a tattoo on the desktop. His glance was held by a copy of an early evening paper. Quaile, although he could not read them from where he stood, saw that the headlines were arresting. McHugh lifted the sheet and thrust it in his direction. Then he saw:

"MYSTERIOUS DEATH IN CITY'S OLDEST THEATRE."

"That will cause talk," Quaile said.

"Talk!" McHugh cried. "You talked too much last night, or else some of the company's been blabbing. All the spook stuff's in here."

"The story was certain to be raked up," Quaile answered. "Brutally, I don't see the harm. It's the first time I've ever known you to shrink from publicity."

"Hang the publicity!" McHugh roared. "The more the better so far as the show's concerned. It's the Bunces."

"The Bunces!" Quaile echoed, seeing light.

"Yes. Josiah's read this. Ethel said he'd just telephoned when we came in. Wants me to trot to his house double-quick."

He brought his fist down with a crash.

"Am I at the beck and call of every Tom, Dick, and Harry?"

Quaile couldn't resist a smile.

"It's obvious you don't have to go."

McHugh stormed to his feet.

"I don't, don't I? That's all you know."

He scattered the papers on his desk. He stamped the length of the room.

"Do you think I'd be annoyed like this if I didn't? That gray-headed, shawl-wearing miser told Ethel if I didn't show up by noon he'd apply for an order vacating the lease. Pretty position for a first-class manager!"

"It's clear the Bunces don't like publicity," Quaile said. "Can't say I blame them in this case."

McHugh took his hat.

"I got to go. I got to quiet them. You come along. I might need a witness."

He summoned his secretary.

"Wilkins, contract is all right," he directed. "See that he signs it, and tell him to report at the theatre by two o'clock."

He struggled into his overcoat. He set forth with the air of an early martyr. During the short journey he refused to be comforted.

A taxicab waited in front of the Bunce residence. Mc-Hugh regarded it with suspicion. The stubbornness of which he had boasted was in full control.

"I'll take it to court if they make me. I've said I would see this thing through, and, by gad, I will!"

Watson opened the door. Evidently, he had conceived no doubt of the manager's prompt response. Without words he led the way to the rear room where the presence of the taxicab was accounted for.

Bunce sat, more wrapped and huddled than at their first visit, in his easy chair. His shawl was awry. His scanty hair had strayed from whatever arrangement it had attempted before. He frowned at McHugh. With an angry wave of the hand he pointed to a sleek figure before the fire.

"Mr. Arbutlmot," the old man announced. "I had my brother, Robert, send up his lawyer. Seemed safer, dealing with theatrical people. Now what have you got to say for yourself, bringing a bad name on our property?"

McHugh's jaw shot out.

"I've got plenty to say, but if there's to be lawyers I'll say mine in court where it'll cost you more than it's worth to hear it."

Josiah curved even farther at the waist. Quaile gathered that the financial aspects of a fight were not alluring.

"Maybe we can settle this out of court," he murmured.

"Not in the presence of a lawyer," McHugh growled.

"Don't get me started on what I think of justice, but you make that fellow walk the plank if you want to talk to me."

Arbuthnot moved toward the door.

"I gather," he said, "that my presence is uncongenial to the cultured dramatic profession. Do you wish me to go, Mr. Bunce?"

"Yes, yes," Bunce answered testily. "I'll hear what he has to say. I don't want to be unjust. We can always go to court."

He picked with diffidence at his shawl.

"I suppose you'll charge for this?"

The lawyer turned at the door, smiling.

"It's customary—wounded feelings and all."

Josiah attempted a cumbersome humor.

"Then you'd better look to Mr. McHugh."

His smile receded into a sly geniality.

"You send your bill to Robert, Mr. Arbuthnot. I don't know much about such things."

The lawyer staged a courtly bow and vanished.

"I wish to the devil your brother was here," McHugh grunted.

"You needn't try to come around Robert because he's easy-going," Bunce warned. "He leaves these things to me, and any fool can see you're hurting my property. I don't like my real estate to get a bad name. I like it kept clean."

"Why do you blame Mr. McHugh?" Quaile asked.

Bunce grasped the arms of his chair.

"Isn't it enough to have another man die on the property? Has he got to manufacture ghost stories to advertise his show?"

Quaile started to interrupt, but McHugh, motioned him to silence.

"I'll tend to this, although you can witness that I told the company last night to keep its mouths shut."

He broke into a loud defense. He expatiated on his own

surprise when his secretary had shown him the paper.

"You come right down to it," he ended, "the shoe's on the other foot. If there's any kick coming, it's from me to you. If the lease is to be broken I have the say, and there ain't a court in the state that wouldn't uphold me."

Bunce signaled a negative.

"I told you about the stories."

"They were gas," McHugh said.

"Yes," Bunce conceded. "Nothing like this ever happened before."

McHugh discarded his fighting manner. He spoke earnestly.

"There's something wrong with that property of yours, Bunce. These stories aren't all fakes. You close the house now and it'll never open again. But if I stay I'll make it clean or become a doddering idiot, believing in spirits. Maybe you don't know what I've been telling Quaile. I was a darned good plain-clothes cop in my day, and I'm at work on this business. I'm more interested in that now than in making money out of the joint. If you love your property, Bunce, you'd better ask me to stay."

Bunce's gray, unkempt brows gathered. He reflected for a long time.

"I want to be fair," he quavered at last. "I thought you were playing advertising tricks with my property. You act as if you meant what you said. I'll give you another chance."

McHugh grasped the hairy hand.

"You're something of a sport after all, Bunce."

The recluse picked up a paperbacked book. Quaile caught a glimpse of the title. It had an amorous pungency. Clearly it was a novel of a remote vintage. Then this crabbed eccentric did actually harbor a streak of romance. To that extent he was, as McHugh had said, something of a sport.

Having rendered his verdict, the old man dismissed them impatiently, and they went, satisfied.

After a hurried luncheon they returned to the theatre.

While Carlton's death very naturally threw a pall of regret over the rehearsal, his successor introduced an air of brisk efficiency which did not fail to impress the company. Things progressed smoothly, yet Quaile, alert for the first alarm, waited with a feeling of dread for the big scene.

There was no alteration in Wilkins' manner as he approached it, but after Barbara's denunciation he hesitated. Suddenly he closed his book and walked down.

"This scene is a mouthful, Mr. McHugh," he said. "Of course, I will have to read the part for some days. If you don't mind I'd rather not rehearse this bit until I'm more familiar with it—until I work out the business."

Quaile didn't stop to weigh the circumstances that had called a halt at this significant place. He experienced a distinct relief that Wilkins preferred not to repeat just now the lines and the action that had preceded Carlton's death and, long ago, Woodford's. Nor did the uncertain light in the actor's eyes compel him at the moment. He was more curious as to McHugh's probable response. He shrank from the possibility of an outburst, an angry command to go ahead. He was unprepared for the manager's indifferent nod, and his voice, pleasant, quite unconcerned.

"Maybe you're right. Skip to 'Mother, now you've had the truth.' Come on, Barbara. You never did like that line. All the more reason for hitting it hard. Jump into it with both feet."

The rest was soon over. In spite of the shadow of the tragedy the company disbanded in better spirits.

"If you've nothing to do," McHugh said to Quaile, "you might drop in at the office after dinner. I got to look over some reports. I'm going to give Wilkins a few pointers now."

As Quaile stepped into the alley something detached itself from the black wall of the theatre and moved forward, startling him. Then he realized it was Barbara, and he was glad, for he guessed she had waited for him. Yet her embarrassment at first made an explanation of her strange behavior seem farther away than before. He tried to help her. He found himself ill at ease.

"I wanted to speak to you," she said.

Her voice was almost inaudible. He could think of nothing to encourage her, because he possessed no clue to the impulse of her rudeness last evening. He saw her hand move in a definite appeal. He forced himself to speak.

"I think I know why you waited. Perhaps that's presumptuous of me—"

"No, no," she broke in. "I couldn't go without saying I was sorry. It was kind of you. It was unforgivable of me last evening."

"Why," he asked, "did you resent my speaking to you?"

"I don't know," she answered. "There was no reason. It must have been sheer hysteria. I've never been a victim of that before."

The alley was nearly dark, but they were very close. He knew that she shook as if a sudden wind had entered.

"I wish I hadn't promised Mr. McHugh I'd stay."

He recalled her response that morning, its color of surprise that such a question should have been put to her.

"I've congratulated myself you had the sturdiest temperament in the company," he said.

Her laugh was abrupt, mechanical.

"Don't discard your good opinion because of this one lapse. You'll not treasure my bad manners?"

He held out his hand.

"I can't when you ask me not to."

The slender fingers in his grasp were not steady. They were soon withdrawn.

"And now if I can find a cab—"

He left the alley with her and summoned one. Thoroughly unsatisfied, he watched her drive away. She had taken the trouble to stop him, to admit her fault, to ask indulgence. She had, nevertheless, explained nothing. Hysteria, he argued, would have welcomed sympathy. Again he was conscious of irritation that an incident so trivial should have progressed in his mind to importance. He tried to thrust it aside. He walked uptown, curious as to his approaching rendezvous with McHugh.

CHAPTER VIII

WHEN, after dinner, he reached the building, he saw that only a single light burned in the upper story. There was no one at the door or in the elevator. He had to feel his way up the long, unlighted staircase. This was an unprecedented freak of McHugh's to brood alone in his empty sanctuary. His interest quickened when he paused on the sill and took in the picture framed by the doorway.

The manager lounged in an easy chair. His feet had found comfort among the litter on the desktop. But the startling fact for Quaile was the choking atmosphere of the room. McHugh's features were made indistinct by a cloud of aromatic smoke. A much reduced cigar lay in the ash tray. Another, still active, gleamed in his mouth. The restraint of years had been cast to the winds. For the first time in their acquaintance McHugh instead of chewing on a cold cigar had lighted one, had smoked it, had started another.

He beckoned Quaile in. With an air of deep content he blew maladroit rings across the fetid air. "Don't look at me that way," he growled, a trifle embarrassed. "You're not my doctor. I had to throw him down. You see, I used to smoke a lot when I worked on cases at headquarters, and I had to think about this case tonight. First one tasted rotten.

Second's not so bad. Have one yourself."

In self-defense Quaile accepted.

"But you didn't bring me up here to see you use a cigar humanly for the first time."

McHugh lowered his feet.

"I wanted to talk things over with you," he said with an air of reflection. "I want to get started on this case. I want to know if there's anything in it a man can handle. I need help for that. Now you've got intelligence. You're a bright boy."

"Thanks," Quaile answered captiously. "Sounds as if you were going to ask me something disagreeable. Tell me first: Do you know anything? Have you found a material basis?"

McHugh considered the curling smoke.

"Let's see what we have," he said. "Our lights have gone out and we don't know how. We've heard footsteps like Woodford's and his cat's. Dolly swears there *is* a cat in the place, but nobody's seen it. Then—the big fact—Carlton talks about warnings and dies the first time he tries the part just as Woodford died, and he told you if anything happened to him it wouldn't be an accident. Then along comes Wilkins, who never had a nerve before, and shies at rehearsing that same scene. And Dolly talks about a perfume like Woodford always used. That is a strong case for the supernatural, but I don't want to be driven out and I do want to do right by Carlton's memory. I've been think-ing up here all alone. I'm getting along in years, Quaile. I'd hate to believe there wasn't something beyond, so that makes me go slow on the proud and haughty stuff. You remember that line Hamlet has about more things in heaven and earth. But I hate to think those things mean murder and discomfort. So, for the present, we pay no attention to the supernatural side, strong as it is. We look at the facts as facts, and they seem to point to danger for the man who plays Woodford's part. I want you to keep an eye on Wilkins. Hang around with him as much as you can and try to keep him cheerful. I believe that will help."

Quaile nodded.

McHugh puffed for some time at his cigar. At last he looked up.

"What's more important, I'm looking for somebody I can trust who has the nerve to hide himself in that theatre after rehearsal tomorrow night."

McHugh's intention was plain enough. Quaile shrank from it.

"That's the only sensible course," McHugh went on. "Somebody has to do it. I would myself, although I'd hate to, but that wouldn't be wise for various reasons. It's simple enough to hide there. It would give the supernatural every chance, but, on the other hand, if there are human devils at work they'd probably expose themselves when the house was supposedly empty. Get me?"

He took a heavy key of an antique pattern from his pocket.

"That's the stage-door key. It's a volunteer job. I wouldn't ask anybody to do it."

"Let's be honest," Quaile said. "You're asking me. I'm ashamed to hesitate."

"No more said," McHugh snapped, and, before Quaile could interrupt, had raised a situation which, on the face of it, appeared cruel, unnecessary, grotesque.

"There's one thing you can do," the manager hurried on. "Keep your eye on Barbara Morgan. Get friendly with her. The girl's worth watching."

Quaile sprang up.

"You're crazy, McHugh. You're off the track. What have you against her?"

The manager's eyes seemed drowsy.

"I get all sorts of queer notions," he said. "Often they don't amount to much. I don't like the way the girl's been acting. I told you I'd had my eyes open. Probably nothing to this idea."

Quaile's hesitation had vanished. He spoke eagerly.

"You didn't give me half a chance a minute ago. You broke in with your absurd suspicion."

He picked up the key and put it in his pocket.

"Of course, you can count on me tomorrow night."

"Good boy," McHugh commented. He yawned. "I'm going home to sleep off this nicotine debauch. Tomorrow my doctor'll give me fits. Ever see such a blame fool?"

In the street Quaile noticed it had turned warmer. Numerous clouds had gathered in the west. They sailed low enough to reflect the city's glare, from which they borrowed the tints of a melancholy twilight.

The unusual heat, the imminence of storm, oppressed him. He was angry that McHugh, within a few hours of his own bewilderment at Barbara's actions, should have voiced such an unjust suspicion. At least he would prove that to the manager. But, as his first enthusiasm cooled, he was a little appalled at the task he had undertaken.

Quaile had never labelled himself as superstitious, but the prospect of secretly invading the dark and empty theatre revolted him. It was folly for him to deny the existence of forces beyond those already chained by a youthful and self-satisfied world. With the rest of mankind he had from time to time received intimations, possibly from over the frontier of the explored—freaks of memory; coincidences, scarcely to be accepted; unaccountable dreams. Perhaps it could be explained on the basis of recollection, but from his own experience he was willing to concede that of strong or unique personalities something stimulating survived at the places where they had lived most actively.

It occurred to him that, from newspapers, running through novels, cutting across club and dinner table chatter, rumors of the abnormal had constantly reached him.

But other people's adventures are light in one's own scales. Now the question had come definitely home to him. His answer was made more difficult by the sudden realization of this almost universal hesitancy before such apprehensions.

He turned in at his apartment, a modern and expensive bachelor establishment. The upper hall was bare save for the house telephone on the wall outside his door.

When he had slipped the key in the lock and pressed the knob he became aware of an unfamiliar sound from his rooms. He paused, surprised, for he knew no one was within. The sound lacked power. He could think only of a bell, heard over vast spaces. It carried the mournful message of a bell heard at night—scarcely heard.

He switched on the light and walked—he didn't know why—on tiptoe down the passage. The sound did not vary. It urged him. He went faster, tracing it to his study beyond which there was nothing but the house wall. Yet even here the sound seemed far away.

He pressed the switch, glancing around. His private telephone on the desk caught his eye. It offered an explanation, yet he took the receiver from the hook doubtfully. The attenuated tinkling ceased. He smiled. Decidedly, he was too imaginative.

"Hello! Hello!" he called.

His hand shook. His eyes widened. His lips remained half parted. All at once he understood Carlton's white-faced trepidation. He could guess at last what he had meant by his warnings from the air. For the voice that answered was like none Quaile had ever heard. Its quality was soft and monotonous, yet it beat against his ears with the urgent blare of a trumpet.

"Don't interfere," it flowed on. "Keep away. I prefer to play my parts to empty seats."

"Who are you?" Quaile shouted.

He could not be sure there was an answer, but for a moment he was almost willing to swear that the name "Woodford" had sighed across the wire. He tried to thrust the suspicion aside.

At least the line was now dead. He waited with a growing sense of helplessness. A remembered voice came to him with its pleasant formality.

"Number, please?"

"No number."

"Then hang up."

He obeyed automatically. The thin, remote sound recommenced.

Thoroughly bewildered, he began to reason vaguely. The medium of electricity through which the warning had come appeared to him significant. With an effort he controlled his thoughts. Surely this was some tactless joke of McHugh's, for they had been alone in the office. No one else could have known of his agreement to secrete himself in the theatre tomorrow night. He reached out again for the receiver, but the unnatural ringing and the memory of that voice made him pause. The telephone in the hall would do as well. He would get the exchange manager and trace that call.

He went, followed by the persistent sound, to the hall. The brisk tones of the manager were reassuring, but the response was not to be believed. There had been no call on his telephone since noon.

He cried back his contradiction.

"Not five minutes ago I answered a call. I want to know where it came from."

The investigation that followed brought the same impossible answer.

"There is no question. Your phone has not been rung since noon. It could not have been rung."

It was only when he realized how curious his insistence

must appear that he gave it up.

He turned away helplessly. He opened his door. His ears were met by the unvarying note of a bell, summoning him with mournful vibrations over vast and lonely spaces.

CHAPTER IX

BARBARA MISSES AN ENTRANCE

QUAILE conquered his repugnance. He entered the passage. He crossed the dark rooms to the lighted study where the unnatural bell sound still quavered. He thrust his hand toward the telephone then drew it back. The thought of exposing his senses twice to that incredible experience was abhorrent. He shrank from hearing again the unearthly voice which, claiming the dead Woodford as a source, had warned him away from the theatre. On the other hand, the monotonous, wayward ringing placed inaction beyond his control. If it persisted he could not remain in the apartment. So he stepped forward, gathering his determination.

The bell abruptly ceased. Its echoes seemed to linger in the silence, but when he placed the receiver to his ear there was no exceptional response. The wire hummed until the central girl cut in with her curt demand:

"Number, please?"

"Sony—a mistake," he muttered.

He hung up and, his hands in his pockets, looked about him helplessly. There was nothing to be gained by calling the exchange again. He had already been told there was no question. His phone had not been rung since noon. That fact destroyed his last hope of a rational explanation that

83

McHugh, indulging in tactless humor, had made the call. Still he clung covetously to the idea that McHugh might offer some interpretation. He would face him in the morning. Meantime, he could examine the telephone box, trusting to find in some irregularity there a reason for the strange tranquility of the bell.

For appearance sake the contrivance had been concealed behind a sofa. He drew the heavy piece of furniture to one side, but, as he stooped to inspect it, the bell itself spared him the trouble. It rang out with its normal racket, and he straightened and ran to the phone, assured by that imperative sound that no unusual summons awaited him.

It was the exchange testing his instrument, for in that ordered place his queer insistence was explainable only through disorder somewhere else. He told the man the phone was all right. He hurried the conversation to an end, then turned wearily to his bedroom.

While he undressed several things became clear to him. The unearthly ringing had evidently been timed for his return to an empty apartment, yet, as far as he could tell, no one had known of his visit to McHugh. Certainly no one could have guessed the arrangement he had made to spend tomorrow night in the old theatre. It appeared equally obvious that whoever or whatever was responsible for the warning had resumed the ringing just long enough to ridicule his temerity in attempting to trace such a call; to convince him, as Carlton had been convinced, that it had, indeed, come from the air.

Quaile would not surrender to such madness, but, in spite of himself, his nerves remained taut. He shrank from a repetition of the lawless sound. When he was in bed its imminence continued to impress him. It held him awake. He tossed fretfully through long hours, aware that his sleeplessness was the worst possible preparation for the lonely vigil he had undertaken for tomorrow night. Once he lighted his bed lamp and tried to read, but his mind revolted, yet during those restless hours the nocturnal silence was broken by no unaccustomed sound. His wakefulness went for nothing. It was as if it had been forced upon him by some external cause, as another warning, as an undermining of his will for his formidable task.

With the first dawn he slept a little, but by eight o'clock he was awake, heavy-eyed and unrefreshed.

He breakfasted without appetite and hurried to McHugh's office. He found the manager chewing as usual on a cold cigar.

"What hit you, Quaile?" McHugh asked, glancing up curiously. "Was it an accident or a party?"

"Neither," Quaile answered.

The words stumbled a little. He tried to hide his confusion behind a laugh.

"Only a warning—out of the air."

McHugh started.

"I mean, I think I can tell you now just how Carlton got his fright."

McHugh took the cigar from between his teeth.

"The devil you can!" he exploded.

He sprang excitedly to his feet. He waved his tortured cigar.

"You wouldn't mix yourself up with fortunetellers, Quaile. Any warning you might get can be traced."

Quaile shook his head. It had become clear enough that McHugh had no interpretation to offer.

"I haven't been near the spiritualists," he said, "but it isn't as simple as you think. Listen. I went straight home from here last night. The minute I unlocked my door I heard a faraway ringing. It was so unusual it didn't occur to me at first it could be the telephone. But it was, and a voice as queer as the ringing came over the wire, warned me to keep away from the theatre, said Woodford preferred to play his part to empty seats."

McHugh paced the length of the room. An increasing excitement recorded itself in his face, grew almost to satisfaction.

"Something to go on at last," he mumbled.

Then Quaile understood. In this sunlight which flashed cheerfully from picture frames and glasses the former detective could grasp only the fact of a telephone conversation, a material thing, susceptible of investigation. Quaile hesitated to destroy his assurance.

"Nothing there," he said slowly. "I got the central and the exchange manager. I kept at them until they thought I was off my head. They said there had been no call on my phone since noon."

McHugh paused in his walk.

"Besides," Quaile continued, "it wouldn't explain that unearthly ringing. I took pains to find out that the bell was all right. And, McHugh—please don't think I'm too gullible—but consider the way this warning came over an electrical appliance, through the means of electricity which in itself is a mystery, which is everywhere—as far as we know—throughout space."

McHugh's belligerency strengthened.

"One thing at a time," he snarled. "I tell you I'll trace that call. I've good friends in the telephone company. I'll turn the whole corporation upside down. I'll lay you golden eagles to rubber dimes I get at that call."

"I pray you do," Quaile said fervently, "but I doubt if you've a chance. You see I went through the thing—at night."

After a moment's frowning consideration McHugh advanced and placed his hand on Quaile's shoulder.

"My boy, when I asked you to hide yourself in the theatre tonight, when you agreed to see what went on there when the place was supposedly empty, I believed that the only one of us in real danger was the man that plays Wood-ford's part. Maybe that's so still. But you've had this warn-ing. Call it off. I'll try to make other arrangements."

His attitude was sacrificial. Quaile smiled.

"I'll see it through," he said. "I'm not as easily frightened as Carlton."

"Carlton died," McHugh reminded him.

Quaile stared from the window.

"I've myself to think of," he said. "I'd be eternally ashamed if my knees were too weak to carry me there."

McHugh's face lightened.

"Heaven knows I want your report," he said, "but if you go it's your own responsibility."

"Any way you please," Quaile answered. "I'm no fool. If this warning promises a dangerous fulfilment I'll get out. But I'll do my best to take care of anything vulnerable. I'll have a revolver."

The hand on his shoulder tightened.

"Good boy! I can't help feeling you'll get some expla-nation of what you might call Woodford's ghost, of the force on that stage that makes people die like Woodford died."

Quaile released his shoulder, stepping away. His face darkened. All night, keeping pace with the mystery of the warning, had run his recollection of McHugh's sudden and undefined distrust of Barbara Morgan. Since he was pre-pared to attempt so much it angered him that the manager should have closed his confidence on such a point. He wondered if McHugh suspected him of too personal an interest in the girl. He scarcely knew himself how little or how much there was to raise doubts on that score.

"So that's settled," he said. "There's one thing more before I go. I've been thinking over what you said last night—about our leading lady. I mean your idea that she might have something to do with the mystery. You know

I'd rather believe in spirits. It would be easier."

McHugh's gravity gathered in a frown. He gnawed at his cigar.

"Seems to me when I told you to get friendly with the girl I might have spared my breath."

Quaile reddened.

"What is it, McHugh? If we're going to work together on this thing we must be frank. We must share our knowledge —ideas."

McHugh's frown died. He spoke gently, with an exceptional feeling.

"You trust me, Quaile. You're young and impressionable. You do as I tell you and let me work my own way. I honestly believe it's the only safe course. There's nothing I can give you. I'm pretty well in the dark. Maybe I ought to have kept my mouth shut."

His expression hardened. His tone was no longer moderate. It carried a quality of derision.

"Just the same, don't you let anybody pull the wool over your eyes."

Before Quaile could speak he had stepped back and raised the telephone.

"I'm getting after that call of yours," he said glibly. "I expect to have news for you at rehearsal this afternoon."

So Quaile went, fighting back his temper with the argument that it was only McHugh's desperate desire to find a rational explanation that had led him to turn in such an unlikely and unjust direction as Barbara.

At any rate he must follow the former detective's instructions. Within the limits assigned him he would do the best he could. He took McHugh's first suggestion. He got Wilkins for luncheon. He would spend as much time as possible with Carlton's successor. And he soon found it would not be an uncongenial precaution, for Wilkins was likable, and, except for an occasional outburst of self-satisfaction, good company. During the meal he displayed none of those symptoms which had preceded his request yesterday to omit the scene during which Carlton had dropped precisely in the manner of Woodford's death. In fact, he didn't once revert to the theatre or the revival of "Coward's Fare."

When they were walking down for the rehearsal, however, he let slip one or two hints that his mind was far from clear of the matter. Yet there was, Quaile noticed, nothing about his manner comparable with Carlton's trepidation on the day of his death.

"Melancholy old hole, Woodford's!" Wilkins said.

And a little later:

"Carlton wasn't a man to go out like that. Funny. Darned good actor, too!"

Quaile could guess that the warning so far had been withheld from Wilkins. He questioned what its effect would be on such a personality.

Then they were in the alley and a moment later had invaded the somber gloom of Woodford's. Quaile breathed again the musty odor which, after a fashion, he had at last been able to name— that disturbing atmosphere of decayed things which Dolly had described as the shadow of the perfume Woodford had used.

He pushed open one of the set doors. McHugh had not yet arrived—a decided variation from his habit. The others sat about silently, their glances directed toward the shadow-thronged auditorium. Involuntarily Quaile's eyes turned to the same point. All at once the desolation there swept him with the futility of McHugh's stubbornness. It seemed out of the question that the man could overcome this depression which had affected them all; or discover and vanquish that silent, unseen activity which had already done for one of their number and which, it was not improbable, might threaten tonight Quaile's own life. The shrouded, empty rows of seats jeered at him. Try as he might he couldn't picture them filled with living men and women, voluble, restless, expectant.

His sleepless night already demanded payment. He turned with a sigh, realizing he must show no weakness before the company.

Dolly moved uneasily about at the back of the stage. The old actress called to him.

"No word from our slave-driver?"

Quaile strolled up.

"I daresay he'll be here presently."

He lowered his voice.

"You're nervous. You feel the—the cat?"

She spread her hands impatiently.

"Always. Always—and close today."

Her certainty chilled him. He shrugged his shoulders and turned to Barbara who sat alone on the sofa. As he approached he studied her intently. It was the first time he had seen the girl since McHugh had advised him she was worth watching. Face to face with her the manager's suspicions borrowed an increased distortion. There was no evil in the quiet figure—only a slight melancholy, perhaps, sprung from sorrow, but more probably to be traced to the gloom of this building and its tragedy.

"You look worried, Mr. Quaile."

"Only sleepy," he smiled.

Dolly had followed him.

"I'm jealous," she said with a false good-humor.

"In the old days the authors always made up to me."

Her glance still roved about the stage. Her manner spurred Quaile's discomfort. McHugh's brisk entrance lifted a responsibility from his shoulders, but he didn't like the manager's expression. It was eloquent of failure. As Quaile had feared, he must have found the telephone company completely mystified.

McHugh clapped his hands. His voice was thin with sarcasm.

"I'm sorry I'm so late. I was detained by a sick friend—or wife—or sister. Take your choice. You see how hollow you sound when you try to hand me that sort of dope. Come on now. Let's get busy. No more nonsense. Things got to go smoothly. Only about a week left. We'll rehearse the first two acts this afternoon. Third act tonight."

He raised his voice.

"Tommy! Tommy Ball!"

The dapper assistant stage manager appeared from the wings.

"Put up a call for eight o'clock. Every night now. Make it big so they won't say they were nearsighted and couldn't see it or deaf and couldn't hear me. Dolly! Barbara! Helen Hendon! Come over here."

When the three women had obeyed he faced them accusingly.

"Clothes all right?"

They nodded. He simulated a vast stupefaction.

"My God! You're not women. You're sorcerers! Then bring 'em down tonight. I'll have photographers. I want to get flashes of half a dozen poses for the Sunday papers, and something big for a poster—maybe that third act scene. Understand, you men? No dress rehearsal, but you'll have to get in costume long enough to give me my pictures. Now then. First act. Come on, Quaile. Over the footlights. Or let's walk through like Johnnies."

With a sly motion he indicated the long, narrow passage which ran behind the boxes, connecting the stage and the auditorium. The ruse informed Quaile that the manager wished to speak to him privately. He had an instant's hope that after all he had learned something.

"Well?" he asked eagerly when the door was closed behind them.

McHugh frowned.

"You were right, Quaile. Your warning's got me guessing. Whole telephone company's been working on it. Not a trace. They say the call couldn't have been made."

Quaile braced himself against the wall.

"I had a sneaking hope, McHugh."

"How do you feel about your night's job now?" the manager asked.

Quaile, as he had done before, fought a stifling sensation in the narrow passage which was nearly dark. He attributed it partly at present to McHugh's announcement. He would have gone on, but there was scarcely space to pass the other.

"I told you I would see it through," he said. "Let's get out of here. There's hardly room to breathe."

McHugh's face confessed doubt.

"It's up to you," he said. "Entirely up to you."

Quaile followed him with a feeling of relief into the wide spaces of the auditorium.

McHugh made a point of catching him after the rehearsal. He drove him uptown in his limousine.

"Don't forget your revolver tonight," he warned as soon as they were alone.

"No danger," Quaile answered grimly.

"And have you a flashlight?"

"No. It might be a good thing."

"You bet it would," McHugh agreed.

He spoke through the tube, directing the driver to stop at a convenient electrical shop. He sprang out there, drew Quaile inside, and from an array of pocket lamps selected a short, black cylinder. He insisted on having a fresh battery inserted. He tested it himself. Even in the brilliant store the lamp shot a brighter ray against the showcase, even to the wall. He nodded contentedly and thrust the lamp in Quaile's overcoat pocket.

"You might as well leave me here," Quaile said when they had returned to the sidewalk.

McHugh spoke thoughtfully.

"Then I may not have another chance to talk to you alone. You can be sure of your ground. I mean every door except the stage entrance has been locked and bolted on the inside. The keys are in safe keeping. All you have to do is to look over the place during rehearsal, then account for us as we go out. So when you go back you can be certain you're alone in the house unless there's another way in or out, and that you'll have every opportunity to see. Honestly, Quaile, even after your warning, I can't see you in any great danger down there. It would be easy to hide from men, and, granted Woodford's spirit, it can't get you where it had Carlton. Besides, if you don't like it you can get out. With the curtain up it's only a couple of jumps across the foots and to the stage door."

"Don't worry," Quaile said. "I'll try to take care of my-self."

He walked on to his apartment. He approached the door unwillingly. Suppose that remote and unaccountable ringing should fill his ears again? But silence greeted him from the dark rooms. Undisturbed, he entered and changed his clothing. Before leaving he took a revolver from his bureau drawer—a six-shooter, not new but serviceable—and examined each deadly cartridge and tested the trigger mechanism. Everything worked precisely. He put the gun in his hip pocket and went out.

He dined in one of Broadway's flashiest restaurants, thinking that the music, the motion, the blatant laughter would fill him with material and cynical thoughts. But always a veil of retrospection drifted between him and the swiftly gliding dancers. Instead of the swaying figures he saw Carlton topple and crash to the stage, and above the music he could hear Dolly crying again and again her

assurance of the proximity of a cat, which, however, remained unseen, unheard.

Into that place he had promised to go alone tonight.

He didn't linger over his cigar. A desire to be at work
urged him to hurry toward his vigil.

In the noisy street he continued to call unsuccessfully on
his logic. He only knew he had told McHugh the truth. His
self-respect demanded the action he was about to take. He
must give the supernatural every chance.

When he reached the blind façade of Woodford's he
realized that the neighborhood at this hour lacked its
afternoon's vivacity. Lofts and offices were for the most
part dark. The restaurant opposite no longer seemed
prosperous. A few stragglers drifted into the motion-
picture house. From its doors came faintly the galloping
measures of a mechanical piano. The alley seemed blacker
than usual. Two photographers lounged with Mike in the
stage door. They said little. They glanced furtively over
their shoulders.

Quaile stepped through, nodding pleasantly at the old
property man. He observed streaks of light escaping from
the antiquated doors of the first-floor dressing-rooms but
Woodford's by the passage, with its faded gilt star,
remained dark. Soon the company commenced to appear
in costumes of the period immediately following the Civil
War.

McHugh's nervous humor, when he arrived, was more
pronounced. He summoned the photographers from the
stage door and led them to the auditorium.

"Pictures!" he snapped. "First act group. Scheming
mother. Obdurate child. Disappointed lover. Come on. You
know your positions. Scheming, I said, Dolly. Buck up,
Barbara. Can't you get a disappointed expression, Wilkins?
Think of your tailor. Your faces would look fine on cigar-
store signs. That's better. Dim your lights, Mike. We'll have

to flash these."

Quaile, from the rear, watched the lights go down, heard the fat explosion, saw the sudden greenish flash transform momentarily the faces on the stage into pallid, unpleasant caricatures.

After a number of the groups had been taken McHugh called Dolly, Barbara, and Wilkins down stage again. His manner was hesitating.

"I've got to have the third act big scene for a poster."

He cleared his throat, glancing apologetically at Wilkins.

"No lines, you understand. Just the posing, and you'll have to center it some. Everybody else off the stage. Out of sight."

Quaile, alert as he was, read no change in Wilkins' face. He fancied, though, that the man's shoulders squared a trifle. On his part he had no fear of this quick posing for a picture. It had little in common with the rehearsal of the complete scene, nor was it reasonable to expect it to approach a similar tragic denouement. Yet that moment during which Wilkins held the candlestick aloft was eventually to impress him with as thorough bewilderment as Carlton's death. For the present, however, nothing extraordinary passed. The powder flashed for the last time. The photographers collected their paraphernalia and disappeared. McHugh started the rehearsal.

This was Quaile's opportunity to follow the manager's directions. He felt his way through the darkness of the staircase to the dress-circle. He searched each corner and repeated the process in the balcony. Neither gallery concealed any living thing. He was glad to descend to the auditorium again, for the musty air seemed thicker in those places as the shadows were thicker.

He paused in the box where he had left his overcoat and took the flashlight from his pocket. Armed with this he descended and explored the insufferably dismal depths of the cellar, turning the brilliant cylinder of light in each direction. Afterward he climbed the iron stairs to the flies where dressing rooms were crowded into odd corners, where the decay of the building was even more impressive than on the main floor. In each of these deserted rooms the past seemed to have gathered with a heavy and tangible melancholy. The shapes of former occupants, long dead, entered his imagination. He pictured them flushed with youth and adulation, clinging avariciously to their fugitive glory, as intent on their success as those others who had supplanted them on the rotting boards below.

He was relieved when he had finished his inspection. As he descended, convinced that the theatre secreted no alien presence, he caught some of the dialogue from the stage. McHugh had gone back to the opening of the act. Therefore, when he looked over the railing he was not unprepared to see Barbara in the wings awaiting the cue for her entrance. Her appearance there was strikingly in harmony with her surroundings and his recent thoughts, for she still wore her costume of the period of Woodford's beginnings, and her face, as far as the insufficient light exposed it, was lifeless, as if she had heard and understood what the old building seemed constantly endeavoring to whisper to all of them.

At his step she glanced up, a rapid alarm altering her expression. She moved back with a little cry, quickly smothered.

He came on down and went to her.

"You're frightened."

"It's you, Mr. Quaile!" she breathed. "You did startle me—because I hadn't thought of anyone coming down those stairs just now. I was dreaming of the people who had worn them away. You see—there on the treads?"

He noticed that her color had gone, that her eyes were anxious and curious.

He smiled.

"I'm sorry I frightened you."

They spoke in low tones to avoid disturbing the players on the stage. The tenseness left her pose. She put out her hand toward him gropingly. Her voice was not quite firm.

"Why were you prowling up there?"

"Just nosing around."

She was oddly persistent.

"I don't believe you'd do that here without a purpose. It's too repellent. I know it makes you uncomfortable as it does me."

"Yes," he said. "It's too old. It remembers too much."

She looked away.

"Then why were you there? And I saw you in the galleries. You're not—you're not preparing to take chances with Woodford's?"

Her anxiety warmed him, but it brought also a less pleasant stimulation. It swung his mind back to McHugh's distrust of her. As a matter of fact, her manner was strange. There had been about it something unusual ever since the moment of Carlton's death. Was that tragedy in itself sufficient reason? He desired to throw aside the cloak of discretion with which McHugh had burdened him. Her adjacence, her solicitude in this wan light were a little intoxicating. With difficulty he resisted the impulse to stumble blindly onto a new and debatable path whose end was thoroughly obscure.

He sneered at himself for a sentimentalist. But she came closer, and he sensed the rigidity of her figure again, the difficult resolution of her mind.

"I don't know what you're planning," she said rapidly, "but you saw Mr. Carlton die, and you've heard Dolly talk about the cat, and you've felt—you must have felt what we all have—"

From the stage he heard Wilkins glibly reciting the cue

for her entrance, but it entered his ears unimportantly, and evidently it had not reached hers at all, for she hurried on in a voice so low that he had to bend closer to catch its eager appeal.

"You won't take chances here, Mr. Quaile, with such forces?"

"You don't believe in them really?" he asked, surprised.

Her response was uncertain.

"I don't know. Does anybody know? Can anybody say they don't exist?"

She broke off, breathing hard.

"No one can deny such forces with confidence," he agreed. "But we have to live in the world we know. We have to act by common sense."

Again Wilkins' voice came, expectant, querulous. It did not appear to concern him or her. He timidly touched her arm. She shrank away.

"Why are you afraid for me?" he asked gently.

McHugh's impatience forbade an answer. He roared from the front:

"Barbara! Barbara! Where the devil—"

She sighed. The entreaty of her eyes increased. Then she turned and ran on. The manager's voice reached Quaile scornfully.

"Been playing with Dolly's cat? What you blushing about, Barbara? On with the play!"

Quaile returned to the box and later to the auditorium, swept finally for a time from his distaste for the night's work. Something fresh and provocative had risen from the gloom of Woodford's. It agitated him in a new fashion. It filled him with, pleasant doubts. During the remainder of the rehearsal he found it difficult to turn his regard from Barbara's graceful figure. Nevertheless, side by side with this growing wonder, the seed of McHugh's suspicion flowered.

He forced his glance away from the girl, but he was glad to turn back, for he saw that Dolly looked continually about the house, and her wrinkled face twitched, as if again she answered to the presence of the unseen cat.

CHAPTER X

THE GHOST OF THE PASSAGE

WHEN McHugh dismissed the company he took out his watch. It was eleven o'clock. Fully half an hour had gone before the players had changed their clothing and were ready to leave the theatre. Meantime Quaile stood where he could keep an eye on the stage door. McHugh strolled over and for a time lingered with him, but he offered no fresh instructions.

"We've covered everything as far as I can see. I've nothing to say except if you want to change your mind it isn't too late."

Quaile shook his head. His brief conversation with Barbara had made him anxious to test his own courage. He experienced a boyish eagerness to prove to her as well as to himself that he was not to be startled by shadows.

As he stepped into the alley she came from her dressing-room and passed him. He felt himself flush in response to her glance, questioning, appealing, almost, he would have said, warning.

He watched Mike lock the stage door after the last straggler and pass the key to McHugh. Side by side with the manager he walked slowly down the alley. When the others had disappeared McHugh pressed his arm.

"Go back now and see what you'll see. I'm running

straight home. If you want me ring me up no matter how late it may be."

"All right. Goodbye," Quaile said, attempting an indifferent tone.

He saw the manager turn into the street. Alone he retraced his steps through the somber alley and faced the stage door. He took the great key from his pocket and noiselessly inserted it in the lock. Although he was as sure as a man could be that the building was empty he had determined to proceed as if it might house a multitude of conspirators. So he turned the key quietly, and gently, to prevent the hinges creaking, drew the iron door back.

The way to the cavern lay open before him.

Its unrelieved blackness, its musty air, revolted him. He stepped through, closed the door, and locked himself in, returning the key to his pocket. Now surely no intruder could enter. He had every assurance that he was cut off from human companionship. That very fact, taken with the appalling night, made it difficult for him to deny the possibility of another sort of fellowship.

The memory of what he had told Barbara was restorative.

"We have to live in the world we know. We have to act by common sense."

That made it easier to approach the stage. His familiarity with the place was useful, but as he passed the switchboard he combatted a desire almost uncontrollable to snap back the switches and flood the cavern with light. Why not if he was so sure the house was empty? Then he remembered McHugh's instructions, and he tried to sneer. He was to give the supernatural every chance.

He decided that the center of the auditorium would be his most advantageous position, but he did not attempt the passage behind the boxes. The stifling sensation he had experienced there, was fresh in his mind. From the first he had instinctively shrunk from the place. He thought he knew why. That link which had connected the audiences of long ago with the beckoning region behind the scenes should be crowded with recollections. Between its constricted walls what anciently flavored romance must have entered, and out of it must have fled what disillusion, what unhappiness! It would be simpler not to use it tonight.

On the stage he paused, breathing deeply the offensive air. His isolation in the black and empty house seemed to have sharpened his senses, for the shadowy perfume the dead Woodford had used detached itself more certainly from the mustiness. He tried to read no significance into the impression; but, in spite of himself, it increased his discomfort.

Without sound he clambered over the footlights and felt his way softly up the aisle. He drew back the cover from a chair and sat down. It was the best he could do. If an alarm should come, which seemed wholly unreasonable, he could conceal himself between the seats, he could move the length of the row beneath the protecting cloth.

He took the flashlight from his overcoat and held it ready in his left hand. He kept his right hand in his pocket, fingering the revolver. He waited, oppressed by the darkness, straining his ears to the silence.

Almost at once he doubted the wisdom of the experiment. His imagination was too lively. Constantly it evaded his control. For it the black building seemed crowded, as if its memories had refused to depart and at this hour disturbed the night with a positive but impalpable activity. A feeling of malevolence nearby grew upon him. The perfumed air became poisonous in his lungs. His breath was shorter. A sense of expectancy increased. In spite of his precautions the building might hold something—

He sprang erect.

A quiet sound, like a breeze over water, had set the

darkness in motion, grew now in volume until it resembled a riotous wind, then snapped back into the sodden silence.

He slipped the revolver from his pocket. He weighed it doubtfully in his palm. Of what use could that be? Even after the sudden noise his reason told him that the house was empty.

Quaile stiffened. Little by little he raised the revolver. He turned warily so that he faced the pall toward the rear of the house. More startled than he had been by the tempestuous sound, he strained his eyes to penetrate the pall. Through the stillness he had received an assurance that he was no longer alone. Somebody, something stared at him from back there—something for whom the night could construct no barrier—something that forced upon him the imminence of a unique danger.

Stubbornly he tried to tell himself it was fancy, but the sensation of a calm and malevolent regard did not weaken. It was only a moment before he received an abominable verification. A new sound, stealthy, calculated, vibrated through the theatre, and his mind went back to that first afternoon when Mike had cried out his terror; and now Mike's state of mind admitted more excuse, for this new sound was of a man walking with a difficult limp, and it came from the dress circle which he had recently searched, which a moment ago he would have sworn was empty.

The one who had stared must have stood at the balcony railing, appraising him who, perhaps, was the real intruder in this desolation.

The steps receded toward the top of the gallery. They turned there in the direction of the stairs and after a moment were shambling down as though each forward movement marked the conquest of a supreme pain. Soon he knew they were on the orchestra floor with him, were dragging along his aisle. Doubtless because of their nearness a new sound, scarcely more than a mental perception, now filled the intervals between their progress. It was the subdued approach of a cat close behind the limping feet.

Taken with his remembrance of that first day it was the final proof. Dolly was right. Of course she had always been right.

Quaile waited hypnotically. There was a fascination about this unseen advance which continued with a measured and unguessable purpose.

He answered to fear. His pounding heart, the shaking of his hands would not let him deny it. But a greater quality than fear held him there. It was for such a moment he Had been placed alone in the theatre. Yet it was for his own sake rather than McHugh's that he waited for this presence he could not see and which had already gathered about itself a legend of supernatural evil.

Steadily the limping steps came nearer. The feline pattering grew more clearly audible. He would wait until both were close before flashing his light in order that at last he might surely see what was responsible for these sounds which approximated the peculiarities of the dead Woodford.

In a moment now—for the footsteps did not vary—if he reached out through the darkness—

He raised the revolver. He pointed the lamp.

"Now! Who are you?"

The words burst forth involuntarily as he snapped the control of the lamp.

The sharp click cut across the black air, but the blackness was not altered. No shaft of light tore through it to the shambling presence and its stealthy companion.

With a feverish haste he snapped the control again and again, recalling the fresh battery he had seen inserted, remembering how short a time ago he had depended on its brilliance for his search.

The footsteps, unhurrying, limped down the aisle,

crossed at the bottom, and entered the narrow passage behind the boxes. In there they ceased.

The useless cylinder slipped from Quaile's fingers to the floor and rolled beneath the seats. Without its light he was helpless. The realization conquered his passionate disappointment. Moreover, he could not doubt that whatever had passed him was, through some unnatural means, responsible for the lamp's failure. Already last night's warning was sufficiently justified. There was no virtue in remaining to combat an enemy who could render useless any material attack or defense he could devise. He had followed McHugh's wishes and his own logic. He had given the supernatural every chance. His logic had for the present been defeated. There was nothing to do but go if he could, for his confidence had not survived the last few moments unscathed.

McHugh had said it was only two jumps across the footlights and to the stage door. Perhaps silence was no longer of value, but he felt his way cautiously along the shrouded seats and tiptoed across the orchestra pit. He raised his hands there to climb to the stage.

He drew back slowly with a choking throat. His hands had touched canvas. Since his entrance the curtain had been lowered. He could not doubt that his escape had been cut off save through the stifling passage from which he had always shrunk, where the footsteps had stopped as if whatever was responsible waited for him.

He cursed the foresight which had made McHugh fasten the doors at the front, for it was impossible to remain here without light, constantly aware of a companionship which could not rationally exist, but of whose actual presence he had had too much confirmation.

He told himself that the limping thing in the passage was no more than human. Armed with his revolver he had no fear of a man. For an instant the prospect of physical struggle stimulated him. He groped his way to the entrance and, his revolver extended before him, stepped into the passage.

Immediately he knew he was not alone. All at once the footsteps strayed close at hand. The purring of a cat was in his ears.

Angrily he gestured at the darkness, as if it were a tangible force, and took a step forward. Then he paused, recognizing the uselessness of ordinary courage. His way was barred, but not by a man.

There was something, not illuminative, but like light in the passage—a half-seen radiance which gathered ahead of him. It faded. It strengthened again. He could not fight that. He shrank back. The footsteps were closer. The purring was more contented. He thought that the nebulous light commenced roughly to assume the lines of a figure. Blind rage drowned calculation. He pointed the revolver at the impossible thing.

"Look out," he muttered. "I'm going to shoot."

He pulled the trigger. The explosion deafened him. It filled the passage with a choking, pungent smoke. But the bullet altered nothing. The footsteps did not falter. The purring increased. Behind the veil of smoke the pallid light grew.

Quaile lowered his arm with the revolver. He shrank against the wall, protecting his eyes with his arm, helpless, no longer able to doubt that the ghastly light was with an extreme rapidity gathering shape to attack him.

CHAPTER XI

THE PRESENCE IN AN EMPTY HOUSE

TRUOUGH interminable moments Quaile remained crouched in the passage, his eyes hidden by his arm, unwilling to look again at the growing splotch of unnatural radiance which he had fancied assuming the outlines of a human form. He was alone in the theatre with this livid thing, and all the pensive memories the place sheltered seemed urging it to some eccentric disciplining of his pre-sumption.

He had reached the point of surrender. Further effort on his part was futile. The ghostly ambush had been too carefully arranged. The failure of his light, the mysterious lowering of the curtain, had driven him too certainly into this choking passage where the limping footsteps still strayed, where the contented purring of the cat persisted. It was useless to retreat to the auditorium whose darkness would unquestionably cloak farther irrational horrors. It was simpler to await the attack here, to resist it here if he could. He wondered if he would be more successful than Carlton who had died. He knew it would come now, for the limping thing was closer.

Without warning a violent pounding reverberated in the meagre space, shattering the silence which hitherto had been disturbed only by the stealthy manifestations of the theatre. It grew in volume. It animated Quaile's frozen senses. For there was nothing immaterial about its urgency. A living person stood in the alley, demanding admittance at the stage door, offering him rescue from his unconformable antagonist. Only a few feet of darkness and the iron door separated him from safety. Somehow he must conquer that journey. He would do it in spite of the pallid thing that blocked his way.

He lowered his arm and opened his eyes. As if it had reacted subtly to the material racket, the luminous mass ahead was dimmer, less shapely.

Quaile's muscles tightened. With outstretched hands he stumbled forward against the fading thing which did not fall back. He had a sensation of walking through a medium scarcely perceptible—less troublesome than the water which opposes a swimmer. As he pushed the passage door back another sound keened in his ears—as nearly as he could define it, the groan of a man abandoned to an unbearable anguish.

He dashed across the wings, thrust the key in the lock, and threw his weight against the stage door which swung back, precipitating him into the alley.

He drank in the cold, clean air. He responded to such a sense of freedom as a man must experience who is reprieved at the edge of the scaffold.

He leaned against the wall of the loft building, staring back at the open door which made a sable scar in the dim glow of the alley. From the street lively and familiar sounds reached him. With the rapidity of a miracle the strain had been broken. The reaction threatened his restraint. For a moment he had an absurd feeling that it must falter into a sob of relief. To save that, since his emotion demanded some expression, he laughed. The sound, uncontrolled, neurasthenic, was restorative. It ceased abruptly, and, although he was still shaken as if by an abnormal cold, he commenced to take stock of his position and to reason.

First of all he was interested in the whereabouts of his rescuer. Surely during the moment it had taken him to unlock the door and stumble into the alley there had been no time for anyone to reach the street unseen. After all McHugh was the only likely person, for who else had known certainly of his intention to remain in the theatre?

"McHugh!" he called in the strained voice with which one addresses a possible emptiness.

No answer came, and it occurred to him that in any case McHugh would have had a key, would scarcely have raised that infernal racket at the door.

He examined the wall opposite more closely. There was just one hiding-place—between the open door and the side of the theatre. Whoever had knocked must lurk there. He took a step forward, grasped the door, and swung it shut. A figure, darker than the wall, shrank back. The light was insufficient to show him more at first than the form of a woman.

"Who are you?" he asked.

The woman did not reply. She was slenderer than Dolly. Then, before he had seen her face, the truth came to him.

"Why do you hide there, Miss Morgan? Come out, please."

She stepped away from the wall, but still she said nothing, and, on his part, words were difficult. Instead of gratitude for the release she had brought him, he experienced a sharp regret. The disclosure of the young actress's identity for the first time offered a substantial reinforcement of McHugh's suspicions. For why should she have come at this hour? How could she have been so sure of his danger? On the other hand, the very fact that she had drawn him from that danger was in her favor. Her proximity, her continued silence, were eloquent advocates. The mystery in there too convincingly approached the supernatural. For McHugh to try to connect her with it was ridiculous. His pulse quickened. Her presence could be accounted for in a happier way. The anxiety she had expressed for him earlier in the evening must be responsible.

"Why are you so silent? Why did you come here at this hour? Why did you knock as you did at the door?"

She shuddered. At last she spoke.

"I heard the footsteps, and a shot, and something like a groan. I've been afraid to ask. I—I—You're not hurt?"

He shook his head.

"No one was hurt as far as I know."

But he questioned if the groan he had heard at the last could have been the result of his shot. If so, plenty of evidence must remain in the theatre. The possibility encouraged him. He began to reach out again for a reasonable explanation of all that he had experienced.

"Then," she said, "you fired the shot?"

"Yes."

"Why?" she asked.

He attempted a laugh.

"An accident."

She turned away.

"You won't tell me the truth."

She faced him immediately again with an air of accusation.

"You don't even thank me for coming when I did."

He was more than ever convinced of McHugh's mistake. She would not have had the courage to assume such an attitude.

"I do thank you," he said, "with all my heart."

"What were you doing in there?" she asked.

With difficulty he made himself follow McHugh's sarcastic advice not to let anyone pull the wool over his eyes.

"Doesn't my question come first?" he asked.

"You mean?"

"About your coming here at this hour."

She gestured impatiently.

"As I told you, I guessed when I saw you prowling about the house during rehearsal that you were planning to take chances with Woodford's. Your manner later proved it. And after the others had gone I waited on the sidewalk some time for a taxicab. When I left you hadn't come out of the alley. Of course it was none of my affair, but at home the thought of any one alone down here obsessed me. I might as well confess it. The place terrifies me as it does Dolly, as it did Mr. Carlton, as it does you and the others. I am sure there's something going on here, Mr. Quaile, that we can't understand. It has proved itself dangerous."

Her voice faltered.

"It has made me say and do things unlike me—coming this way for instance. But I couldn't bear the thought of any of you alone here, taking chances with what frightens me so."

His heart responded to her halting confession, but she hurried on defensively.

"It made no difference who was here, I felt I had to come. And you found danger. I know. Something happened that made you afraid, or why did you fire your pistol?"

He tried to see her eyes in order that he might read a denial of the impersonal grounds on which she had based her interference. It was too dark.

For the second time that night he answered to the magnetism of her personality. Now he offered less resistance. Their detachment from the rest of the world in this secluded place, veiled by a half darkness, gave to the present a false and galvanic value. The obscurity of the future ceased to interest. He longed to throw reserve to the winds. He wanted to talk now at random about an emotion he scarcely understood. His answer was pitched low. His tone, he felt, was an avowal.

"Suppose I was afraid? Isn't it unkind to remind me of my cowardice?"

"Would a coward have gone in there alone at night?"

He reached out quickly and grasped her arm. Uncalculated words were in his mind, crying for expression.

She sprang back, freeing her arm. Her quickened breath was audible.

"You understand—" he began.

Her laugh had a desolate ring. It trailed away.

"I understand," she said, "how foolish my coming here must appear to you. If you don't mind I shall go now."

He repented his precipitancy.

"Wait," he urged her. "I was about to say things— You're probably right. They're better unsaid now. Perhaps you'll try to explain my impulse by gratitude. Something did happen in the theatre. I was glad enough to get out. You gave me my opportunity. By every law of reason there's a man inside. As you say, he's dangerous. I don't pretend to understand his magic, but that door is his only way out, and we haven't seen anybody leave."

"You're not going back!" she said quickly.

He did not yield again to his impulse.

"Not alone."

"Then why should I wait?"

"Because," he answered, "I want you to help me."

"You're too sure of a man," she said. "You're forgetting Mr. Carlton."

"I'm doing my best to forget everything except common sense," he answered. "I'm going to try to find the source of all I heard and saw in that house."

"I've no faith," she said, "but I'll help you. What do you wish?"

"As you see, I can't leave here. I want to watch that door. Would you mind telephoning McHugh for me? Tell him to hustle right down."

She nodded.

"That isn't bad. Let him take some of the responsibility."

"Then," he directed, "I want you to bring back the first policeman you can find. We'll put it up to him. We'll switch on every light. We'll search the place from top to bottom for that limping trickster and his cat, and, by gad, we'll find them. Don't you see? We must find them."

But she failed to share his enthusiasm.

"You won't go in until I get back with a policeman?"

He was honest.

"I've no desire to enter that place alone again."

She turned and walked away.

"Then I shan't be long."

He watched her graceful figure go down the alley and into the lighted street.

He braced himself against the wall opposite the iron door, and, his hand on his revolver, waited.

It was pleasant to recall the girl's recent companionship. The new problem she had brought to him had a little modified the horror he had experienced in the theatre. He could look forward with a real hope to the approaching search. If his bullet should have struck a man!

On the whole he did not regret his romantic impulse or the revelation it had given her of his feelings. He was, perhaps, glad that nothing definite had distilled from it. Yet her response, half angry, had been unexpected. It troubled him.

It was nearly a quarter of an hour later when Barbara conducted into the mouth of the alley a policeman—an elderly man, a relic, Quaile guessed, of the less sophisticated days of the force. He came up to Quaile and looked about with a slightly confused manner.

"You sent for me," he said. "The lady didn't quite make herself clear. Talked about a man hiding in there, then didn't seem so sure."

"It was difficult," Barbara put in. "Maybe you can make him understand."

Quaile attempted to explain.

"I've had a queer experience," he began.

He nodded at the closed door.

"I was alone in there—quite alone, I thought. I heard someone walking around."

"Couldn't you see who it was?" the policeman asked.

Quaile cleared his throat.

"There were no lights."

"That's funny," the policeman commented. "What were you doing in there without light?"

"It makes no difference," Quaile said irritably. "The fact remains that I was in the dark, and when I heard this—this man I couldn't get to the lights. It rather frightened me, because I had been so sure of my solitude. I started for this door when—when—well, I know somebody tried to stop me. It all seems very vague, but you must take my word that there's a man in there who has no business. I fired a shot at him. If you'll help me bring him out I'll make a charge of trespass or whatever you think necessary."

The policeman considered.

"This is Woodford's Theatre," he commented as if he had said a great deal.

"What of it?" Quaile asked.

The man lowered his voice.

"I read in the papers about that actor Carlton's dying inside. First and last I've heard a lot of talk about Woodford's. Now let me get it straight. You didn't see this man, but you must have felt him when he tried to stop you."

Quaile knew what the policeman was driving at. It was difficult to believe that the dread of Woodford's had run so far.

"I didn't feel him," he answered, "and, if you don't mind,

I prefer not to be put on the witness stand before I get to court."

"Then," the policeman said bluntly, "the only evidence of a man is footsteps you thought you heard in the dark?"

"Is it the dark that makes you hesitate?" Quaile flashed.

Barbara held up her hand.

"It would do no harm to look around," she said to the policeman.

"That was stupid of me," Quaile apologized. "The switchboard isn't far in. We can light the place up. You stand in the doorway while I go—"

Barbara reached out to him.

"No!"

Her voice failed. The policeman looked from one to the other curiously.

"Seems to me," he said good-humoredly, "we're three nervous people. I don't mind saying I've heard too much about this building to like it. That's all talk. As the lady says, it'll do no harm to go in and take a look around for your man."

He grasped the handle of the door and pulled. He turned, a little surprised.

"You must have locked it when you came out. Where's the key?"

Quaile could not believe.

"What are you talking about?"

"This door is locked," the policeman said.

"Nonsense," Quaile cried.

He sprang forward and tugged at the handle. He stepped back, bewildered.

"You didn't lock it?" the policeman asked.

"No, no," Quaile answered, "I left the key on the inside."

He remembered how the door had stood open until he had swung it shut to discover Barbara's shrinking figure. It offered testimony apparently beyond dispute that there was, indeed, a man in the building. He spoke of that to the policeman who could only agree.

"Then you'll have to break the lock," Quaile said. "Try your nightstick."

But the policeman shook his head.

"You don't own the building?"

"No."

"Or hold the lease?"

"No."

"Then you'll have to get me authority. I won't break in without it."

Quaile started to urge him, but Barbara interrupted.

"He's right."

"Then what about McHugh?" Quaile asked her. "You got him?"

"Yes. He hadn't gone to bed. He said he would start right away. He shouldn't be long now."

"Arthur McHugh, the manager," Quaile explained to the policeman. "He holds the lease. He'll give you all the authority you want."

"Then we'd better wait," the policeman said.

They stood in a group opposite the puzzling door, and minute by minute Quaile's impatience grew to search the place for the one who had harassed him, had driven him out, then had silently turned the key.

McHugh didn't keep them long. He stormed through the mouth of the alley. He paused just inside.

"It's dark as Egypt. Quaile! You there? Come lead me up."

Quaile resented the shallow stratagem. He knew that the manager desired to talk to him apart from Barbara. It was wiser to obey, so he hurried down.

"Well? Well? Quick! What's happened? What's the girl doing here?"

In a few words Quaile told him of the sound, as of wind,

of the limping footsteps through the darkness, of the failure of his light, of the lowered curtain, of the pallid ambush in the passage.

"It was like a figure in cold, white flame. Then she came or I don't know—"

"She came, eh?" McHugh snorted. "How did she guess?"

Quaile paid no heed to the question.

"I fired at the thing, McHugh. A few minutes afterward I heard a groan. I thought it was meant to frighten me, but I might have hit. The queerest thing—the door's been locked from the inside as we stood in the alley."

McHugh found a cigar and commenced to bite on it.

"Fine! Fine! Then I guess maybe you did hit. I knew you'd do well, my boy. Now we'll get somewheres. Who's that? There's somebody with the Morgan girl."

"A policeman," Quaile said.

"That's good. You're bright, Quaile. Come on. Looks as if we had something up a tree at last."

He grasped Quaile's arm and strode to the policeman.

"I'm Arthur McHugh," he announced. "Break that lock if you can. Maybe you can't unless you've got some loose dynamite about your clothes."

"Do my best," the policeman said.

He raised his night stick and took hold of the door handle. He started back, crying out. The door swung lazily back.

"Thought you said it was locked," McHugh grumbled.

"Tricks!" Quaile muttered. "Deliberate mockery."

"I didn't hear any key turned," the policeman said, "but we know he's there."

The strange and derisive incident angered Quaile.

"Then let's get him."

But as he sprang forward McHugh caught his arm.

"Easy!" he cautioned. "Make way for the law. Haven't you any manners?"

He beckoned the policeman.

"Come ahead. I'll find the switchboard. Quaile, you hold the doorway. We'll keep our friend bottled."

He stooped and struck a match. Its light flickered on the serious, set face of the old policeman.

Confessing an unwillingness equal to Mike's on that first day, the policeman followed McHugh across the threshold.

Quaile stepped to the sill. Barbara after a moments hesitation joined him.

"You needn't, you know," he said. "If you'd rather go—"

"I want to stay," she whispered. "I want to see."

CHAPTER XII

THE ANTICS OF A LAMP

THEY watched the match cast huge, distorted shadows. The progress of McHugh and the policeman made a hollow sound which loosed many echoes. It had little in common with the limping steps Quaile had heard. Then the manager was at the switchboard, and light flashed against the tawdry walls and exposed the void of the auditorium. Quaile took a step forward.

"The curtain, McHugh!"

"Why, yes," McHugh drawled. "Seems to be up just as I left it."

He directed the policeman to search the auditorium and the galleries.

"Try every door," he said. "Go through every corner."

He strolled back to Quaile.

"Thought you said the curtain was down. You been dreaming?"

"The whole thing seems a nightmare," Quaile answered, "the door, too, but I've witnesses of that."

"So you have," McHugh mused. "That's no dream anyway."

For the first time he spoke to Barbara. He faced her with a brutal abruptness.

"What you doing here?"

Quaile studied the girl anxiously, expecting an awkward and insufficient excuse. The rapid ease of her reply, therefore, astonished him. Its color of prevarication seemed a worthy defense.

"I guessed Mr. Quaile was coming ghost-hunting to-night. I couldn't resist the temptation. I hoped he might let me join him, but I got here too late."

McHugh chewed thoughtfully at his cigar while he considered her face. It expressed only surprise at his manner. At last he took the cigar from his lips and smiled genially. His attitude no longer threatened an inquisition. Quaile had an uncomfortable feeling that both Barbara and the manager were masked.

"Nervy girl!" McHugh grinned. "I like nervy girls myself. Glad to know there's one in the company who isn't afraid of Woodford's spook."

She smiled placidly back at him.

"I'm much more afraid of you—naturally."

"What's that? Oh! Now maybe you'd better run home and get your beauty sleep."

He waved his cigar.

"Not that you really need it."

"I'd like to stay and see the excitement," she said.

With quick daring she placed herself on unassailable ground.

"Then, perhaps, somebody will see that I get home."

McHugh didn't disguise from Quaile his gesture of distaste.

"If that's the way you feel, all right."

He drew the stage door shut, locked it, and removed the key. He examined the key closely before dropping it in his pocket.

"Just the same," he said, "this door's worth guarding. The cop doesn't seem to be finding much out there. Suppose you run through the dressing-rooms and the lofts,

Quaile. Maybe I'd better do it myself. You stay by this door."

It was obvious that the manager wished Barbara kept under observation as much as the door. Quaile nodded. McHugh took a handful of matches from his pocket and climbed the iron staircase.

Barbara's face had lost its vivacity. She watched the man go with a troubled frown.

"He makes me feel that I'm in the way. Why? Do you know?"

Quaile wanted to throw reserve to the winds. It seemed only fair to tell her of McHugh's suspicions. He forced a laugh.

"The riddles of the sphinx are simple compared with a manager's whims."

"I suppose I'm a fool to stay," she said.

All at once she had grown very tired. He brought a chair. She sat down, sighing.

"Thanks. I'm stubborn enough to wait. I do want to see what they'll find. It's all so queer."

She rested, half closing her eyes. For a long time they waited without words, listening to McHugh and the policeman as they prowled about; constantly on the alert for an alarm.

At last the two searchers met on the stage and with puzzled faces descended to the cellar.

"They've found nothing yet," Barbara said.

Quaile clenched his hands.

"Then they will. Surely down there—"

But McHugh and the policeman returned empty-handed. The protagonist of the supernatural illusion had left no trace.

"But I heard a groan after I had fired," Quaile insisted.

"There's no blood," McHugh answered. "Every door's locked. We've been in each rat hole."

"Except the passage," Quaile reminded him.

He went forward and glanced through. McHugh peered over his shoulder.

"Where did you stand when you fired?" he asked.

Quaile entered and at a distance of several feet faced the manager. In the narrow space the acrid odor of the powder still lingered.

"And where was the figure?" McHugh went on.

"A little in front of where you're standing. Just inside."

McHugh turned and hurried to the rear of the stage where he supplemented the vague light with a number of matches.

"Come here, Quaile," he snapped.

Quaile walked over, the policeman at his heels.

"No dream about that," McHugh said.

He indicated a groove in one of the iron steps, then led them to the brick wall which in one place had been newly flaked.

"Your bullet's there," he announced.

He thrust his finger in a small orifice.

"I can feel it."

Quaile moved uneasily.

"Then it wasn't a man in front of me. He would surely have been hit."

The policeman sniffed.

"Funny smell here. Why don't you air the place out?"

McHugh glanced at him doubtfully.

"Entire case is beyond me," the policeman went on. "Somebody locks and unlocks that door from the inside, then we find there was nobody to do it."

With a motion of significance McHugh put his hand in his pocket.

"Say, you'd look like a fool, wouldn't you, if you reported this case at headquarters?"

"Nothing else to do," the man answered. "Suppose I've

been caught off post?"

"You just let me know and I'll fix it with the commissioner," McHugh said.

Quaile looked considerately away, but he suspected money passed between them. McHugh at least was being honest with the Bunces who owned the building. As he had promised, he was doing his best to keep the ugly scandal from spreading.

"Best not to mention it at all," McHugh advised.

The policeman's voice rose on a note of gratitude.

"I'll do just as you say, Mr. McHugh."

His good night was cheery. He did not attempt to disguise his relief at leaving the building.

Barbara had watched and listened restlessly. McHugh glanced at her. Quaile knew the manager wouldn't catechise him as to the details of his experience in the girl's presence.

"Suppose you'll have to see her home," McHugh said under his breath. "So come to the office the first thing in the morning. I want every little detail that happened while you were alone."

He raised his voice.

"I'm stumped, Quaile. Who locked that door? Who raised that curtain? Not here now anyway. So we might as well all go home and sleep on it. Better pick up that lamp of yours."

Quaile vaulted the footlights and walked up the aisle to the seat where he had waited for the thing that limped. The cover was pushed back as he had left it. He glanced at the dress-circle from which the thing had first imposed its nearness upon him. The whole adventure during the last half-hour had been placed upon such an insecure foundation that he found it difficult to realize he had actually sat there and suffered its elusive phases. The flashlight, however, was sufficiently confirmatory. He stooped and found it where he had remembered hearing it roll beneath the seats.

As he arose he exerted a perfunctory pressure on the control. He braced himself heavily against the seat. A brilliant path of light tore across the auditorium to the farther wall. He snapped it off. The shadows jeered at him.

"McHugh!" he shouted.

The manager sprang from the wings, scrambled over the footlights, and ran along the aisle.

"What's up now, Quaile?"

Quaile saw Barbara step on the stage and look anxiously in his direction. He held up the cylinder.

"This," he said. "I told you when the limping thing went by it wouldn't work. Just now when I picked it up—Look!"

He pressed the control. The light glared. McHugh snatched the cylinder from his hand.

"You found it exactly where you dropped it?"

"Yes."

"Then you were too excited. You couldn't have worked it right."

"Don't think that, McHugh. You can't do any more than snap the button back as far as it will go. I did that time and again."

"This is the strangest thing yet," McHugh mused. "I'm glad you came anyway, Quaile. You've given me a lot to think about."

"For heaven's sake," Quaile cried. "Have you any ideas?"

"Mighty few that you haven't handed me," McHugh replied.

He pressed the control a number of times. The light gleamed, died away, flashed forth again.

"What are you doing with that light?" Barbara called.

McHugh took his cigar from his mouth.

"Maybe signaling Mars," he answered dryly.

"Easy, McHugh!" Quaile warned.

McHugh grinned.

"You've a lot of imagination, Quaile," he said enigmatically. "An awful lot of imagination."

"None about what happened here," Quaile answered hotly.

"We'll make up our minds about that in the morning," the manager said.

Quaile, uncertain, a good deal hurt, followed him down the aisle.

"Can we go now?" Barbara asked as they climbed to the stage.

"In a hurry?" McHugh wanted to know.

She shivered.

"It's cold here. I—I'm afraid. I want to go."

"All right. You and Quaile open the stage door while I put out the lights. Here's the key."

Quaile took the key and led Barbara to the iron door. He unlocked and opened it while McHugh threw the switches. The darkness lowered its black pall as if it had been expectant. McHugh hurried to them.

"It can be dark in here," he said with an uncomfortable laugh. "Got me guessing. No one's gone out, so no one could have been here."

As if in defiant contradiction through the darkness behind them came the sound of limping footsteps.

For a fleeting moment Barbara shrank against Quaile. McHugh stiffened.

"Good God! You hear that?"

Close beside them Quaile caught a gentle padding. From out the pit-like night of the theatre a tiny, lean, black body glided past him, slipped into the alley, and, before he could touch it, before he could convince himself that it had actually been there, had slunk from sight close to the wall. At the same moment the limping footsteps ceased.

Barbara faltered into the alley. Quaile and McHugh

followed. While the manager slammed the door and turned the key Quaile ran up the alley as far as the fence. He found no sign of a cat. He came back, speaking with a decided reluctance. His eyes had had no chance to accustom themselves to the new darkness. The thing had been so rapid, so unexpected, he wasn't confident the others had seen what he had.

"I thought I saw—" he began.

McHugh nodded.

"Then I did, but it went by so quick."

"A shadow," Barbara whispered.

No doubt remained, but like the assistant, Tommy, who had imagined a cat that first afternoon, none of them could be quite sure of having seen a living thing.

"Can't we go? I want to get away from the place," Barbara cried.

Quaile realized the futility of entering again the building which he had twice assured himself was empty, yet which had just given them fresh proof of an habitation, mysterious and not to be accounted for.

"We can't do anything more tonight," McHugh agreed.

He led the way down the alley. In the brightly lighted street Quaile appreciated that the manager was a good deal more moved than he had been even at the time of Carlton's death, yet it was in a different way. As McHugh stood on the sidewalk, gnawing at his cold cigar, he seemed to have grown old, to be actually at the point of surrender to the supernatural.

He turned from an unseeing stare at the arc light on the corner to Barbara. His manner toward her, which had been harsh and contemptuous, altered. He attempted a rough kindness.

"You look sort of sick, Barbara. Remember you're a nervy girl. If old Woodford is walking around inside he's got nothing against you. Don't you worry. And, until we find out what went on in there tonight, you keep your mouth shut. Don't you let any of it get to Wilkins."

Her answer conveyed a reproach.

"You can trust me, Mr. McHugh."

"That's all right," he said. "Now run along home. Quaile will see that nothing troubles you."

He made a wry face.

"What's there to be afraid of out here except trolley cars and automobiles and confidence men and thugs? That's nothing much to be afraid of, is it?"

She took him seriously. Her lips trembled.

"Not much."

"Then I'm walking home. Need a little air. First thing in the morning, Quaile."

He jerked his hand in farewell and started up the street.

"What does it mean?" Barbara demanded hysterically, "the steps like Woodford's, the cat, the things that happened when you were alone—of which you won't tell me?"

"What would be the use?" Quaile said. "You've heard and seen enough. McHugh has sworn to find out for us all, but I think he's a good deal shaken now. That's a taxi over there. Come. We'll rout the driver from his slumbers."

He glanced at his watch.

"It's after one o'clock. A useful hour for all that's happened."

She had controlled herself. She followed him silently across the street and entered the cab. When he was seated beside her the girl's attitude urged on him an increasing sympathy.

"You *are* nervy," he said softly. "Most women would have screamed—made a scene."

Her hand moved, but she didn't answer. During most of the ride, in fact, she remained withdrawn in her corner, and, he fancied, a more profound emotion than fright held her so. He became a trifle ashamed of that unguarded moment in the alley, yet even now he fought back a temptation to break down her reserve with a rapturous materialism.

In a sense he was glad when the cab drew up in a quiet side street before a large apartment house. He helped her to the sidewalk.

"You'll let me thank you again for coming down."

She sighed.

"How odd it must have seemed!"

"Everything," he answered, "has been unusual tonight. I'm glad you've given, me one pleasant surprise to recall."

"I'd rather you didn't remember. I'm a little ashamed."

"I wonder, if you hadn't come—" he said. "Will you promise me not to brood over what you heard and saw?"

She pulled at her gloves.

"It is easy to ask promises."

"You must try."

Her mood changed. She laughed mirthlessly.

"We were all like children tonight—looking for buga-boos. If only we hadn't found them! Now goodbye, and you have had warning enough, haven't you? You won't take any more chances with Woodford's?"

"That really concerns you?" he asked quickly,

"One such tragedy—"

But he wouldn't take her literally.

"I'd rather think your anxiety less general."

She didn't let him go on. She moved away, but he followed her to the door, glancing up at the facade of the apartment house, a new building, evidently expensive.

"This is where you live."

She nodded.

"I wonder," he went on hesitatingly, "if some time I might—"

"When things are a little more settled," she interrupted. "Perhaps after the opening. I'd like you to come to tea."

"You make it too remote," he objected. "So much has happened to throw the opening into doubt."

"Then soon, if you wish," she said, and frankly offered her hand.

It was cold and lifeless in his grasp. She drew it away and walked past the waiting hall boy at the door.

Quaile returned to the cab, and, as the chauffeur drove him rapidly off, fell into a reverie, discontented, almost morbid. At first his latest memories crowded his mind. He no longer questioned that tonight a new element had entered his life. He was not at all sure it was welcome, that its ultimate resolution wouldn't mean unhappiness. For he could not think of Barbara without recalling McHugh's misgivings. They served to remind him, too, that he really knew nothing about the girl except that she was beautiful and possessed a personality which had always appealed to him as provocatively out of the ordinary. With whom she lived, about what interests her non-professional life centered, he had no idea. At the first opportunity he would accept that invitation which he had to all purposes forced from her.

Somewhere there must be an explanation of her moody and undependable actions. He had a sudden fear that the past might harbor it. Carlton's death had altered her. Did that suggest an answer? Could there have been between Barbara and him a sympathy concealed from the rest of the world?

He tried to put her from his mind. He told himself that the reaction from his experience in the theatre, the dusk of the alley, the strangeness of her presence there, the anxiety it had suggested for him, had all combined to fill him with a sentimental folly without real foundation, which consequently could not survive. He was glad it had not carried him too far. Nevertheless, it worried him that her bearing had forecasted an unfavorable response.

At least the incident had served for a time, druglike, to deaden the mental pain of his vigil in the theatre. That surged back now with its impossible details, its impotent horror. He gazed at the streetlamps and the thinning crowds with unbelieving eyes. With a supreme effort of the will he refused to give himself up to the madness of conviction, but the facts slyly whispered that Woodford's was the abode of a mystery, abnormal, perilous, and unconquerable.

He entered his apartment with callous indifference. So much had happened within the last few hours that the prospect of the occult bell had ceased for the moment to terrify him. Silence, however, pervaded the place.

In his bedroom he faced a mirror. His hands tightened on the edge of the bureau. The countenance that stared back was gray and marked by unfamiliar lines. The eyes were bloodshot. The lids twitched. Suddenly the face broke into a cynical smile. The time-worn simile had flashed into his mind—"Like a man who has seen a ghost."

He was glad that the others had in one way or another experienced the manifestations of the house. Otherwise, standing there, his brain turbulent with incredible memories, he could easily have doubted his sanity.

He hurried to bed, and, thoroughly exhausted, slept.

The vivid life of the street awakened him. He gazed from his window at the dawn of a perfect day. His will was stronger. He would not argue the merits of last night's adventures, which had the savor of a bitter dream, until he had talked with McHugh.

Early as he was at the office the manager waited for him. He sat at his desk, staring at the wall with an expression suggestive of a new bewilderment. He seemed, however, surprisingly fresh. Those signs of age and discouragement which had followed the straying of the footsteps and the appearance of the cat, had vanished. The fact was a tonic for Quaile.

"You seem to have slept well, McHugh," he said.

The hand that held the customary unlighted cigar shook.

"I thought I had hold of myself," the former detective said. "I was beginning to use my thinker again when just now—"

He broke off. He fumbled among a pile of photographic proofs on his desktop.

"I've just got the prints of those pictures we took last night."

He glanced up, a trifle ashamed, Quaile thought.

"They're good?"

"All but one," McHugh answered slowly.

He passed Quaile a bundle of proofs, but his hand covered one which remained on the desk.

"These are clear enough," Quaile said, beginning to suspect. "But where's the one of the big scene? You had it taken for a poster."

McHugh raised the picture he had withheld, but he kept its face hidden.

"You don't mean there's something wrong with that?" Quaile cried sharply.

McHugh nodded.

"Who was on the stage when that picture was taken?"

"Why, Miss Morgan," Quaile answered, "and Dolly, and Wilkins."

"You'd swear there was no one else?"

"Certainly. You could see as well as I. You know as well as I do."

"I thought I saw. So did Tommy and Mike and the photographers. Just take a look at this."

With a quick gesture he turned the proof of the big scene—that same grouping that had seen the death of Woodford and, forty years later, Carlton's similar end.

Quaile snatched the picture from McHugh's hand and bent close above it. It challenged his reason as deliberately as the figure in cold white flame had done last night. For it contained, where he knew there had been only three, a fourth form, standing close to Wilkins, indistinct, scarcely outlined, as if out of focus; and crouched at its feet was a small black ball like a cat.

"Look at this," McHugh said hoarsely while Quaile's eyes widened.

He passed him a faded cabinet photograph of a dark-faced, repellently handsome man.

"That's Woodford," he said, "made the year he died."

Quaile compared it with the unaccountable figure in the picture taken last night. Although that was nebulous, like a thing seen through fog, its resemblance to the jealous Woodford's forty-year-old likeness was arresting, imperative, on no account to be denied.

CHAPTER XIII

THROUGH THE DUSK

FOR some moments Quaile stared at the old photograph of Woodford, contrasting it with the dim figure in the group posed last night.

"Woodford!" he muttered finally. "It's the shadow of Woodford."

McHugh bit at his cigar. He took the photographs from Quaile and placed them in the desk drawer.

"Thought you'd see it."

"I didn't want to see it," Quaile answered dully. "You must have heard of spirit photography."

McHugh leaned back in his chair.

"Oh, yes. I've heard of it. That looks like a shining example."

"I've never thought of such things seriously." Quail burst out. "Yet last night I heard and saw what is explainable as nothing but Woodford's spirit, and now this—"

"Brace up, Quaile. It looks bad, but it's a fine day out."

Quaile gazed from the window.

"New York!" he said. "If it had happened in some lonely, rotting house in the country! But in the heart of New York, within a few feet of Broadway!"

He turned.

"McHugh, this affair is making me a moral coward."

"We're all apt to be that at times," McHugh said dryly.

"Last night you were on the point of surrender," Quaile reminded him. "What about it now?"

"It's a fine day," McHugh repeated, "so fine that I still want to weigh the facts. I'll give it to you without frills. When I first saw that picture you could have knocked me over with a feather. But the sun kept coming in, and the racket out there was like a bracer. Always gets me that way. So I'm going to look the new facts all over. You've only told me about the high spots of last night. Get down to cases— every little thing, no matter whether you think it's important or not."

Quaile sat on the edge of the desk and rehearsed each detail of his terrifying vigil in the theatre from his first impression that someone was looking at him over the gallery railing, through the approach of the limping footsteps and the cat, to that final moment in the choking passage when a figure had seemed about to materialize before him in cold white flame.

After he had finished McHugh considered for some time. Quaile watched him, praying that the former detective had found a flaw in the illusion of the supernatural. At last the manager shook his head.

"If I hadn't gone down myself," he said, "I might have been a lot cockier. But I heard the footsteps, too, right after I'd sworn the house was empty, and I saw that black cat. Take it all in all, it looks like a clear case of a haunted house. Seems as if Woodford's spirit was as jealous as the man was in life, as if he was using all the evil powers in hell to keep us from reviving his play and stealing his glory. Good Lord! Have we got to fall for that? Have we got to let Carlton's death remain a crying mystery?"

He looked up.

"There's one thing we can be pretty sure of. That noise you heard like wind must have been the curtain coming down."

"Surely," Quaile agreed. "I couldn't believe it at the time, and, as a matter of fact, who was there to lower it or to raise it again?"

"Anyway, you're certain," McHugh went on, "that you've told me every little thing?"

"Quite."

"You didn't smell that perfume again—what Dolly says is the ghost of the perfume Woodford used?"

"Yes," Quaile said. "I noticed it more than usual as I walked through the darkness across the stage."

McHugh grunted.

"And you'd take your oath you really pressed the control when your flashlight wouldn't work?"

"I snapped it time after time," Quaile assured him.

Again McHugh grunted. He traced odd and meaning-less patterns on his blotting pad. Quaile still watched him, guessing that the old detective wasn't thoroughly frank, perhaps concealed any real ideas he might have formed. If that was so, Quaile argued, it was because McHugh distrusted his friendship for Barbara. He arose. He leaned across the desk, determined to test his suspicion.

"See here, McHugh, after last night and this—this mad picture, are you going on with the revival? Will you pro-duce 'Coward's Fare' in Woodford's Theatre?"

McHugh glanced up with an air of childlike surprise.

"Why, of course—if my health lasts and I can put it over in spite of old Woodford."

That settled it for Quaile. He knew that McHugh had not surrendered unconditionally to the supernatural. His de-termination to carry the project through indicated that he was working definitely ahead like the real detective he was. Yet Quaile could imagine no profitable line of reasoning, and he knew it would be useless to ask questions now. From the man's attitude, however, he drew a degree of comfort. Even after his experiences in the theatre, he would admit nothing as long as McHugh in his secretive way held out a hope.

He straightened.

"Then I'm off," he said. "I'll try to get Wilkins again for luncheon. I'm remembering your advice to keep an eye on him as far as possible."

"Good boy!" McHugh approved. "We can put it down as settled that, playing Woodford's rôle, he's the one in the worst danger. Say, you haven't got an extra bedroom in your flat?"

"I have. Why?"

"Might ask Wilkins up to stay with you until the play opens. He's probably living alone in some hotel or boarding house."

"Certainly, if you wish," Quaile said, "but wouldn't he think it queer?"

"I'll make it all right with him," McHugh answered.

"Don't think I'm trying to raise objections," Quaile hurried on, "but there's the telephone in my apartment. One warning has already come over that, and Wilkins is inclined to be nervous."

"If he's due for a warning," McHugh said softly, "it won't make any difference what telephone he's near. Shall we consider it settled?"

"Naturally."

"Then don't ask Wilkins for lunch today. I want you to feed with me."

"Honored, I'm sure."

"I did a heap of thinking when I got home last night," McHugh said. "That business down at the theatre had got pretty far under my skin. Ever hear of Raleigh Joyce, the English high-brow that's lecturing up at Columbia?"

"Yes. What about him?"

"I've asked him to lunch with you and me."

"What's the idea?"

"Seems," McHugh answered, "he's made a life study of spooks—is a big guy in that spook society. What do they call it?"

"The Society for Psychical Research?"

"That's the very lodge. This fellow's scientific, and he's studied spooks the way young ladies study botany—torn 'em to pieces and indexed 'em. I've got an idea of putting Carlton's death and what happened last night up to him. No harm getting at all sides of a matter."

"No harm," Quaile agreed, "but where's the good?"

"We'll see," was all McHugh would say. "I want to get after Woodford every way I can."

Quaile left, uneasy and resentful in face of this new arrangement. Joyce, he had no doubt, was a vacant-eyed, aggressive fanatic who would endeavor to reduce every variation from the normal to terms of his own unhealthy vocabulary. More than ever, since the supernatural had so convincingly strengthened its case, he wanted the contrary shouted at him even against the evidence of his own senses.

He was astonished and relieved, therefore, to find the Englishman a well set-up, middle-aged man, smooth-shaven and scrupulously tailored. He would have impressed a stranger, in fact, as more probably a product of the cricket field than an expert in psychical subtleties.

He seemed captured by the racket and the color of the restaurant where they lunched. McHugh, over the coffee, had to drive his attention to the purpose of their meeting. Joyce smiled tolerantly, uninterestedly.

"One finds it difficult to suspect spiritual manifestations in this country of yours. It is so wholeheartedly young and alive."

"We get old young here," McHugh grinned.

He prefaced his account of what had happened at

Woodford's with a demand for secrecy. Joyce met it, displaying, however, a good deal of astonishment. It became clear to Quaile, as McHugh went on, that the Englishman really expected nothing of uncommon interest. His attention sharpened with the recital of Carlton's death, but it was completely captured only when Quaile gave his testimony as to the shadowy perfume and told his own experience of the footsteps, the cat, and the vision in cold white flame.

"Really a remarkable case," he said then, "particularly so in its details. There are plenty of people like your old actress, Dolly. I mean, you mustn't lay her confidence in the presence of a cat to fancy. I know epileptic types who are consistently thrown into convulsions by the mere unseen approach of the animals. So you may take the cat for granted whether it is substantial or not. The perfume fits in very well. Odors connected with particular people are frequently accepted as proof of the spiritual proximity of such personalities. As for the footsteps and the vision, it is hard to believe you could have imagined all that, Mr. Quaile. Moreover, you have the evidence of the futility of the light and the pistol. It's only fair to tell you at the start, there's nothing you've said that hasn't its counterpart in the records of the Society for Psychical Research or other similar organizations."

This statement affected Quaile all the more because it came from a student who was not, in fact, a crank. McHugh's response varied astonishingly from his own. While the manager's frown persisted, dark and unrelieved, his belligerent expression had increased.

"What about Carlton's death?" he snapped.

"That is very tragic," Joyce answered, "and I shan't try to deceive you for your own comfort. I am holding no brief for ghosts. I am only reminding you that our sins—and why not our other idiosyncrasies?—live after us. That theatre was the focus of Woodford's mature life. His jealousy, its ruling passion, centered there. It is not impossible that that jealousy should remain, perhaps wholly undirected by Woodford as Woodford. This evil thing might have accumulated at the very point where it caused Woodford's death in such force as to make a repetition of the tragedy, under precisely similar circumstances, altogether possible."

"You talk well," McHugh said, "and I've been intending to eat a dictionary for some time. Are you trying to say it would be murder to send another man on in Carlton's place?"

"A great deal," Joyce answered slowly, "would depend on the resistance of the individual attacked. This actor, I gather, was impressionable, expectant of some unfortunate occurrence. And he'd had these warnings over the telephone. I only suggest that electricity as a medium for spiritual communication is worth a good deal of thought."

"I've got a strong man for the part," McHugh muttered, "and I want to put this revival over in spite of Woodford, in spite of the devil himself. You're not telling me it can't be done?"

Joyce smiled, shaking his head.

"I am only saying, after years of investigation, I accept the supernatural as a fact. Constantly things happen that admit only of an occult explanation. I give you my judgment freely on the general question, but I withhold my opinion of this particular case which I have at second hand. The responsibility is too great. A man has been killed. As long as the possibility of a human crime exists we must seek to discover and punish. Let me look the theatre over, then. Let me talk to these people. Go ahead for the present, but on no account rehearse that scene until it is absolutely necessary. If we are dealing with the supernatural it would be dangerous in the extreme."

McHugh arose. The corners of his thin lips twitched.

Quaile had been puzzled by his bearing throughout the entire interview. He could not account for his having sought it at all. From now on he studied the other minutely, growing more and more convinced that the manager had never had the slightest intention of permitting Joyce's opinion to alter his course. Why then had he summoned the man? Why had he involved Quaile in such a curious enterprise?

They drove quickly to the theatre and entered the alley. Mike was outside the stage door, his face recording a sharper perturbation than usual. McHugh presented him to Joyce.

"Talk to him, if you want," he said. "He was with us the first day, and he knew Woodford. So did Dolly. Come on in when you're through, and I'll steer you up against her."

Quaile and he entered the shadowed theatre. McHugh called Dolly. As the old actress came to them Quaile was struck by an alteration in her appearance—a change decidedly pleasant. Her wrinkled face smiled. Her voice, when she spoke, had a ring almost cheerful. McHugh evidently noticed these things, too.

"What's up, Dolly? I haven't raised your salary that I know of."

Her smile widened.

"You ought to. Every actress, even at my age, knows she's worth double what she gets."

McHugh watched her out of narrow eyes.

"I've got a spook doctor outside, Dolly. He's talking to Mike. When he comes in, I want you to give him all the dope you can about Woodford's jealousy and the cologne and the cat."

Dolly laughed. She spoke happily. The amazing cause of her cheerfulness became apparent.

"The cat! It isn't here today."

Quaile guessed that McHugh's mind had gone back with

his to the moment last night when the lithe black body had slipped from the theatre to the sound of limping footsteps. Consequently, he could not share Dolly's relief, nor did McHugh.

"How are you so sure?" the manager asked.

"I know," she answered. "I don't feel it near anymore."

A sudden resolution animated McHugh's features.

"Mike!" he called.

The old property man entered, followed by Joyce.

"Come over here, Mike," McHugh demanded. "Why are you looking so upset today?"

Mike's hands worked fretfully at his hat. He flushed.

"I know you don't believe me, Mr. McHugh—"

"He's heard the footsteps again," Joyce put in.

"That was easy to guess," McHugh said. "Well? When? Where?"

"When I first came down," Mike answered. "No matter what you think, Mr. McHugh, I'm sure. He seemed looking, sir—looking everywheres. I ran out and waited until the others came. Then there were no—no more footsteps."

"The cat?" McHugh asked.

Mike looked up, surprised.

"It wasn't like the other afternoon, sir. The cat didn't seem to be with him."

McHugh's glance met Quailed. It did not conceal his trouble.

"You remember what we told you about last night, Joyce."

He swung on Mike, attempting his old tone of banter.

"You've got so darned much imagination it's a shame you aren't a playwright like Mr. Quaile. You go on talking to this gentleman and he'll straighten you out. Sit in a box, Joyce, when you're through with him, and I'll send Dolly to you at the first opportunity Quaile stepped to the stage where he had seen Barbara lounging on the sofa. In a way he shrank from their first meeting after last night's fears and uncertainties. As he crossed she did not meet his eyes, and before he could speak to her McHugh summoned him over the footlights and commanded the company to commence rehearsing.

In the auditorium the manager threw aside his pretense.

"It's as queer as the rest of it," he said, "because, Quaile, we did see something go out of the door and disappear."

The rehearsal, indeed, offered further proof that the theatre was, temporarily at least, rid of one disturbing agency. Scene followed scene with an unfamiliar smoothness. Quaile saw Dolly enter the box where Joyce had made himself comfortable. He watched her cheerfulness diminish as the Englishman questioned her. For Joyce himself, evidently, the rehearsal meant nothing encouraging. His bland good-humor of the restaurant had gone. He no longer smiled. He appeared relieved when Dolly left him and McHugh, at the commencement of the big scene, arose, and, following his custom, clapped his hands and called out:

"All right, Wilkins. That will do. Come on, Barbara. Skip as usual to, 'Mother, now you have the truth.'"

Quaile was anxious for Joyce's verdict, but McHugh carried the man off, almost pointedly, in his limousine, and it wasn't until the next afternoon that he had an opportunity to ask questions. McHugh was oddly reticent then. Joyce, he admitted, however, had found the atmosphere of the theatre depressing and malevolent.

"I thought he'd be a better man than you to hide here for the night. Gave him his chance, but he took water—a great big, upstanding guy like him! Said there was a feeling of too much evil. Thought you were lucky Barbara raised that racket when she did. Probably pulled you out of a bad hole."

"What was his opinion?" Quaile asked. "Did he advise getting out?"

The former detective evaded the question.

"I don't have to take the advice of every schoolteacher I talk to, do I?"

"Then why did you go to him at all?" Quaile asked flatly.

"Wanted every angle," McHugh muttered, and that was all Quaile could get from him.

As if the retreating black shadow had carried with it a large share of the theatre's menace, the rehearsals for several days proceeded successfully. Even Mike had nothing new to report, and his eyes followed McHugh with gratitude.

Each day the manager questioned Dolly. Quaile could understand that, for to him, too, the old actress had become a barometer. From her manner he had learned to forecast, not only the course of the rehearsals, but the reactions of his own mind to the gloomy building. Constantly she reported the absence of the cat, but the wraith of the perfume lingered, reminding her perpetually of the passion and cruelty of her old director.

Frequently Quaile tried to contrive a few minutes uninterrupted conversation with Barbara. His lack of success pointed the fact that she was avoiding him. Since the night she had come to his help, drawing from him a response not confined to thankfulness, she had assumed an artificial hardness. Constantly she piqued his curiosity, making it impossible for him to jeer at the amorous promptings he had experienced in the alley and afterward in the cab. For a long time she gave him no chance to accept her invitation for tea. Circumstances conspired to make that possible only on the afternoon before the dress rehearsal.

Before dismissing the company that day McHugh called the members down stage and faced them, a little embarrassed, Quaile thought.

"Things have run smoother than I expected," he said, thrusting his thumbs in the armholes of his waistcoat. "You deserve a little vacation, so I'm going to give it to you tonight—all except Dolly and Barbara and Wilkins. You three stay. The rest run along and be here at ten-thirty in the morning. And don't forget. Dress rehearsal tomorrow night. We're going through the whole piece from start to finish for the first time, and there'll be some people in the house. Letter perfect, every one of you."

While the others strolled out Quaile climbed to the stage and waited with a growing discomfort. He had been wondering how long McHugh would put off the rehearsal of the big scene. He was curious to know if Joyce had told him he might go ahead. He shared the doubt Wilkins could not hide. He realized it would be necessary to play the scene on this stage tomorrow night, but there would be a small audience then, more light, costumes, an air of activity and excitement. He shrank from attempting it now, bathed in this air of loneliness and age. He saw Barbara pulling at her handkerchief. Dolly's face was startled. McHugh reassured them.

"I got a date uptown. We'll have to do this trick tonight, and it's scarcely worthwhile opening up for that little bit. Where can we all get together?"

Then Joyce hadn't told him it was safe to go ahead here.

"You live uptown don't you, Barbara?" McHugh went on, a trifle self-consciously. "Dolly can't live far off, and Wilkins, Quaile, and I will manage it at eight-thirty if you'll have us."

Quaile guessed the manager had a purpose in choosing such a rendezvous. He accepted it as additional proof of McHugh's doubt of the girl. She flushed. She didn't quite meet McHugh's glance, and the warmth of her acceptance lacked spontaneity.

"Certainly, if you wish. I have a large room."

"Settled," McHugh said. "I expect you've been there already, Dolly."

Surprised, Quaile saw the old actress shake her head.

"Then," McHugh directed, "everybody'd better put down the address."

Barbara gave them the number and street, turned, and started for the stage door. Since Quaile had been standing nearby it was natural he should leave the theatre with her. She had an appearance of restrained flight as she went down the alley. He knew that tonight would offer no chance for quiet talk or for those questions he felt he must put to her. She hurried from the mouth of the alley and crossed the sidewalk.

"There's a cab. Until half-past eight, Mr. Quaile."

He caught her at the curb.

"We're free so early today," he said. "Isn't it a splendid hour for tea?"

She glanced helplessly at the cab.

"You're reminding me of my invitation."

He reddened.

"If I've been tactless I'm sorry," he said, "but lately we've seen so little of each other."

She moved away.

"Come by all means, and perhaps you'll understand why I haven't been more cordial."

"I'm not forcing my welcome?"

She shook her head, so he followed her to the cab. During the ride to the apartment she chatted with a gayety almost feverish.

The hallway, the elevator, the service, all had an air of gentility. The house was reserved, in a sense, forbidding. A maid opened the door of Barbara's apartment for them. The immobility of her face attracted Quaile's interest. Her movements as she took his coat and hat were smooth, repressed, noiseless. He was uncomfortable beneath the curiosity of her glance.

"You'll bring tea at once," Barbara said, and led Quaile to a large living room.

The fading light entered through wide, small-paned windows. It was sufficiently strong to outline the quiet luxury of the furnishings. Barbara hesitated before the electric switch.

"Shall we have more light?"

Quaile could not understand her obvious reluctance to press the switch. It was unlike her. It gave him a queer, uncomfortable feeling that there might be something here she wished the dusk to veil.

"It is pleasant and restful as it is," he said.

He lounged in an easy chair, seeking answers to those doubts which his own heart and McHugh's antagonism had dictated. In the corners there were shadows his glance could not penetrate, yet the room, he felt, sheltered nothing more important than her proximity and his un-studied response.

The servant, treading softly, brought tea on a wheeled tray. They lingered over it while the dusk thickened, while Barbara's face and figure became less and less distinct; and, as the night slowly shrouded her, the caution with which McHugh had impressed him lost its significance. He felt himself back at the point from which he had recoiled— on the verge of sentimental surrender to a woman of whom he knew nothing beyond the elusive charm of her manner, and her personality, unique and inscrutable. He broke a long silence.

"You live here alone?"

It was too dark to see her eyes.

"Perhaps you see why my invitation lacked warmth."

He arose and strolled to the window, lighting a cigarette. He stared at the sky in which a wan color, still survived. He felt himself an intruder here, seeking selfishly to learn more about her than she was willing to tell. One thing he had found out and it made no difference.

"It was good of you to let me come," he said. "After all the excitement and uncertainty down there—"

Her voice was low.

"It has been restful," she said, "but I shouldn't be glad you are here."

He heard her arise. He didn't turn, but he was tinglingly aware of her approach. He knew she had reached his side. He turned then and saw that her eyes also had been drawn by the pensive afterglow which gradually diminished above an uneven line of chimneys and cornices.

"It's almost like a view across a foreign city, that bit," he said. "There's actually a chimney pot. Do you see?"

She nodded. Her voice had no resonance.

"I lived abroad once—when I was very young."

"Do you ever wish to go back?" he asked.

She looked straight ahead. She might have forgotten his presence.

"I don't know," she mused. "Go back? I don't know."

It was clear the conversation held for her a meaning beyond his comprehension. He wondered. Then a greater wonder grew upon him. Her nearness in the dusk was too provocative. The melancholy afterglow seemed to surround them with a solitude, limitless, beyond the reach of conventional restraints.

"How lonely everything is!" she whispered. "Fall sunsets fill one with loneliness."

His hand crept toward hers, touched hers, carried to his brain an intoxicating content. The contact for the moment made words inexpressive, unfit.

She drew her hand slowly away. She turned and walked across the room. He heard her sigh. The sound was a reproach, an awakening. It sent the blood to his cheeks.

The beating of his heart was as pronounced as it had been before the approach of the limping footsteps.

"What are you going to do?" he asked.

Her answer wasn't quite steady.

"You've reminded me why I didn't want you to come."

Her tone strengthened.

"It is dark in this room. I—I hate the darkness."

"Don't," he cried. "It was all perfect until—"

Impulsively he started forward.

"You'll let me tell you?"

The maid stole in.

"Mr. Quaile is going," Barbara said indifferently. "Will you please bring his hat and coat?"

"A—a permanent dismissal?" he asked.

"You are coming with the others tonight," she said.

He saw the light flash on in the hall. A passionate dissatisfaction swept him.

"We are always misunderstanding each other. Will you never care for my justification?"

"I would rather not hear it," she answered.

The maid stole back with his coat and hat. Barbara shook hands frankly, but her fingers had no warmth for him.

"I am glad you could come," she said with a formal unconcern clearly intended for the maid.

In the presence of the servant he had no reply, so he walked through the lighted hall and out of the apartment.

CHAPTER XIV

WOODFORD'S LAUGH

AT LEAST his visit had solved one problem. Walking disconsolately, angrily, home, he acknowledged that the emotions Barbara had aroused were infinitely stronger than McHugh's suspicions. Sooner or later he must reach a definite understanding with her. Had it not been for the prospect of seeing her tonight he would have tried to shape that unfavorable moment to his uses. He might have bared his heart then.

His impatience urged him rapidly downtown. Always, he reflected, he carried from his interviews with Barbara a sense of something unexplained, something disturbing, something unhappy. He wondered why his casual comparison of that mournful prospect with a foreign city had thrown her into a humor, withdrawn, retrospective.

He was grateful for the entertaining appointment he had for dinner. Then he remembered Wilkins. He knew that McHugh would want him to cling to the actor tonight, to dine with him, to make sure that he reached Barbara's safely and on time. He was glad when Wilkins, already dressed, told him he would dine alone in the apartment and go straight to the rehearsal in a taxicab.

"You know, Quaile," he said, "I've come to look on you as my guardian. Don't think I resent it. On the contrary a feeling of protection's not to be despised. But don't fret yourself about me tonight. Nothing can happen up there, and things have been going along smoothly enough at the theatre."

But Quaile was not convinced. He could only recall that they had never gotten through that scene. He glanced at the telephone. It was clear from the other's manner that so far he had been spared one of those warnings, purporting to come from the dead Woodford, which had startled Carlton, and, later, Quaile himself.

Wilkins had not spoken so frankly before. His words opened Quailed eyes to a change in the man. His cheeks were not so ruddy. A slightly restless manner had replaced his ready assurance. Quaile guessed that his misgivings focused on tomorrow night. Certainly, as he had said, nothing could happen at Barbara's. It was quite all right to leave him now.

"Then," he said, "I'll see you up there, Wilkins. I may be a few minutes late, so if McHugh gets feverish tell him not to wait for me."

Wilkins nodded and picked up a book.

Quaile kept his appointment, but he was in no mood for the entertainment he had anticipated. The dinner for him was a dreary affair. He hurried through it, finding it hard to believe his anxiety for Wilkins could have reached such a pitch. At the first opportunity he called a cab and drove uptown to the apartment which, he knew now, housed a mystery for him almost as impressive as the theater's tragic one.

As he stepped from the elevator he glanced at his watch. He was scarcely ten minutes late.

The quiet, emotionless maid opened the door. Immediately he heard a stir within, but no voices. Then McHugh stood in the doorway of the living room, glancing across the hall out of narrow eyes.

"Wonder you'd come at all," he snarled. "Where's Wilkins?"

Quaile's heart sank.

"Surely he's here."

"I'm just asking you to train my voice," McHugh sneered.

He strode forward. He watched the maid go. His lower tone indicated a desire for secrecy.

"Where the devil is he? I thought I told you to keep an eye on him."

"I've done it as far as possible. I had an appointment for dinner tonight."

McHugh's disapproval increased.

"You ought to have broken it."

His manner opened Quaile's eyes to the gravity of the delay.

"After all, he's only ten minutes late."

"Where'd you see him last?" McHugh, asked.

"In my rooms," Quaile answered, "not two hours ago. He said he'd have a bite to eat there and come straight up."

McHugh frowned.

"Then he wouldn't be late. Why in the name of heaven couldn't you stay on your job tonight?"

"Give him a few minutes," Quaile said. "Things have been going so well I didn't think—Perhaps, the telephone— He might have got one of those warnings and funked it. Suppose I call up my apartment?"

McHugh shook his head.

"We'll wait till nine o'clock. There's nothing to do but wait."

Barbara appeared in the doorway. She smiled at Quaile quite as if their latest parting had been constrained by nothing unusual.

"What is it? Mr. Wilkins isn't with you?"

"No," Quaile said with an attempt at ease. "But he ought

to be here any time now."

They entered the living room. Quaile examined it more closely in the light of candles and lamps. Its comfortable good taste was merely accented. As far as he could see— and the corners were exposed now—it held nothing Barbara would have had a purpose in hiding. There were only two doors—the one from the hall and another at the side which probably led to a bedroom.

Dolly, stretched in an easy chair, appeared rather pleased at the delay.

"Hello, Mr. Author!" she greeted Quaile. "Why aren't we always rehearsed as pleasantly as this?"

For a moment the smile left her lips.

"How much better than a gloomy ruin full of sickly memories!"

"You shut up, Dolly," McHugh commanded.

The white-haired actress smiled again.

"Excuse me. I didn't know I had to be so careful when our leading man wasn't present."

But before long she, too, confessed surprise and uneasiness at Wilkins' strange delay. Quaile tried to bolster the conversation, but memories of his afternoon's visit conspired with his anxiety to keep him quiet. When the silence in which they sat now, alert for the sound of the doorbell, had continued more than a quarter of an hour, he caught McHugh's attention and indicated the telephone questioningly.

The manager arose and commenced to pace up and down the room. At last he paused and glanced at his watch.

"All right, Quaile," he said. "Call up your joint and see if he's left."

Quaile walked to the telephone, glad to be actually making an effort to explain Wilkins' absence. The connection was quickly arranged and he recognized the voice of his hall-boy.

"Yes, sir," the boy said in reply to his questions. "Mr. Wilkins had his dinner upstairs and left at eight o'clock sharp."

Quaile replaced the receiver, glancing at McHugh.

"He left at eight."

McHugh snapped his watch shut.

"And it's nearly nine."

Barbara looked up.

"Where do you suppose—"

Her voice trailed away. She strained forward. Dolly half arose. McHugh stared incredulously at the telephone. Quaile, who had started to return to his chair, stopped short.

He knew what it was, this new sound that had slyly invaded the place. It was as if it had little by little detached itself from the very body of silence, and still clung, undecided. Then the attenuated tinkling, the precise sound he had heard the night Woodford's spirit had seemed to warn him, reached a higher note and held it.

"Quaile!" McHugh murmured. "Is that it?"

"Yes," Quaile said hoarsely. "Perhaps we'll have news of Wilkins now."

He returned on tiptoe toward the telephone. He stretched out his hand with a distinct hesitation. McHugh sprang forward and grasped his arm.

"Wait!" he cried, and his tone was round with excitement.

"Don't you touch it, Quaile. Dolly! You answer that call."

The old actress raised herself slowly from the chair. Her feet were uncertain.

"Is it the telephone?" she asked blankly.

"What do you suppose?" McHugh grumbled.

"That bell! I've never heard a bell like that. Barbara! What a queer bell! It makes me shiver."

Barbara looked helplessly around.

"It is not my telephone bell."

The insistent, far away calling continued.

"It's the—the ghost of a bell," Dolly said.

"I told you to answer it," McHugh muttered.

Quaile watched her take the receiver from the hook. They waited motionless while she placed it at her ear and in her pleasant voice, sharpened by astonishment, called into the transmitter:

"Hello! Hello!"

Quaile kept his glance on her face. He saw it whiten, saw her eyes widen with unbelief and fear. She started back. The receiver slipped from her hand and clattered against the table. Her mouth opened, but she remained mute, gripped by some stem emotion, evidently, for the moment, beyond expression.

McHugh thrust her aside and raised the receiver to his own ear.

"Yes, yes," he said while disappointment marked his face.

"No, no," he said after a moment. "A mistake. No number."

He faced Dolly. Quaile appreciated his effort at control. The man spoke almost casually.

"Well? Who was it? You look as if it must have been a pet creditor, Dolly."

The old woman stirred. A little color returned to her wrinkled cheeks.

"God help me, Mr. McHugh. That was Woodford's voice."

The manager placed his hand on her arm.

"Get hold of yourself, Dolly. What you talking about? You look as if you'd seen a spirit."

Quaile knew he was leading her.

"It comes down to the same thing," she said. "I—I've heard one."

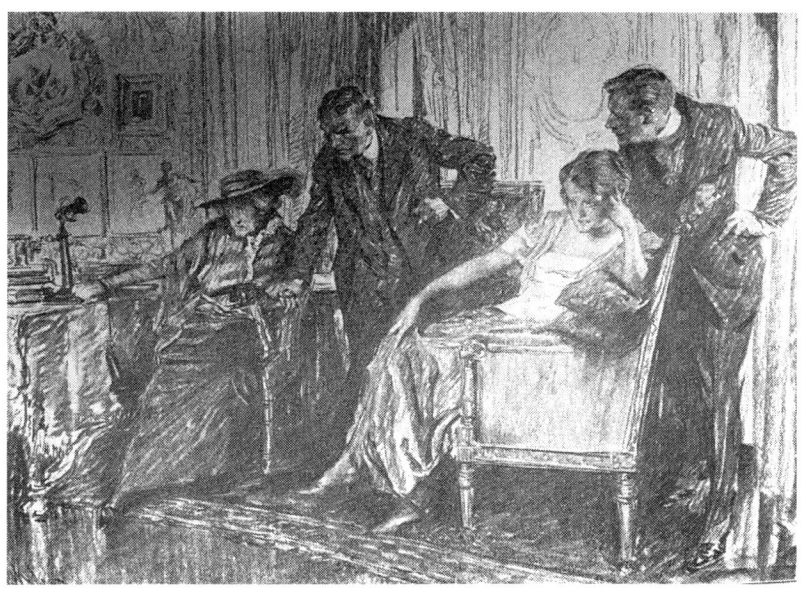

Quaile kept his glance on her face. He saw it written, saw her eyes widen with fear. The receiver slipped from her hand and clattered against the table.

"You don't mean it!" McHugh scoffed. "And what had it to say for itself?"

"It said Mr. Wilkins wouldn't be able to rehearse the big scene, and it laughed, I tell you—Woodford laughed."

She raised her hands to her face and sank on a divan.

"Now wait, Dolly," McHugh said gently. "Let me get this straight. You'd swear the voice sounded like Woodford's?"

"I know," she answered. "I'd remember that laugh."

"And that's all you heard? Give me the exact words."

She struggled bravely to steady herself.

"He said: 'This fool is ill. He can't rehearse my part tonight or any night.' Then he laughed. That laugh—that laugh! How we all hated it!"

"Never you mind," McHugh said. "It's some joke."

Barbara spoke unexpectedly.

"No!"

Quaile swung in her direction. Her face was whiter than Dolly's. She was more moved than the old actress who had actually received the message. She had braced herself against a chair back. Apparently she forced herself to speak.

"You must realize," Mr. McHugh, she said rapidly, "that something strange or terrible has happened every time we have tried to rehearse that scene. First, Mr. Carlton's death. Even the day of the reading he was affected at that very point. Then Mr. Wilkins stopped there without any reason. And now this— But, Mr. McHugh, how do you dare speak of a practical joke? Dolly ought to know."

"I know, I know," the old woman sobbed.

"So you've suddenly become a ghost worshipper, too? I'll run my own business just the same, thank you. We'll rehearse that scene with the rest of the play tomorrow night or my name isn't Arthur McHugh."

"And Mr. Wilkins?" Barbara asked.

McHugh's temper ran away with him.

"I'll see about Wilkins. I'd play the part myself. Come

ahead, Quaile, let's get out of here. I'm no use with a pack of sniveling women. Let's find Wilkins, if he's to be found."

"If he's to be found—" Dolly whimpered.

Quaile got his hat and coat from the quiet maid and followed McHugh to the hall.

"Wilkins," he suggested when they were in the limousine, "uses the Stage Club a good deal. Since we know he left my apartment—"

McHugh approved. He directed the chauffeur to drive to the club.

"And pretend the cops are street ornaments," he ordered. "I'm in a hurry."

At the club, however, nothing was known of Wilkins' movements. He had not been there during the day or evening. Friends of his in the lounge had not seen the actor.

"We'll go to your apartment on a last chance of his having returned," McHugh decided. "Or he might have left some word."

They made a thorough search of Quaile's rooms without finding any message, any clue as to Wilkins' destination.

When they were in the lower hall again McHugh questioned the boy.

"Did any one call for Mr. Wilkins?"

"Not that I know of, sir."

"He left alone at eight o'clock? You'd testify to that under oath?"

The boy, amazed at such insistence, nodded.

"And no one called him over the telephone?"

"No, sir."

McHugh handed the boy a coin and walked out, beckoning Quaile.

"Drive to the nearest drug store," he directed the chauffeur.

And when they were in the car he explained.

"I want a telephone booth where I won't be overheard.

I'm going to put the czar of the company to work tracing that call."

Quaile felt completely helpless. He saw nothing to be gained by such a course.

"You've tried that once," he said. "You *are* stubborn, McHugh."

"Got to be," McHugh muttered, "or go to night school with Joyce. If I didn't keep on trying I'd lose my mind."

He entered the drug store and five minutes later returned, perspiring and irritable. He spoke to the chauffeur in tones Quaile could not hear, then climbed in.

"There's just one thing left to do," he said as he slammed the door.

"To get the police after Wilkins?" Quaile asked.

"Naw. Do I seem as rotten a detective as that?"

He hesitated. He found a cigar and placed it in his mouth, chewing at it reflectively.

"I mean," He said slowly, "to go back to Barbara's."

Quaile started.

"Whatever for? What are you driving at, McHugh?"

"Needn't come along if you don't want to," the manager grumbled.

Quaile tried to hide his eagerness. He didn't want McHugh to see that under such conditions nothing could keep him away. He couldn't guess McHugh's purpose. He couldn't understand what he expected to find there, but a fear grew upon him that it would mean unhappiness for Barbara and, consequently, for himself. Nor would the other explain. Quaile gave it up.

"Are you afraid," he asked later, "that when we find Wilkins he will be like Carlton—dead?"

"The old scratch," McHugh grunted, "wouldn't know what to expect in this affair—unless He's engineering it himself."

He relapsed into a moody silence.

When they stepped from the elevator at Barbara's floor McHugh's manner became transformed. He walked stealthily toward the door and grasped the knob. He glanced back at Quaile, his lips working.

"I took the precaution," he whispered, "of snapping the latch when I came out so I wouldn't have to disturb anybody."

"You're going to spy," Quaile flashed.

McHugh put his finger to his mouth. He moved his head negatively.

"Just a small surprise for Barbara."

He turned the knob and noiselessly opened the door.

Immediately Barbara's voice reached them, high-pitched, appealing, alarmed.

"Don't try it," she was saying. "Oh—don't. Give it up. It's mad to go on with it. Mad—suicidal."

McHugh leered. Quaile pushed by. He put a period to McHugh's triumph. He called out:

"We've come back."

McHugh made an angry gesture. Barbara's frightened voice stopped short. Unwillingly it came into Quaile's mind to whom she had been speaking, yet surely that was out of the question. He flung back the curtain and stared at Wilkins' face, white and bewildered.

Dolly had gone, and the man sat, as if he had collapsed, in her chair. He held his open watch in his fingers as he looked at Barbara who stood nearby, her hand raised, her lips still parted.

"Wilkins!" Quaile breathed.

McHugh came in.

"Thank the Lord you're here, Wilkins."

Quaile swung on the manager.

"Did you expect to find him?" he asked hotly.

"Didn't know," McHugh answered. "Can't say that I did."

And in his face Quaile could read no denial of his words.

Barbara had relaxed. She leaned against a chair, staring at the others. McHugh examined the actor closely.

"Brace up, Wilkins. What's happened? Where the deuce you been?"

Wilkins tottered to his feet. He glanced at his open watch. His voice jerked.

"Heaven knows, because I left your apartment at eight o'clock, Quaile. I drove straight here in a taxi. I arrived after you had left. I—I thought I was in plenty of time, and I asked Miss Morgan if I was the first. She told me, and I looked at my watch. It was half-past nine."

His voice rose. It groped. It cried his dismay.

"I tell you I came straight, and nothing happened, and it isn't only my watch. It's the clock at your place, Quaile, and the clock here. An hour's gone out of my life. But it couldn't have gone, f-for nothing happened—"

Quaile and McHugh went to him. They looked at his watch. They compared it with their own.

Wilkins sat down heavily. He raised his shaking hands to his head. The watch, forgotten, slipped to the floor where it lay, face up, exposing its testimony, unreasonable and lawless, to their startled eyes.

CHAPTER XV

THE SEXLESS CLAMOUR

McHUGH, frowning and eager, bent over the actor.

"Try to think, Wilkins. You got to remember. There must be something if you can only remember."

But Wilkins' face remained blank, and, even after he had fought for and won a semblance of control, he had nothing more to offer than that statement beyond the bounds of reason, yet verified by his watch and the clocks, that he had left Quaile's apartment at eight o'clock, had, as far as he knew, come straight, nevertheless had taken an hour and a half to complete the twenty-minute journey. Certainly the man had no purpose in lying.

"That hour's gone out of my life," He said. "It—it makes me feel—sick."

He arose and faced Barbara while McHugh watched him closely.

"Could I have a glass of water?"

Barbara rang. McHugh continued to study the actor. The maid slipped in with the water. Wilkins drank it thirstily. He tried to smile. The effort twisted his features unpleasantly.

"Maybe you're suspicious of my habits, Mr. McHugh."

The manager's glance did not waver.

"You say you ate dinner at Quaile's apartment?"

"Yes."

McHugh turned away.

"Must have rotten food at your joint, Quaile, if it puts a man out like that."

The material thought the remark suggested did not convince Quaile, yet he failed to understand why McHugh did not question the other closely along that line. He made an effort himself.

"You didn't stop at the club for a drink, Wilkins?"

"I've had nothing to eat or drink," the actor answered, "since I left your rooms."

Quaile questioned if McHugh didn't purposely prevent his quizzing Wilkins. At any rate the manager straightway approached Barbara whose attitude had been tensely observant, almost, Quaile fancied, apprehensive.

"What's become of Dolly?"

Barbara sighed. At last her hands left the chair back.

"Dolly was no use," she answered. "We were sure there wouldn't be a rehearsal, and she wanted to go home. She was afraid of the—of the—"

She broke off, glancing at the telephone.

"What's the bluff for?" McHugh asked harshly.

"I don't understand."

"I guess you understand," McHugh said. "Aren't you trying to give me the impression you don't want Wilkins to know about Dolly's scare with the telephone?"

The protective instinct to which Quaile had answered before urged him to interfere, but Barbara gave him no opportunity. Her cheeks, which had been as pale as Wilkins', flushed.

"Wasn't that your wish?"

"A lot of good my wishes do!" McHugh scoffed. "See here, Barbara, we've come to a showdown, you and me. What you mean by begging Wilkins to throw over the part—talking about madness and suicide? Eh? What's the idea? Time I knew something about it, too."

Her tone colored with an anger that failed quite to hide its perturbation.

"You saw Mr. Carlton die. You've more knowledge of what's happened in the theatre than I have. You know as well as I do that it does seem mad and suicidal to play that part. If you're too selfish to tell Mr. Wilkins so yourself, I'm not. Well, I've told him."

Quaile, expectant of a riotous outburst on McHugh's side, saw only a growth of the man's determination before this unforeseen defiance.

"I'm the best judge of how to run my own business," he said mildly.

"Then tell me," she answered, "how you happened to overhear what I said to Mr. Wilkins."

McHugh grinned sheepishly.

"Your door was unlocked. I walked in."

"And how did it get unlocked?" she demanded. "You arranged that in order to eavesdrop."

She spoke more rapidly. In her eagerness the words stumbled a trifle.

"It really is time we had a showdown, as you say, Mr. McHugh. You've gone out of your path to be rude and unfair to me. You almost make me believe you suspect me of something. Can't you be honest? What is it?"

"Now come. Now come. I never said I suspected you of anything, Barbara."

"But I know you do," she answered. "After what you've said and done tonight we can't go on together. If my leaving the company puts you to inconvenience you've only yourself to blame."

Wilkins started forward.

"I'm sorry, Miss Morgan, if I've had anything to do with this."

Quaile stared. He had never fancied Barbara capable of

such calculated temper. The fact that it was justified, however, made him glad of her response. No more than at the
beginning could he sound McHugh's attitude toward her.

The manager laughed shortly.

"Hoity-toity. Come off your high horse, Barbara. I never
knew you were so darned high strung. That's worried me
from time to time, because you're a first-class actress and
I'm a first-class manager, so if we don't fight like cats and
dogs we aren't doing business normally. We ought to be on
better terms than ever after this spiff. Hear the girl! Leave
my company!"

She appeared no less dumbfounded by his humor than
Quaile.

"I take water," McHugh went on. "If I heard anything
that wasn't intended for my ears I'm sorry, let's forget it."

She hesitated.

"I prefer to drop out. If you're doing this simply because
you can't get along without me—"

McHugh winked at Quaile broadly. Quaile felt that the
man deliberately wheedled her toward a goal he already
had in mind.

"—don't you charge me with anything like that, Barbara."

"I mean," Barbara said determinedly, "this sort of thing
can't occur again. I shan't stay on if I'm to be treated like a
criminal."

McHugh's face became serious again.

"Tell me one thing, Barbara. Do you, or don't you, know
anything about Woodford's ghost?"

She laughed, a little hysterically.

"It's hard to believe you're serious. Of course not."

"No more said," McHugh muttered.

He grasped Wilkins' arm.

"The girl's got some reason. I've no business taking risks
with other people's lives against their will. You're a strong
man, Wilkins, and I don't believe afraid of much, but just

now you're upset by a bad scare. Understand, you're to do as you like about the part, but if you want to please me you'll sleep on it. You won't make up your mind until morning. Then, if you want, I'll steer you up against a spook doctor. Quaile's talked to him. He'll tell you he's got a lot of horse sense."

Wilkins nodded.

"I don't want to seem a quitter, but this is a queer business, Mr. McHugh. I will sleep on it. I'll let you know in the morning."

"We'd better be off," McHugh said. "Time Barbara got quiet. Don't you hold anything against me, young woman. What I've just said to Wilkins is fair enough, isn't it? Come on, Quaile. I'll run you and Wilkins downtown."

But Quaile had decided not to leave with the others. Barbara's alarmed appeal to the actor had startled him no less than it had McHugh. Moreover, he was not restrained by intriguing policy, as McHugh apparently was, from pressing his curiosity too far. His interest in the girl, which he defined unconditionally now as love, made him unwilling to leave without a resolution of those doubts McHugh's suspicions and his own observations had posed. He must remain after the others. He must force her, if possible, to an explanation, also, perhaps, to that final sentimental understanding he craved with all his heart.

In answer to Barbara's summons the maid entered stealthily and waited until McHugh and Wilkins had put on their coats. Quaile studied her with an increased curiosity, realizing that she had not once spoken in his presence. A somber quality about her face, its lack of expression, harmonized with her dark uniform for which the apron and the cap seemed merely accents.

"Coming, Quaile?" McHugh asked.

"A few minutes after you," Quaile answered, attempting to hide his discomfort. "I want to speak to Miss Morgan about another matter."

"It is very late," she said.

The presence of the others made a more active objection impracticable, but Quaile saw clearly enough that she recoiled from the prospect of such an interview. McHugh glanced at him curiously. Quaile did not meet his gaze. He had a sensation of placing himself on an enemy side. Try as he might, he could find no forgiveness for McHugh's recent treatment of the girl. The manager shrugged his shoulders.

"Hustle on, Wilkins. Quaile seems to have a lot of irons in the fire these days."

The two went. The quiet maid slipped out. Quaile and Barbara faced each other, alone. She would not raise her eyes.

"After what happened this afternoon—" she began.

He gestured impatiently. He stepped impulsively closer to her. She drew back until she leaned against the wall.

"All the more because of this afternoon," he said. "But that isn't the only reason I stayed. Listen, Barbara."

And, as he saw her shrink back.

"I shall call you that. The time has come for the destruction of a lot of pretense between us. We're dealing with too grave issues to dare veil what little truth there is."

The emotion her reluctance to meet his eyes confessed affected him profoundly. He was aware again of the staccato pounding of his heart. He wanted to touch her, to draw her so close that he could no longer see, and feel his purpose scattered by, the uncertainty and the discontent of her pose. He made himself go on quickly.

"I think you know already that I—I—"

She would not look up. In spite of her shrinking he reached out and grasped her hands.

"Barbara," he said huskily. "Let's be frank. If I displeased you the other night and again this afternoon, it was because I love you. Surely you've seen."

She tried to tear her hands away, but he crushed them tighter.

"No. You'll listen to me. You have to answer."

She held her face averted, so that he couldn't see her eyes, but her cheeks were pallid again, and her lips twitched.

"Each day I've been surer of it. I've fought it, but tonight when McHugh sprang his brutal third degree I knew there was no use."

Her head moved slowly, so that at last she faced him. Her eyes were wide. They were like eyes that are about to fill with tears. In spite of their proximity, in spite of their actual contact, her voice scarcely reached him.

"No—no—no."

And her shrinking, her inability to speak plainly, that evident imminence of tears, destroyed for the moment his doubt of her eventual response.

"You can say what you please—" he began triumphantly.

She straightened. With misdirected efforts she struggled wildly to free her hands. Her hair escaped a little from its orderliness and strayed with a provocative abandonment about her temples and her neck. Then the tears appeared in her eyes and fell to her cheeks, more eloquent than anything she could have said, anything she could have done. So Quaile had to let her go.

She raised her hands to her face. The crimson marks of his fingers on her wrists appalled him.

"I'll lash myself for a blundering fool," he said, "if you'll tell me you've nothing to offer me—no hope—"

She moved slowly away toward the window, his gaze following her. He was no longer sure of himself. He was swept by the conviction that without her the future could hold no romance, no shadow of amorous content.

After a time she turned, lowering her hands. The pallor of her cheeks still carried the souvenirs of grief.

"Will you go now?" she asked quietly.

It was difficult for him to speak.

"You don't doubt what I said. Nothing can alter that. Surely you can give me a little hope that someday you will marry me."

The quick trembling of her body was like a shudder.

"We mustn't talk of that," she said. "I only want you to go."

"Without a word?"

"What word do you want?" she cried. "Very well. You shall have it. You came back with Mr. McHugh. You played his spying game, too. And—oh, I know—you came here as a spy this afternoon. You saw that I didn't want you. And when you found that I lived alone you spied and—and touched my hand. It—it was Judas-like. Will you go now?"

He walked to her, but this time she did not shrink from him. Her defiant attitude had a pitiful bravado.

"You shan't say such things," he said, "because you don't believe them. Or are you only trying to make me angry so I'll go? I did come this afternoon to learn more about you—with whom you lived. I didn't know you lived here alone. Is it unnatural I should do that when I love you?"

The simplicity of his question for a moment relaxed her defense. Her face did not quite hide a swift response. He fought the desire to take her hands again, to urge that response into words.

"Barbara," he burst out, "what is it? I believe if it were only yourself you wouldn't shrink from me, you wouldn't say things I can't accept. I told you it was a time for truths. Perhaps I am disloyal to McHugh, but I owe no one the loyalty I do you. I trust you. I believe in you. I couldn't love you any other way. Then McHugh does suspect you—has suspected you for a long time of knowing something about the mystery at Woodford's."

"What has he told you?" she breathed.

"Nothing. That's just it. Not a definite word. Can't you guess how that puzzles and hurts me?"

She spoke coldly, with a slow deliberation.

"You acknowledge you suspect me, too."

He moved his hands helplessly.

"I don't want the woman I love surrounded by mystery. Nor am I blind. Since Carlton's death you have altered. I did hear you tonight warning Wilkins to give up the part. Your eagerness suggested a downright assurance that what happened to Carlton would happen to him if he went on. I'm only human. I want to know why that was."

She shook her head.

"So you ask me to marry you, and you expect me to believe in such a love."

As he was about to defend himself he started. Every muscle tightened while the blood rushed to his face and he listened with a vast incredulity.

For a voice had risen beyond the door he had imagined leading to a bedroom. It vibrated from a low and mournful keening higher and higher into a scream which abruptly ended. After a moment, out of the new silence, sobs followed one another, sharp and unnatural. But the strangest quality about the scream and these sounds of a violent sorrow was their complete lack of physical character. He did not know, and, as he listened, he could not tell, whether the cry and the sobs had issued from the throat of a woman or a man. The choking, sexless clamor wandered into silence. Hastening feet pattered in the hall, and, turning quickly, Quaile saw the black-robed maid pass. It was not she who had cried out.

He looked at Barbara. She gazed at the door, an expression of horror in her eyes. She took a few steps in that direction, then paused and glanced at him.

"What was that?" he asked sharply.

She didn't answer. The pain from the tight clenching of

his hands was restorative.

"Those sounds—you told me," he whispered, "that you lived here alone."

"I didn't tell you," she whispered back. "It was your own conclusion. I didn't deny it."

"Then who is in there? What do those sobs mean?"

She seemed seeking some manner of escape from him.

"No one," she answered incoherently. "No one—as far as you are concerned. You're to forget you heard anything. It will not occur again. You heard nothing. You understand? There was nothing to hear."

He shook his head savagely.

"That's nonsense. You will tell me what that was, why you have kept the presence of that—that person here a secret, why that cry terrified you."

Answering to an intention, unjustifiable, except in so far as it was instinctive, he walked toward the door behind which the cry had keened. He paused, aware through the confusion of his thoughts that Barbara's hand was on his arm, that she was drawing him back with an unsuspected strength. Recklessness was expressed in her face which had suddenly flooded with color.

"What right have you to ask that?" she said.

He stared at her, dazed by her unexpected change of front. He stammered a little.

"My—my love. Doesn't that give me a right?"

Her color deepened.

"Not unless I—I—Don't you see. Only I can give you such a right."

She moved away from the door toward the window, beckoning him. He followed her uncertainly. She drew back the curtain and for some time gazed at the rooftops which were definable only for a little distance, burying themselves toward the horizon in a dismal mass of swollen clouds. The dreariness of the prospect impressed him more than its forerunner had done that afternoon. It was disturbingly appropriate to the abnormal events of this evening. It occurred to him that more than once the wider aspects of nature had combined to reinforce the manifestations of this mystery which convincingly obscured itself beneath the supernatural.

He could not understand Barbara's silence. It had followed suggestive and impetuous words. It became unbearable.

"Why did you bring me here," he asked. "I thought for a moment, perhaps, to give me the right—"

She turned slowly. Her face was in shadow, but he could see that there were tears in her eyes again. Suddenly she stretched out her hands, and he grasped them and tried to draw her closer.

"If I should give it to you," she said, "the right to ask those questions?"

He wanted his arms about her, but she shook her head.

"Wait."

She bent back against the heavy folds of the curtain, but she permitted him to retain her hands.

"You leave me no choice," she whispered. "If I should tell you one truth would you trust me and let the others go?"

"Barbara! You mean—"

She nodded.

"I will do that, because what you have heard here tonight must be your secret and mine."

Still she resisted him.

"Then," he asked, "you'll tell me who is in there?"

"No, no," she answered quickly. "I only tell you that I love you. Isn't that enough?"

The quiet words swept him beyond denial, but she guarded her lips.

"No. Because in the long run this only means sorrow for

us, and it isn't fair. You must see that. It isn't fair to me."

Nor would she tell him anything more.

"I only want you to go," she begged, "asking nothing. If you can't trust me you must never talk of love again."

"I'll say nothing," he promised. "I'll ask nothing until you are willing to answer."

She tried to smile.

"You won't misunderstand then? You won't credit me with manufacturing ghosts? You'll believe I am afraid of the theatre—oh, how horribly afraid? Not for myself. It is because I am afraid that I came to your help the other night, that I warned Mr. Wilkins just now. You believe that?"

"Yes," he said, "but that cry? Is there any connection between that and—"

She placed her hand on his lips.

"Your faith," she said wistfully, "is not very strong. If your love is no stronger!"

In spite of her quiet tone he appreciated the existence of a crisis. It was necessary for him to throw logic to the winds, to obey her wishes, strange and disturbing as they were, to deny his natural impulse to remain longer with her.

"Then I shall go," he said, "but you must never talk again of sorrow in the future for us."

"Yes," she said eagerly. "Don't let me talk of that. Try not to let me remember that."

She walked swiftly away from him to the bell. He followed her.

"Don't ring," he said. "Your maid—I can't explain it. She is too quiet. She makes me feel uncomfortable. And tonight I want to see no one but you."

He couldn't disguise his discontent and unhappiness. With a sudden movement she bent and raised his hand to her lips. Before he could recover from his amazement she had run across the room and turned with her hand on the knob of the door from behind which the cry and the sobs had reached him. She gestured him away. Her voice thrilled him.

"I shouldn't have done that. I should never have loved you."

She opened the door and disappeared, but she could not close the door quickly enough to smother the sounds of a difficult and stertorous breathing.

He walked to the hall, his heart beating rapidly. What hideous or unnatural thing did that door protect? Without a clue as to its nature his sense of its presence sickened him.

He walked slowly homeward, one moment elated by his recollection of Barbara's beauty and her furtive caress, the next, responding to a sense of futility and fear, born of the shocking cry which had forced her surrender as the price of his silence and his departure. If he had been disloyal to McHugh he could not regret it even after that.

CHAPTER XVI

AFTER FORTY YEARS

WHEN he reached his rooms he was relieved to find Wilkins had gone to bed. He was in no mood for a conversation which, from its nature, could have led to nothing useful, nor did he wish to have any share in Wilkins' decision. At the moment he rather hoped the actor would drop out and halt the revival. But he realized what that would mean—the retreat of McHugh, the victory of the supernatural against which he had struggled so desperately.

The next morning, indeed, McHugh showed no interest in the white flag. He came to the apartment early and burst without ceremony into Quaile's bedroom. He perched himself on the foot of the bed and bit at his inevitable cold cigar.

"You don't look tickled to death to see me, Quaile."

"I suppose I ought to be," Quaile answered wearily. "This is condescending for a manager."

"Hang the fluff," McHugh answered. "I'm running no cut and dried production, and don't forget things may come to a head tonight. We go through that scene at dress rehearsal if Wilkins sticks, and, by my own advice, he's thinking it over. Honest, I haven't the nerve to ask him how he's jumped, because, Quaile, if Woodford's ghost, by any chance, isn't doing all this damage, the only way I've got to prove it is to bring this production off."

"I suppose you've been working on a definite idea," Quaile said. "I must say, I resent your lack of confidence in me."

McHugh arose and strolled about the room.

"What I've just told you is confidential," he answered. "That's the way I feel about it. The production's got to go through."

He paused.

"Did Wilkins say anything last night? Or maybe you've seen him this morning?"

Quaile yawned.

"I haven't, and he'd gone to bed when I got home. Any word from the telephone company?"

"Yes, and no better luck than I had with your warning. They say that the call that scared Dolly couldn't possibly have been made. As far as they're concerned it was Woodford's laugh she heard."

Quaile sat up, throwing back the covers.

"McHugh," he said, "if you could only tell me that the thing isn't spiritual!"

"Well I can't," McHugh answered. "Wish I could. Wish the first night was over and we were all out of the woods. Look here. I've got to find out about Wilkins sooner or later. Which is his room?"

Quaile told him and arose. He heard McHugh knock and enter. From time to time the subdued murmur of voices reached him.

After he dressed he met the manager in the hall. It was not difficult to read Wilkins' decision in McHugh's sparkling eyes, in his face, broadened by a smile, in the jaunty angle of his cigar.

"So he's going on?" Quaile said.

"Nervy boy, that!" McHugh commented. Same class as

you."

Quaile questioned if McHugh had urged the favorable resolution with facts he had withheld from him. A moment later, when the manager left, he was almost sure of it. He followed him to the door. McHugh faced him there with an unaccustomed restraint.

"Say, how long did you hang on at Barbara's last night?"

Quaile was glad so little daylight entered the hall. He tried to answer unconcernedly.

"Really I don't know. Maybe fifteen or twenty minutes."

McHugh appeared to search for words.

"I don't suppose— There's no earthly use my asking what you talked about?"

"There isn't," Quaile answered firmly. "That's one point on which we disagree. I've told you often enough I won't spy on Miss Morgan, and I—well, no matter what you have in your mind—I trust her."

"All right," McHugh said. "I was young myself once. Too bad youth and dam foolishness trot along hand in hand. Still it's great to be young."

"Just what do you mean?"

"What a blind man could see," McHugh said, "that you've fallen hard for the girl."

"That scarcely concerns you," Quaile flashed. "But suppose I had. Wouldn't it be the decent thing for you to explain your absurd suspicion of her?"

McHugh grunted.

"Just why I won't."

"Then please don't draw inferences from my friendship for her. In any other direction I'll do what you wish. Heaven knows I want to help, for I am afraid for Wilkins."

McHugh opened the door.

"Then we'll hope, Quaile, we won't have to say any more about it. And don't think I'm an old busybody. I got to do my job as I see it, no matter who gets stepped on."

Quaile closed the door, more worried than he cared to admit by McHugh's parting words. His reason cried that a menace lurked in them for Barbara and himself. Wilkins' manner, when he came from his room, troubled him further. Although the actor appeared tired and haggard, Quaile could get nothing illuminating from him as to McHugh's arguments.

"I'm going through with it," was all he would say, "because I can't bear the thought of cowardice. Yet I'm afraid."

"It's the wrong attitude," Quaile argued. "For instance, if Woodford's spirit was responsible it could injure you chiefly through your own fear. It's worth recalling that Carlton, when he tackled that scene, was terribly afraid."

"Joyce's dope," Wilkins guessed. "McHugh's arranged for me to meet him this morning, though I don't see for the life of me what good it can do."

They walked to the theatre in a silence neither cared to break. The moment he stepped on the stage Quaile saw Joyce in the auditorium. The psychist sat with McHugh who straightway beckoned Wilkins. The three talked then for some time in low tones while the anxiety of Wilkins' face increased.

Again Quaile was puzzled by McHugh's interest in the Englishman. Why should he bring him here a second time? Why should he wish him to talk to Wilkins except as a defense against the supernatural? That, as always, seemed the only logical solution of the case.

There was more light and a new activity in the theatre today. The entrance to the foyer and several fire exits stood open. Cleaning women, stout, slow in their movements, bent in grotesque and dejected angles, scrubbed and dusted. The shadowed daylight appeared not to diminish the familiar gloom. The whirling dust increased rather than smothered that mysterious and persistent odor of a perfume used years ago by Woodford.

Quaile searched anxiously for Barbara. He asked Mike if she had come. The old property man had not seen her enter. Disconsolately Quaile returned to the stage. For the first time he noticed Dolly who sat alone in a corner. He joined her, answering to a new mistrust, for not only did she carry deeper scars of last night's fear than the rest of them, but her old uneasy manner had returned, her eyes were ominously restless.

"Why do you glance around like that?" he asked. "Not because—"

She nodded. She tried to hold her eyes steady.

"It's here again," she said, "and tonight we go through that scene."

Her fingers pulled at her handkerchief.

"I saw Woodford die. I saw Mr. Carlton die during that scene, and it was there both times. The first time, I saw it, because it was alive. But it was there just the same the other time, even though I didn't see it. I can't bear to look at Mr. Wilkins. It is like looking at the dead in a dim nightmare. I tell you that the cat is here. It is ready, too, for the big scene."

Quaile wanted to reassure her, but he couldn't hide his own belief.

"Your nerves after last night."

"We'll see," she said dully.

She put her handkerchief to her eyes.

"But I don't want to see."

"Have you told McHugh?"

"Yes, and he doesn't doubt. The Englishman believes it. It's wicked of them to let Mr. Wilkins go on. You didn't sneer at me when I said it was Woodford's laugh I heard over the telephone."

McHugh called to him, and he turned and hurried to the footlights. Joyce, he saw, had left the theatre. Wilkins strolled up and down the aisle, his hands in his pockets. McHugh glanced at his watch.

"Half-past ten," he muttered, "and no sign of our leading lady. At least, Quaile, you might tell me if you've any reason to think she's going to throw me down."

"You heard what she said last night," Quaile answered. "That's all I know, but from what I've seen of her I think she'll keep her word."

Mike came from the wings. He was clearly angry.

"Mike may have heard from her," Quaile suggested.

As a matter of fact, Mike brought a message from Barbara. She had just telephoned she was suffering from a headache and would have to cut the morning rehearsal.

"Say anything about tonight?" McHugh snapped.

"Yes, sir—that she would surely be on hand for the dress rehearsal."

"Then what you looking so glum about?" McHugh demanded. "Much you care if our morning's wasted."

"It's the newspapers," Mike answered. "There are four reporters at the stage entrance, and I can't drive them away, sir. They try to pump me and they laugh at me. They say they won't go until they see you."

McHugh flushed. He sprang over the footlights.

"They'll get their wish," he cried.

Quaile followed him.

"Easy, McHugh. We can't afford to make enemies of the papers."

"Ferrets!" McHugh growled. "Wish I could switch Woodford's spook on them. I've no time to waste today smoothing Josiah Bunce."

Nevertheless he faced the four pleasant but persistent young men with a fair amount of restraint. They displayed copies of an early edition of a sensational newspaper. McHugh snatched one away and glanced it over with Quaile. Its leading story elaborated the revival and the strange difficulties which had threatened it. Most astonishing of all, it contained hints of the vision Quaile had seen, of the flight of the cat, of Wilkins' unaccountable adventure last night.

"Nothing to say," McHugh announced. "Where did all this fairy-book stuff come from?"

But the reporters did not choose to be interviewed. That was their business. They wanted a verification and fresh and dramatic details.

McHugh turned away in disgust.

"I told you I had nothing to say. You youngsters better see the owners of the building, Robert and Josiah Bunce."

One of the reporters laughed.

"A swell chance we'd have with Josiah! They say the old miser hasn't been out of his house for fifteen years."

"Maybe I'm to blame for that," McHugh said. "So long, boys, I'm more interested in a theatrical production than ghosts."

"I hope that's right, Mr. McHugh," a reporter dared.

McHugh refrained from answering. He reentered the theatre with Quaile and dismissed the company.

"All on hand at seven-thirty sharp," he shouted. "There are reporters in the alley. Don't open your mouths to them. I'll run the publicity for this concern, and I'll see that you get plenty of the right kind."

When Quaile and he were driving uptown McHugh reverted to that astonishing article.

"I never told anybody about the cat slinking out. Did you?"

"That's an absurd question, McHugh."

"All right," the manager took him up. "Then it looks a whole lot like friend Barbara. And why couldn't the rest of it have come from her?"

Quaile wouldn't answer, but he acknowledged the justness of McHugh's conclusion. On the other hand, he could imagine no motive that would have urged Barbara to talk in defiance of the manager's command. He did his best to cover his chagrin.

"No matter where it came from the publicity will bring a line a mile long to the box office."

"So it will," McHugh mused. "So it will."

A closed car of a foreign pattern stood in front of the entrance to McHugh's offices. As Quaile and the manager stepped to the sidewalk the distinguished figure of Robert Bunce emerged from the hallway. McHugh cursed under his breath.

"I knew it. Trouble's breaking already."

Robert, however, revealed no excitement, and only the mildest disapproval. Having been told McHugh was out, he explained, he had been about to seek him at the theatre. He appeared to find an element of humor in the situation, but it was sufficiently patent that he accepted his eccentric elder brother's belief that McHugh was making advertising capital out of Woodford's history. But Robert, Quaile appreciated, did not share Josiah's sacred regard for real estate. As an extraordinarily successful business man he must grasp the manager's fancied point of view. He shook hands formally.

"I daresay you know why I'm here," he said to McHugh. "I come from my brother. He's read this miserable drivel in the papers, and, foolishly, he's let it throw him in a passion. But it is the second time it's happened, and consequently, he says, the last. In a word, Mr. McHugh, he wants to recall the lease and get you and your damaging publicity off our property. I must say I agree with him, but he says you were a trifle offended the last time he talked with you. So, I volunteered to see if I couldn't straighten things out— perhaps get your promise to muzzle your press agent."

McHugh cried out.

"As the Almighty's my judge, Bunce, I've had nothing to

do with these stories, and they're true—gospel. That theatre of yours holds a mystery that's turning me gray, making me doubt my own senses."

Bunce moved back.

"It's inconceivable, Mr. McHugh," he answered in a puzzled tone, "yet you seem to believe what you say. I don't want to be unjust. Suppose you go talk to my brother and see if you can persuade him. He handles our real estate, and I promise you I won't interfere as long as my interests are reasonably protected."

"I'll go right away," McHugh accepted. "Get back in the car, Quaile."

"Good," Robert said. "I'll probably be there myself before you leave. We'll talk things over and try to get at the truth of the matter."

"He's got some sense," McHugh said as they drove off.

"Too much," Quaile answered, "for us to make him believe half we've experienced at Woodford's."

"I shan't worry about him," McHugh said, "until I've been through the fiery furnace of another interview with Josiah. Old fool! I'd rather try to borrow money from a country banker."

They had only a few blocks to go. They alighted in front of the Bunce mansion which, in this bright sunlight, had a dingier, more disreputable appearance than ever. Its large, heavy front door had the aspect of a portal raised against cheerfulness and youth.

McHugh's ring brought no response. He pressed the button again impatiently. At last the Scotch butler, Watson, threw the door wide. His face was white. His hand on the knob trembled. For once he had an air of welcome.

"Oh, sirs," he quavered, "come in quick. Thank the Lord you're here."

"What's up, Watson?" McHugh wanted to know.

But Quaile, sufficiently startled by the servant's manner,

went through into the twilight of the hall. From the rear he heard a groan, low pitched, prolonged. Then Josiah's frightened voice arose.

"Watson! Watson! Don't you leave me!"

"It's the old man," McHugh cried.

Quaile ran along the hall. At the moment he suspected nothing more than Josiah's sudden illness, but on the threshold of the library he paused, aware of his mistake, yet unable to interpret the scene before him.

The shades were no more than half raised. The brilliant sun was not permitted to enter here. Josiah had left his customary chair. He stood in front of the fireplace, his uncouth figure silhouetted against the flames, swaying back and forth, back and forth, while the tatters of his dressing-gown flapped about his ankles. His scanty hair was in disorder. His face was vacant with alarm. He held the fire tongs loosely in his knotted hand. As McHugh pushed past Quaile he groaned again. The tongs slipped from his fingers and clattered on the floor.

McHugh strode to him and grasped his shoulders.

"What's happened here, Bunce?"

The hermit fumbled at McHugh's coat. His voice whined, evidently overcoming a difficulty in his throat, suppliant rather than accusing.

"This is your work, Mr. McHugh."

The manager's grasp tightened.

"What work? That's what I want to know."

"You did it," the old man broke out. "Tell me that you tried to fool me, and I won't be mad. I won't say anything. Didn't you try to frighten me?"

McHugh stepped back, releasing the other's shoulders.

"Sorry, Bunce. Now you tell me what frightened you."

Quaile had a feeling that McHugh could forecast the answer.

Bunce relaxed. He stumbled forward and sank in his

easy chair. He sprawled there, his knees shaking, his jaw fallen, in an attitude of complete exhaustion.

McHugh turned to Watson who had followed him in.

"I found him standing that way by the fire, sir," the man whimpered, "it's not five minutes ago."

"Watson's no use," Bunce gasped. "And he left me alone. Not a soul in the house."

"It's the cook's day off, sir," Watson said defensively, "and Mr. Josiah sent me on an errand."

"I didn't think," Bunce groaned. "How could I think of that?"

McHugh bent over the awkward figure in the chair.

"What was it, Bunce? Are you going to tell me?"

And again Quaile received the impression that the manager could guess.

Josiah motioned toward the hall. His lips moved. He scarcely made himself audible.

"The—the thing that—limped out there."

In the close and insufferable atmosphere of this room Quaile felt suddenly cold. McHugh straightened.

"That limped!" he shot out. "What do you mean? What was it like?"

Bunce wet his lips.

"Like—like Bertrand Woodford."

With an unexpected gesture McHugh snatched the cigar from his mouth, broke it in half, and flung the pieces on the fire. Quaile, looking at him, saw purple rage in his face.

"So like," Bunce went on, "that I forgot for a minute it's been forty years since I heard him limp in this house, and I—I called his name, but no one came in, and, when I got to the hall, it was empty."

He grasped the arms of his chair and drew himself up. His voice rose shrilly.

"If it wasn't your trick it must have been Woodford, because I heard. His—his cat was with him."

"Quaile," McHugh snarled, "get upstairs. I'll search this floor. Watson, go through the basement with a fine-tooth comb. Hurry now."

Josiah indicated his approval. Quaile sprang up the stairs and ran through rooms filled with decaying, old-fashioned furniture. He opened closet doors. He peered behind curtains and under beds, convinced of the fruit-lessness of his efforts. He entered the last room, a small apartment, evidently unused, for the blinds were drawn, and in the tranquil green light the dust lay thick on furni-ture and floor, and cobwebs waved in the angles of the ceiling. He went on and opened the closet door.

He stiffened, choking back his cry. He closed his eyes that he might not see, but the picture became more terrible in this self-imposed darkness. So, he opened his eyes and gazed again at Barbara Morgan, cringing in the shadows of the closet, trying pitifully to hide herself where there was no longer any concealment from him of her atrocious presence. He wondered that the contortion of her face did not destroy its beauty.

"I don't know anything about it. For God's sake don't let them know I'm here. I'd rather kill—"

He couldn't look any longer. He drew away. As her voice failed a quiet rustling reached him. He glanced back. She lay face downward on the floor of the closet.

CHAPTER XVII

McHUGH LOSES HIS TEMPER

QUAILE conquered the numbness which momentarily had held him from thought, from action. He advanced slowly toward Barbara's motionless figure. The main fact, the shameful truth, was beyond contradiction. She had concealed herself in a remote part of this house after the limping footsteps had frightened Josiah Bunce. But he couldn't cry out her guilt as long as a chance remained that she might explain her presence here. He would give her that chance if he could keep the others downstairs.

He stooped and raised her wrists. The flesh was cold under his touch, but she stirred almost immediately, opened her eyes, and endeavored wildly to get to her feet.

"Barbara!" he said. "What are you doing here?"

She had struggled to her knees. She paused there and leaned back against the wall, breathing harshly.

"You mustn't ask that."

"You will tell me," he said.

But she shook her head. She made herself go on with odd, uneven pauses between the words.

"You've not forgotten that you love me—that you—promised to trust me? You won't let them know I'm here?"

For a time he was certain she held the explanation of Woodford's ghost—a solution infinitely more abhorrent than that spectral one from which he had always shrunk.

"Then you did that," he breathed. "It was you who made the limping footsteps that frightened Bunce."

She glanced up with unstudied bewilderment.

"How can you think that? No. I heard them. They frightened me, too. I ran here."

"Did you see anything?" he asked.

"No. I was frightened. You won't let anybody know I'm here?"

"I want to believe you," he began.

He broke off and grasped her elbows.

"Tell me," he begged. "Don't you see you've got to tell me?"

With an impetuous vehemence she tried to free herself. He grasped her closer. He could not let her go until she had answered that question. But she held herself rigid. All she would say was:

"I can't tell you. I can never tell you."

"You know the Bunces?" he asked.

She shook her head.

"Answer me," he urged her desperately. "Then what are you doing in their house?"

Her breath caught.

"Let go my arm. You hurt. You lied last night. You are going to tell—"

McHugh's shout reached them from the lower floor.

"Quaile! Quaile! You found something up there?"

"What are you going to answer?" she whispered.

He made one last effort.

"You won't explain?"

"No, but if you tell them—"

He let her arms go. He steadied his voice and called.

"Nothing, McHugh. Nothing. I'll be right down."

She braced herself against the door jamb and hid her face.

"I can't wait," he said. "Will you be able to get out un-seen?"

Her head moved affirmatively. He looked back from the door.

"Barbara! Barbara! Why did you come here?"

She gave no sign. She did not move. So he went slowly along the hall and down the stairs. He sought no excuse for his action. She had challenged the fairness of his own attitude toward her. He had kept that clean. He had responded to the trust she had placed in him last night. His reward seemed removed forever beyond his grasp. He mustn't think of that. As far as possible he must strangle thought, for McHugh waited for him at the foot of the stairs, and the former detective had sharp eyes.

"You been gone long enough to find a regiment of ghosts, Quaile."

Quaile managed to answer.

"I wanted to make sure. You and Watson found nothing?"

McHugh spread his hands.

"Never anything but shadows where those footsteps limp."

Quaile at his heels, he walked into the library. Josiah had drawn his rug about his knees. Now and then he shook as if he experienced a sharp chill. Quaile was grateful for the lowered blinds which kept a too-revealing light from his face.

"What am I to do?" Josiah sniveled. "I can't sit here night and day waiting for him to come back."

McHugh sat down.

"Let's get to cases. There's nobody in this house except us four. You've said there was no one here—no servant even—when you sent Watson on the errand."

"Yes. I'm sure."

"How long before we came in did you hear the footsteps?"

"Not more than five minutes. Watson got back right away."

McHugh glanced at the butler.

"You saw nobody, Watson—nobody coming down the steps or from the kitchen entrance?"

"No, sir."

McHugh frowned. He spoke, Quaile thought, with a pronounced reluctance.

"What had you been doing, Bunce—I mean, just before you heard this thing like Woodford walking?"

The recluse reached out and lifted from the table a copy of the newspaper containing the ghostly story of the theatre.

"I remember. I was reading this again. I had sent Robert some little time before to find you and bring you back. I was pretty hot, Mr. McHugh. I was going to give you the devil."

McHugh cleared his throat. His irresolution became more noticeable.

"Were you by any chance talking to yourself?"

Quaile caught the trend of his questions.

"Maybe I was," Josiah said.

"Try to think what you talked about," McHugh urged.

"I don't know," Josiah said reflectively. "I was pretty mad. I—I think I said Woodford's ghost would have a fine chance on my property."

He seemed to appreciate the significance of his words. The ashen shade of his cheeks increased. McHugh glanced at Quaile.

"Bunce," he said solemnly, "get over your temper with me. The only place to lay that ghost is right in your theatre. Dress rehearsal's tonight. Things are coming to a head. We're all worked up enough. I don't want any interference tonight or tomorrow."

"You seem honest," Josiah muttered, "but if I hadn't heard that thing—"

He looked up with a certain slyness. His tone was uncomfortable.

"I'd like to be there myself tonight."

McHugh grinned.

"You, Bunce! They tell me you haven't been out of this house for fifteen years."

The unkempt head bobbed up and down.

"But I don't want to sit here waiting for that thing to limp back."

His sinewy fingers strained about the chair arms.

"You are straight, Mr. McHugh, aren't you? You're not playing tricks on me? It isn't advertising?"

"Don't be a fool," McHugh grunted.

Josiah closed his eyes.

"I'd like to be there just the same."

Quaile could approximate what was going on in that narrow, ineffable mind. Those footsteps had undoubtedly started a renascence of old and supposedly forgotten habits. They must have filled Josiah's brain with the promptings of a youth he had deliberately strangled.

"I'd like to be there," he mused. "I'll send Robert anyway. I wish he was here now."

"He spoke of returning before we left," Quaile said. "When he's heard your experience he may be less doubtful about trusting us."

"We'll wait," McHugh said, "for I want to have a free hand from this minute."

It wasn't long before Watson answered Robert's ring. The younger brother's tolerant smile faded into curiosity before the timid air which still filled this faded and stifling room. He walked to his brother, took his hand, and for some time looked anxiously into the distrustful eyes.

"You're not ill, Josiah?"

Josiah wagged his head from side to side. Robert straightened, a little bewildered.

"Have these people been bulldozing you?"

He laughed shortly.

"Or have they forced one of their publicity spooks into your presence?"

McHugh held up his hand.

"Cut the comedy. Tell him the facts, Bunce."

Josiah recited in detail his experience of the footsteps and the cat while Robert listened, taking no pains to hide his incredulity.

"Sounds like Woodford as I remember him," he said, "but—"

He walked to the mantelpiece and for a long time stared at the fire. Quaile, fighting his own thoughts, felt no impulse to interrupt his reverie. McHugh, however, grew restless.

"I got to be running along," he announced. "So if you've anything to say, better get it off your chest."

Robert turned to his brother.

"What have you told this disciple of Shakespeare, Josiah?"

"I've told him," Josiah answered, "to go ahead and try to find out."

Robert nodded.

"That's sensible, if he's honest, but frankly I don't believe in footsteps without feet."

"That's what I want to get at," McHugh muttered.

"And you're to be there, Robert," Josiah said. "The dress rehearsal's tonight. They won't play any tricks on you."

"Yes, I'll go," Robert answered. "At any rate, we'll be honest with each other, Mr. McHugh. If somebody's trying to play tricks on you as well as on us, you'll find me a strong ally. But please don't blame me if the tremendous benefit you're bound to derive from these stories keeps coming back to my mind."

McHugh started for the door.

"I don't blame you. I only hope you'll get a few of the jolts we've had in that theatre. Then you'll be begging me to stay and fight it out."

But Robert, Quaile saw, would not be easily convinced by any appearance of the supernatural.

"It's high time," he was saying, "that somebody with common sense took hold of the case."

McHugh's temper ran away with him.

"Much obliged," he roared, "but don't you try to interfere with what common sense I have got. There's enough trouble without the people in whose interests I'm working stirring up more."

Robert covered his ears.

"I'm glad to say, Mr. McHugh, in spite of my years, my hearing's quite unimpaired."

McHugh lowered his voice.

"I want to pump into you that I'm working on the level."

He faced Josiah.

"You believe that, don't you?"

"I don't know," Josiah groaned. "I'm worried about my property, and I don't want to be left alone in this house any more. I leave it to Robert to judge you."

Smiling, Robert held out his hand to McHugh.

"If you're on the level, as you put it, you will find me a lenient judge."

"Then you'll be one," McHugh grunted.

"Robert's too practical I'm afraid," Quaile said when they had reached the sidewalk. "It does look to any practical man as though you were manufacturing this stuff to assure a financial success."

It struck him as curious that McHugh failed to meet his eyes, but he had little time to consider that, for the manager straightway recalled to him the necessity of concealing his own emotions.

"You look," McHugh said, "more upset than Josiah."

"It does worry me," Quaile answered.

He knew the uselessness of trying to make excuses. He refused to accompany McHugh to his office. He pleaded the necessity of rest and hurried home.

But when he had stretched himself on the bed, his need of sleep was vanquished by his turbulent recollections. It was comforting to realize that the evidence supported Barbara's assertion that she had had nothing to do with the illusion of the footsteps. Certainly, she had not been in the theatre that first afternoon when the limping and the surreptitious patter of the cat had startled McHugh, Mike, Tommy, and himself. And the footsteps had strayed near him the other night when she had stood beyond the iron door, pounding for admittance. Moreover, she had been with him and McHugh when the unconfirmable sound had pursued them from the theatre.

He reached out also to his memory of her warning to Wilkins last night. Was it possible she had gone to the Bunces to urge them to break the lease? But that was not curative. It argued too clear a conception on her part of the nature of the danger. Nor did it explain her hiding herself away, her abominable terror that McHugh and the Bunces might know she was in the house. And it sharpened his remembrance of the cry from behind the closed door in her apartment, the horror with which she had greeted it, the deliberate destruction of her reserve in order that he might hold it secret. What suffering, he asked himself, lurked behind the door, nearly always silent, but now and then unexpectedly gathering strength for a spasmodic and uncontrollable outburst?

Such reflections placed inaction beyond his power. He abandoned the effort to rest. Wilkins, stimulated by more personal and menacing doubts, evidently shared his agitation. Quaile had heard the leading man moving about in the next room. He went in. A pungent fog of cigarette smoke whirled in the draught from the door. Wilkins, without his coat, paced up and down. A neglected book lay on the bed. He swung around as Quaile entered.

"Perfect rot my not being able to rest when I know McHugh will probably keep us up most of the night!"

"I can understand," Quaile answered, "but all that smoking's beastly for your nerves."

"Confess I'm doing it to keep them up," Wilkins said. "Wish to the devil Joyce hadn't ordered me to approach the big scene without a sense of fear. I'm to forget that Woodford fell dead playing it, and that Carlton dropped the same way forty years after. You know, that's the deuce of a proposition to put up to a man."

Quaile agreed.

"It is nervy of you," he said, "to take it on at all."

"No," Wilkins answered. "I might have thrown McHugh down, but I'm dashed if I could treat myself that way."

Quaile acknowledged that he, too, had found rest impossible. He suggested that they go to his club and cut in a bridge game.

"Something to think about," he said. "I mean, if we don't keep our minds on the game our partners will give us plenty to worry over."

Wilkins accepted eagerly. They struggled along, as Quaile had prophesied, to the wrath of their partners until it was time to return to the apartment.

While he dressed, and during their hurried dinner, Quaile's ears were alert for the telephone. He prayed that Wilkins would be spared that unnatural warning before attempting the scene. The bell remained quiet. He closed the door and walked to the elevator thankfully.

When they reached the theatre Wilkins went through the alley to the stage door, but Quaile paused on the sidewalk, gazing with a feeling of wonder and encouragement at the transformed facade of the old building. It seemed impossible that where there had been so much darkness, so much dinginess, there should have sprung up such light, such motion, such eagerness. He recalled his reverie the afternoon he had stood opposite, trying to imagine the theatre in its youth. Already Woodford's made a brave attempt to resume the mantle of its ancient glory.

The iron railing, which had guarded the filthy emptiness of the lobby, had been removed. The cracked and weather-stained display boards at either side were concealed by new and colorful posters, advertising "Coward's Fare," calling attention blatantly to the fact that it had been the famous Bertrand Woodford's greatest play. Workmen had polished the brass railings, and to an extent had removed the dripping grime from the walls. The violet rays of a new arc light softened the scars too deep for healing. Most amazing of all, those rays bathed a long line of men and women which curved along the sidewalk, up the steps between the slender columns, and to the open box-office window. Such an advance sale was without precedent. Whether McHugh wished it or not, the publicity centering about the occult was bearing golden fruit.

He saw Tommy, the assistant stage manager, watching the line with eyes that sparkled. He climbed the steps and went up to the small, trim figure, resplendent with the latest sartorial caprices.

"Geest, Mr. Quaile!" Tommy greeted him. "Ever see such an advance sale? We'll need a platoon of cops to hold 'em back tomorrow night. I hate to carry the figures to the boss—they're so big."

"Where is Mr. McHugh?" Quaile asked.

"Back—where I ought to be."

The stained-glass doors glowed with a subdued light from within. For the first time Quaile realized that he no longer need use the somber alley through which many times he had walked reluctantly to face the old building's manifestations. He followed Tommy through one of those pleasant doors. He paused, while the assistant went on to the passage behind the boxes, and took in with a quickening pulse the new appearance of the auditorium. Hitherto the abode of suggestive shadows, it stretched away from him now flooded with light. The linen covers, which he had found comparable with shrouds in a huge mortuary, had been removed. The staircase, down which the limping footsteps had shambled the night of his vigil, radiated an air of comfortable warmth from its dull red carpet. He glanced at the seat on the aisle where he had awaited that terrifying approach. The curtain, whose lowering then had startled him through a darkness almost palpable, was down. The house was quite ready for a performance. Its former aspect was one with a morbid dream. Its manifestations assumed the same unreal quality. Surely the unhealthy influence of the place was in retreat before these pretentious changes. Surely things would proceed normally tonight. Surely Wilkins would come through.

Such thoughts, however, survived only as far as the passage to the stage. They armed him with no new strength to enter that constricted space where he had faced the vision in cold white flame. Moreover, as soon as he started through he became aware of that customary, repellent odor, the shadow, as Dolly always said, of the perfume Woodford had used.

There was more beyond to destroy his fugitive contentment. McHugh, Dolly, and Mike stood in the center of the stage. The flashing borders and the brilliancy of the new scenery pointed the contrast of the drawn faces and the distrust of these two who had known Woodford.

"What's up now?" Quaile asked as he joined them.

"The brainless idiots!" McHugh muttered with an artificial scorn. "They've been seeing and feeling things again."

Mike's face worked.

"But I did see it, Mr. McHugh."

"What?" Quaile asked.

"A figure, sir. Like him. Like Mr. Woodford, except that it was white fire."

Quaile's jaw set. Here at last was the verification of his own vision. The affair was back on its old impracticable basis.

Dolly placed her hand on the property man's arm. He shook from head to foot. He could not keep his mouth still. He was a picture of unconditional fear.

"Just my luck, Quaile, to have you hear that," McHugh lamented. "I won't have a steady pair of knees in the house. You've done enough, damage, Mike. Chase back to your job if your legs'll carry you."

"He's right," Dolly put in. "I warned you this morning, and tonight the cat is closer."

She looked swiftly around.

"As close as the day Mr. Carlton died."

McHugh flung up his hands, but behind his bluster Quaile saw the real extent to which his anxiety had been spurred.

"Shut up, Dolly, and get to your dressing-room. Mike, do as I tell you. Back to your door."

Dolly went, with an extreme unwillingness, her eyes searching—searching—

McHugh met Mike's appealing glance with an angry wave of his hand.

"It's taking too big chances," Quaile said when the property man had gone.

McHugh shifted his weight.

"Maybe so, but I got to take them."

"How did Mike see the—the thing?"

"It was when he came down to open up," McHugh explained. "He says he saw the thing like what you saw come out of Woodford's old dressing-room between the stage door and the passage. It took the starch out of him. He ran to the alley and wouldn't come back until the crew arrived to shift the new scenery. Of course, those birds have been whispering. Got their heads together now. But there aren't any union rules about ghosts."

"And Woodford's dressing-room?" Quaile said. "Surely you haven't put Wilkins there?"

McHugh glared.

"You think almost as well of me as Robert does. Certainly not. Wilkins is where he dressed the night we took the pictures. Dolly and Barbara were together that night, but now I've made them all comfortable."

Quaile could guess the point of McHugh's circuitous announcement.

"You mean?"

McHugh cleared his throat.

"That I've assigned Barbara to Woodford's old room."

Quaile flushed, tempted to take issue with McHugh on that arrangement. He did not like to think of Barbara there. It was obvious that the manager wished the girl where he could watch her comings and goings. But did that cover his purpose? Had it any deeper significance?

"You think it safe, McHugh?"

"Why not? Nothing's been after Barbara but you that I know of."

It wasn't easy for Quaile to press the point. His recollecttion of Barbara hidden in the Bunce house smothered his resentment. He tried to speak indifferently.

"Is she here yet?"

McHugh's frown was sufficient answer. He glanced at his watch.

"Quarter of eight. If that girl throws me down—"

He snapped the case shut.

"I thought you might know something about her movements, you're so darned friendly with her."

"I know nothing," Quaile said.

"Don't you suppose she understands," McHugh asked fiercely, "that if she fails me I'm beaten?"

"You mean," Quaile asked with dry lips, "that you would accept that as the final proof against her?"

McHugh's tone was ugly.

"I usually mean just about what I say."

He crossed the stage in the direction of Wilkins' dressing-room. Quaile deliberately chose the other side and walked toward the alley door. He was glad to leave McHugh. He knew as he stood in the shadows of the wings that his face recorded his mental suffering. His misgivings were all the more profound because McHugh had based his enmity for the girl on reasons he cherished stubbornly. He could not tell, therefore, how serious the manager's threat was. But Barbara had answered to the desperate necessity of concealing in her home a person whose incoherent, sexless cry had brought a color of guilt to her appearance and her actions. She had gone stealthily to the Bunces' and had hidden there in a panic of fear. These facts suggested that there were, indeed, angles from which McHugh might attack her with a vicious assurance of success. The impetus for such an attack, he had made it clear, would spring from her absence tonight or her refusal, if she came, to play the part.

He paced rapidly among the new litter of scenery. He was scarcely conscious of the burly, shirt-sleeved members of the crew who jostled him without ceremony. He could not wholly censure McHugh. The man's nerves were raw. Barbara's defiance last night gave him no cause to spare her. On his own part, in face of all that had happened, Quaile clung to his faith in the girl. That helped urge him to his final, delicate resolution. If she came here he would see to it that she played her rôle. If she failed to appear he would use every means in his power to bring her. He clenched his hands. Perhaps she had not left the Bunce house unobserved. Suppose Robert, Josiah, or the butler had discovered her and turned her over, as those men would, to the authorities for punishment? He strode, lashed by this fear, to the stage door.

"Mike," he said, "you're sure you've had no word from Miss Morgan? She couldn't have telephoned without your knowing it?"

Mike glanced from the door.

"Who's that coming now, sir?"

Quaile stepped out. A furtive figure had entered the mouth of the alley. Although the place was very dark the figure clung to the thicker obscurity of the theatre wall. It approached slowly. Once or twice, Quaile thought, it stopped altogether. Mike drew back.

"I think, sir, it is Miss Morgan."

Quaile turned away, not wishing to believe, yet convinced that Mike was right. She came up, breathing as if she had been running. He spoke gently to her, but she seemed not to hear. As she hurried through the stage entrance he saw that she was dressed exactly as he had last seen her in her sanctuary at the Bunces'.

"You got out," he whispered, close to her.

McHugh slipped from behind a piece of scenery. To all appearances he had been waiting as anxiously as Quaile. Barbara stepped back.

"Maybe better late than never," McHugh grumbled. "You hustle, Barbara, or you'll hold the show up."

She bowed her head. Quaile scarcely caught her voice.

"I can't go on, Mr. McHugh."

"The devil you can't!" McHugh snarled.

"I can't. I can't," she repeated dully.

She was very tired. She grasped the doorknob of Woodford's dressing-room. She leaned wearily against it.

McHugh didn't disguise his temper. In a way, his excuse was valid. Quaile knew he had staked his reputation as a detective on the solution of the mystery. That, he had said more than once, depended on the production of "Coward's Fare." Now this girl threatened to make it impossible.

"You cut the temperamental stuff," he cried, "and get in your clothes, or you'll never play on Broadway again, and that's only the beginning of what will happen to you."

"Don't, McHugh," Quaile begged.

"I can't blame him," Barbara said, "but it makes no difference. I won't go on with it."

"Maybe you'll tell us why?" McHugh sneered.

For the first time she looked directly at him.

"Because I'm afraid."

"What of?"

She continued to stare at him with the air of one whose vision is not limited by the visible world.

"Of this place," she whispered. "Of the thoughts—of the ghosts in this place."

The dead level of her tone, which expressed an absolute sincerity, shocked Quaile. Nevertheless, it could not destroy his resolution. He didn't give McHugh time for another outburst.

"Keep quiet," he said, "and let me talk to her alone."

Her glance was alarmed.

"And what will you two say?" McHugh scoffed. "Maybe something like you said last night, eh?"

Quaile turned to Barbara.

"Will you wait here for a moment?"

"What for? It's no use."

"Will you wait?"

She nodded indifferently, so he drew McHugh to one side.

"You'll let your temper carry you too far someday," he

said. "No. Don't break out. We're all too highly strung, but we all want to see this thing through. You ought to know your threats won't move her an inch. You've resented my friendship for her. At least it gives me a better argument than yours. If I talk to her alone I may change her mind."

McHugh's jaw receded. His flush died away.

"Do that, Quaile, and we'll forget the harsh words all around."

His smile was whimsical.

"I'm an old fool, and you're a young one. Wish I knew what was going on between you two."

"It's of small consequence now," Quaile said, and went slowly back to Barbara.

CHAPTER XVIII

THE CLAWS OF THE UNSEEN CAT

"WHAT is it you wish?" she asked. "You won't be long? I want to go home. I want to get away from this place."

"You must stay."

"Oh, no," she said wistfully. "I shall not stay."

"The future means nothing to you?" he asked.

She laughed harshly.

"The future! That amounts to very little. It's the present I'm afraid of."

"You mean?"

"The shadows here, and what has happened on that stage; and what may happen again."

He looked at her closely.

"Yet you say you know nothing about it. Then you will do this for my sake."

Slowly she shook her head.

"It was you," he said, "who didn't tell the truth last night."

She turned away.

"There's no use talking of that. We must never talk of that again."

He failed to hide his bitterness.

"Think of yourself. I warn you McHugh has his reasons for putting the production through. If you stop him his resentment will go farther, perhaps, than you think. Remember he might still interest the police in Carlton's death."

But that threat had no more power with her than McHugh's.

"I am only afraid of the things I can't see."

Then to spare her, equally whether she had told the truth or not, he forced himself to state his ultimatum.

"Barbara," he said, "you are going on tonight, and, if we rehearse that scene without another tragedy, you are going on for the opening tomorrow night."

She stammered:

"Yo—you're commanding me!"

"Since there's no other way."

She cried out angrily:

"And I refuse!"

He spread his hands.

"Your refusal sends me to McHugh. A man has died. Another is threatened. I must give what information I can."

Her lips parted.

"You'd tell him—"

"About your secret presence at the Bunces' this afternoon. If necessary, about that hidden thing that screamed in your home last night. You force me to do it."

His words might have had a tangible power. They repelled her step by step. The expression that unnatural scream had brought last night he read in her eyes now.

"You shan't," she breathed.

"You mean you'll go on."

"No. No."

She shuddered.

"I tell you I'm afraid. You wouldn't make me go on?"

His victory was less palatable than defeat would have been.

"McHugh!" he called hoarsely.

There was a stir at the rear. The manager hastened toward them.

"I hate you!" she said. "I hate you!"

Her laughter was harsher than before. It had the quality of a sob.

"And they want me to mimic tragedy—on the stage."

"Well?" McHugh asked as he came up.

Quaile looked away.

"She will tell you."

"What's the word, Barbara?"

Quaile would not glance back. He wouldn't face again her fear and her uncertainty. He heard her speak. He had not realized how vital her answer had become to him.

"I'm going on, Mr. McHugh."

McHugh exploded joyously.

"Good girl! I knew you'd come to your senses. You'll be a Mrs. Siddons yet."

She spoke through chattering teeth:

"In which dressing-room did my maid leave my things?"

"I've put you," McHugh answered, "in Woodford's dressing-room."

She stiffened. She raised her hands defensively.

"You won't make me go there!"

McHugh touched the faded gilt star on one of the panels.

"Say, you're hard to please. I'm giving you the star dressing-room. Actresses cry for it."

"Woodford's room!" she murmured.

"Sure. Wasn't he a star? No more talk now. We're losing time."

McHugh's stubborn manner furnished further proof that he had a subtle purpose in forcing her to use that cheerless room.

"There are plenty of places upstairs," she said.

McHugh frowned.

"They're not ready."

He opened the door and stepped past her into the blackness of the little room. Quaile heard a click, and light
flashed on stained and desolate walls. The only signs of
occupancy were a number of bottles and boxes on the table
and Barbara's clothes, arranged by the maid in the closet
whose door stood half open.

She glanced in once. Holding her breath, she crossed the
threshold.

"After all," she whispered, "what difference does it
make?"

She closed the door.

McHugh turned to Quaile, about to question, perhaps to
accuse. Quaile could not face that now. Before the manager
could speak he had slipped into the passage. He hurried
through, aware of a new, strange humming sound which
echoed in the narrow space. But the memory of the last
words Barbara had addressed directly to him filled his ears.
"I hate you!" she had said. "I hate you!" Yet he had guided
his course by the single beacon of her welfare.

As he stepped into the auditorium the explanation of the
new sound challenged him to a saner mind. At last a small
audience had collected in Woodford's. There were managers or their representatives, critics, friends of McHugh's
and the company's, a group which held itself aloof and to
which Quaile was attracted by one or two nods of welcome.

Robert Bunce was in the midst of the group. Probably he
had brought these people, for they were wealthy, of assured
social position. With their evening dress and their laughing
chatter they gave an added touch of cheerfulness to the
auditorium.

Quaile couldn't very well avoid them. He went over and
spoke to the few he knew. Robert shook his hand, impressed no doubt by his acquaintance with friends of his
own.

"Well, young man," he said pleasantly, "things are normal enough out here. How about the mystic regions back?"

"I wouldn't venture to prophesy," Quaile answered.

The trepidation he failed to hide had no effect on Robert's good humor. The lights and the liveliness had distilled a sufficient antidote for the talk of the supernatural the man had heard from McHugh.

Robert glanced around retrospectively.

"Many, many years since I've seen a dress rehearsal here. Not a rehearsal, I believe, since Woodford's last revival of this play. My Lord! Am I that old?"

"I've read about it," one of the women cried. "Woodford fell dead in the third act."

Robert put his finger on his lips.

"*Sh-h*, my dear. Mustn't recall unpleasant memories tonight. I was no older than you when that happened. You know, Mr. Quaile, my brother was tempted to leave his shell. He would have appreciated this. I must say it surprises me to see how much life there is in the old place."

Quaile turned at a quiet footfall behind him. Tommy approached the group. Quaile could guess his purpose, so he stepped aside to meet him.

"Sorry to tear you away from your swell friends," Tommy said, "but the boss is raising cain and wants you. We're nearly ready back there. I'm going to give 'em the first call in a jiffy."

Quaile excused himself and followed Tommy down the aisle and through the passage. McHugh and Joyce waited for him at the other end. The presence of the psychist added to Quaile's uneasiness.

"You'd better get yourself settled, Joyce," McHugh was saying. "Stay back here or go to the auditorium—anywhere you think you'll be most useful."

Joyce's face was heavy and serious.

"I've done my best with you," he said. "I've told you it is

wretchedly unsafe to do that scene. But you're your own master. I'll sit in the box I used the other day if you don't mind. That will put me quite close to the stage. You think it won't be long now?"

"Not over five or ten minutes," McHugh answered.

"Then I'm off."

Quaile regretted the Englishman's departure. It left him, in a sense, at McHugh's mercy, vulnerable to questions for which he had no answers. Nor did McHugh hesitate.

"Why did you rush off?"

"Because I didn't feel like talking."

"You'd better talk now," McHugh snorted. "Seems to me I have a right to know why one of my actresses throws the glove in my face, then turns around and takes water from you."

"You would have aroused the antagonism of a Quaker," Quaile answered, ill at ease. "And, as you've guessed yourself, there was more reason why Miss Morgan should have listened to me."

McHugh flushed.

"That means nothing. You know something about that girl you haven't told me."

Quaile laughed outright.

"I can certainly fling those words in your teeth."

"We're going to have it out," McHugh went on. "You'll give up what you know or—"

Barbara's cry from behind the closed door of Woodford's dressing-room cut across the manager's angry accents, brought them to an abrupt pause. It vibrated with a shrillness, demonstrative of an uncontrollable terror. It ceased.

"Barbara!" McHugh cried.

As Quaile sprang for the door he heard Tommy's feet clattering on the iron stairs, his monotonous voice sing-songing the first call. The cry, then, had not penetrated to the other dressing-rooms. It seemed incredible to him that the routine of the theatre should continue.

He raised his hand, and, afraid to forecast the response, rapped on the panel beneath the faded star. Through the silence that followed he heard a gasping sound. There was no other answer.

"Get in," McHugh ordered.

Quaile grasped the knob, turned it, and opened the door on complete darkness. The gasping sound was more audible. He entered, groping with blind gestures through the obscurity.

"Who put out this light?" McHugh roared.

Quaile heard him stoop and strike a match. The flame glimmered on Barbara. She sat in front of the dressing-table in the costume of the period of Woodford's youth. Her head had fallen forward. Her difficult breathing persisted. Her right hand hung limply at her side. Immediately she raised it and hid it in the folds of her gown.

McHugh reached up and snapped the control of the electric fixture. There was no response.

"Mike!" he shouted. "Mike!"

The match expired. He struck another one as the property man paused on the threshold, glancing in with frightened eyes.

"This light's burned out. Get a new bulb here."

Mike wouldn't enter.

"I put a new globe in this morning," he said.

"It was a frost. Get another double-quick."

Mike turned, shaking his head. Suddenly the room was full of light. The globe burned brightly again.

"The devil!" McHugh muttered. "Go away, Mike. Don't try to argue with me now."

He closed the door. He advanced to Barbara. Her breathing was quieter, but the chalky whiteness of her face made Quaile afraid to speak. McHugh had no scruples.

"You make all that fuss just because the light went out?"

At first she did not answer, but, if that were all, it furnished sufficient excuse for Quaile.

"None of the other lights in the house were affected," he said. "There was no reason for this one to go out and come on again."

Barbara turned slowly. The hatred she had expressed earlier survived in her voice.

"It was your fault," she managed to say.

McHugh was insistent.

"What for besides the light?"

"Because," she said with that same effect as of chattering teeth, "when the light went out I knew—I wasn't alone in this hateful room."

She bent forward against the table, burying her head in the curve of her left elbow. Her right hand, Quaile noticed, still remained hidden in the folds of her gown.

"How were you so sure," McHugh asked, "that there was somebody in the room?"

"I heard footsteps," she said. "The footsteps we heard the other night—footsteps that limped."

McHugh placed his hand on her shoulder.

"Go on," he said more gently. "Then you screamed."

But she shook her head.

"Not then."

McHugh started.

"What more could have happened?"

Her voice gathered strength.

"Something sprang at me. I couldn't see it or feel it, but I knew it was there, lithe and—and black."

She took her hand from the folds of her dress. Glancing up, she slowly raised it, exposing the underside of the wrist.

Quaile stooped swiftly, and, without touching it, examined the white skin. In one place it was scarred with a long, jagged scratch, and, against the pallid flesh, one or two drops of blood stood out, redly eloquent.

She hid her hand again. Quaile looked at McHugh.

"A cat!" he said. "That was done by a cat."

McHugh nodded.

"No question."

Quaile saw his unfriendliness and antagonism for Barbara replaced by a bewildered pity, a genuine remorse. To him, too, unquestionably, this attack suggested Barbara's total ignorance of the theatre's mystery, destroyed beyond a doubt his suspicion of her connection with it. The manager, in fact, hurried Quaile's thought into words.

"I'd bet a house and farm you're not acting now, Barbara. And that door's not been opened since you first came in. I own up I've had my eye on it all the time. That cat has got to be in this room still."

"And whoever limped," Quaile said.

He spread his hands toward the bare, stained walls and the closet whose door stood open, permitting a thorough view of its interior.

"Spookier than ever!" McHugh mused.

Barbara raised her head.

"I didn't want to come in here. I didn't want to go on."

McHugh took her hands.

"You forget what a cross old cuss I've been, Barbara. Remember I've got a lot on my mind. I'll make it up to you. I'll star you on Broadway in letters big enough to make Sarah Bernhardt look like a chorus girl."

"You mean," she whispered, "that I have to go on?"

"Sure. You're nervy. You're not going to let me be beaten by a pack of shadows."

"Oh, I can't! I can't!"

She glanced appealingly at Quaile. He, as thoroughly as McHugh, after what had just happened, answered to an unaccounting ambition to avoid defeat.

"McHugh is right," he said softly. "You must go on."

She commenced to fumble among the makeup para-phernalia on her dressing-table.

"My maid," she said wildly. "I had Mike telephone her. Why isn't she here? And I won't stay in this room. I can't do that for you."

"All right," McHugh agreed. "When your maid comes have her move your things. Double up with Dolly, and I'll have another room fixed for you in the morning."

There was a discreet tapping at the door. Quaile opened, and the silent maid of Barbara's apartment, dressed as always in black, stalked in. Quaile could not conceal his repugnance. He left the room. After a moment McHugh followed him.

"Makes me feel like a criminal, Quaile. Every manager ought to be a slave-driver at heart. I guess I'm a bum man-ager after all."

"This has upset your calculations?"

McHugh didn't answer directly.

"Wouldn't it yours?" he flashed.

"If you'd only be frank, McHugh! If you'd only been frank from the beginning! Tell me what's in your mind."

McHugh kept his face averted.

"I'm wondering if it isn't empty," he said. "There's nothing I can talk to you about now, Quaile. Maybe later. I wish tonight and tomorrow night were over. I wish Wilkins was safely tucked in his bed."

He took a cigar from his pocket and fingered it absent-mindedly.

"Don't think hard of me because I'm a clam. I'm trying to be as good a sleuth as I know how, but no detective ever went up against a proposition like this."

He walked away. His step faltered. He did not once look back.

CHAPTER XIX

AS WOODFORD AND CARLTON

QUAILE remained for some time, staring at the panels which divided him from Barbara and the stealthy maid. Tommy's banging at the doors, his raucous voice, aroused him. He watched the company assemble in the wings. Barbara's door opened. She walked out. She passed close to Quaile, but she failed to glance at him. She hurried by and took up her position at the entrance she must use in the first act. Her makeup, skillfully arranged as it was, did not cover the drawn lines of her face or its pronounced mistrust. Her maid followed her out and, bearing an armful of clothes, glided across the wings to the iron stairs. McHugh's voice came, extraordinarily repressed for him:

"All set. Curtain in two minutes."

Quaile walked through to the auditorium and sat apart in the last row. The spectators were scattered in little groups now among the seats, expectant, almost silent. He envied their ignorance of what he had just experienced. His fingers worked nervously. He watched the curtain, shrinking from its first fluttering. He had the feeling of one who stands on the edge of a precipitous descent before a hurrying and violent pursuit. Joyce, even at this distance, patently displayed his anxiety. The Englishman's glance, too, was steadily attracted by the curtain. He sat well forward in the box, one hand grasping the railing.

Quaile stirred. He tried to fix his attention on less disturbing objects, but the lights and the well-dressed men and women no longer seemed a defense against the manifestations of the house. He had experienced those too convincingly. It occurred to him that they had come to seem as much a part of the building as its ancient walls, its rusty furnishings.

The footlights blazed. The curtain waved and rose with a deliberate smoothness. The stage was exposed. The rehearsal commenced. Quaile watched, absorbed by the picture.

Little by little as the play progressed a curious idea took possession of him. The surroundings, the archaic costumes worn by these actors and actresses, who revived old passions and old humors, seemed to his sensitive imagination actually to have brought back to the theatre its atmosphere of half a century ago.

The illusion captured him. He realized he was a spectator of the very gestures, an auditor of the very words which forty years past had thrilled and horrified the vanished audience that had witnessed Woodford's death.

Barbara alone retained the power to draw him back to the present. She played with a feverish haste. Her movements were uneven. Once, when she cried in Dolly's arms, he knew her grief was real.

There were no interruptions. The first act hastened to its close. The curtain fell. Quaile glanced at his watch, computing the brief time that would elapse before they faced the big scene of the third act. He saw Joyce leave the box and go back, but he remained where he was. He didn't want to go back. He didn't want to greet Dolly with her assurance of a cat, or Barbara with its marks upon her arm, or Wilkins who ran the gravest risk and constantly confessed his understanding of it.

The guests were noisy in their approval. Robert

strolled up and sat with him during a portion of the entr'acte. He was warmly congratulatory.

"You've kept the spirit," he said. "There are very few changes, still it doesn't creak. McHugh must realize—and that's the best argument in his favor—that the play doesn't need such ridiculous publicity. Anyway, things seem to be going smoothly enough. You know, Mr. Quaile, it rolls the years back. This place seems to me as it was then."

"I've been thinking something like that," Quaile answered moodily.

The curtain rose. The second act ran its course. Now the players were not so sure of their lines. From time to time the voice of Tommy, prompting, reached Quaile. It was clear that the strain increased.

Quaile counted the minutes during the second entr'acte. He watched hypnotically as the curtain rose on the third act. The piece ran quickly toward the big scene. He longed for McHugh's power to stop the play before it should be too late. He had seen Carlton die precisely as Woodford had died. Now Wilkins for the first time would follow those directions, would repeat those lines. It wasn't to be borne. He agreed with Barbara and Dolly. It was like murder to drive Wilkins to that point.

With an effort he restrained his desire to cry out. He recalled McHugh's cleverness. The man must know what he was about.

Wilkins made a brave defense, but the panic against which Joyce had warned him was frequently discernible in his voice and his actions. His control, however, was greater than Carlton's had been. Nevertheless, his strength seemed to have evaporated. He was like one who has suffered from a destructive fever.

Dolly's eyes sought again—perpetually sought something she never saw. Barbara's steady watchfulness of Wilkins was no less disturbing. As if her glance included nothing else, she stumbled about the stage, supporting herself when she could against pieces of furniture, clinging now and then to the draperies across the doors.

This increasing apprehension, this unwillingness to proceed, impressed itself upon the audience. Men and women made restless movements, glanced at each other uneasily, commenting in low tones. But more than anyone else Joyce appeared moved. He was bent far forward over the railing of the box. His fingers were white and tense against the red velvet. His glance was absorbed by Wilkins.

Almost before Quaile realized it the company, for the first time since Carlton's death, had entered that tragic scene. It was the genuine anguish of Barbara's denunciation that aroused him. As Wilkins strode to the mantelpiece and snatched up the heavy candlestick, his gesture had the abandonment of a blind despair. Dolly screamed her line.

"Marjorie! Look out!"

Quaile started from his chair. The cry had the broken ring of a dreadful sincerity. Its warning was for Wilkins rather than the girl.

Barbara, however, continued with the directions Quaile had copied from Woodford's yellow script. She backed to the wall, raising her hands against Wilkins. Her gasping voice scarcely carried across the footlights.

"Be careful! What are you going to do to me?"

Wilkins turned, lifting the candlestick, about to spring for her. His open mouth had an appearance of gaping wonder. The line, which death had forbidden two men to speak, started from his lips in a hoarse whisper.

"Pay what debts I can. Kill you, if the strength—"

The candlestick slipped from his fingers and clattered on the boards. His whisper failed. Like a man already dead he crumpled and fell to the stage, without a cry, without a saving gesture.

Quaile, halfway down the aisle, paused, crushed by the sudden blackness which descended upon the house. And through this rapid and unexpected night tore screams and the incoherent movements of panic. But, above it all, from the stage he could hear the measured beat of limping footsteps.

CHAPTER XX

BARBARA'S FLIGHT

QUAILE waited only a moment—that brief moment during which the limping steps trailed across the stage and died away. Their cessation cleared his mind for the actual crisis. Wilkins had fallen as Carlton had died, as Woodford had been stricken forty years before. The only variation had been this invasion of the theatre by a darkness, thick almost to fluidity. That was also impressive as disciplining his momentary confidence in the new brilliancy of the place. Its shadows were still triumphant—still held the power to gather quickly for the destruction of light and tranquility. Somewhere in that darkness sat Joyce who had warned McHugh not to attempt the scene, who, by means of specious formulas, proved the existence of the supernatural. Beyond him lay Wilkins on the decayed flooring of the stage. Quaile had no doubt that he, as the other two had gone, was dead.

The screams of the women in the auditorium were less restrained. The stirrings about him—from the stage. It was as if the repetition of the occult tragedy had imposed upon its previous witnesses a mute and helpless fatalism.

Then, as Quaile started to feel his way down the aisle, McHugh's voice came huskily out of the sable pall:

"Light here! Mike!"

The old property man's broken accents followed.

"Mr. McHugh! He's here! His dressing-room! I knew all along—"

A match scraped on the stage. A blazing spot appeared in the center of the pall and appeared to smolder, leaving ragged fringes of darkness. McHugh's face was lighted—a face as grim as it was alarmed, and the black shroud was destroyed a little above the quiet heap that Wilkins made.

Before Quaile could understand, the house was brilliant again. It was as if the pall, after smoldering, had sprung from the match into a sudden and consuming conflagration.

He scrambled across the footlights. McHugh bent over Wilkins, fumbling about his heart. Dolly had sunk in a chair. Her face was hidden by her wrinkled hands. She muttered to herself, shivering, something about a cat. Barbara was braced against the table, staring at Wilkins' motionless figure.

As he ran toward McHugh Quaile glanced at the auditorium. The rush for the doors had a little subsided. White-faced men and women here and the rustling of skirts, the undirected stumbling of anxious feet—increased; but at first there was no sound there had paused and looked back, clinging to the arms of seats as though their scarcely begun flight had exhausted them. Joyce had climbed to the railing of his box and, crouching upon it like some strange animal, was about to spring to the stage.

McHugh glanced away from Wilkins.

"Ring down!" he cried.

The curtain remained suspended. Quaile guessed that Tommy had fled to the alley. McHugh arose.

"Tommy!" he shouted. "Mike! Will somebody ring down?"

Mike's haggard face appeared at the side. He grasped the cable which controlled the curtain and commenced tugging at it with jerky and nearly futile efforts. Quaile wouldn't look at him, for his features had become distorted. He had surrendered himself to that difficult and unspeakable grief of an old man. His sobs retched through the new stillness. They seemed to mark time for the uneven lowering of the curtain.

The dirty canvas imprisoned them closer with their fear. Quaile, who had been the first to make sure of Carlton's death, had no instinct to examine the huddled shape at his feet. McHugh had done that. Behind those narrow eyes the truth lay. Quaile touched his arm. His question seemed unnecessary.

"He's—dead?"

The tight lips parted.

"Not dead."

A laugh rang out. Its shrill mirth was brutal, nearly blasphemous.

Quaile swung around, revolted. Barbara had not altered her tense and spellbound attitude, but there was no doubt. It was she who had laughed. Her mouth was still open. Her face was without emotion. It was the face of one temporarily stripped of reason. So the apparent mirth of her laughter disclosed its real meaning, and Quaile went to her with a swift concern.

Before he could touch her, before he could speak, a black figure with an indifferent and expressionless face stole from the wings and grasped her arm. Quaile answered to a hot anger against this silent maid whose features and bearing furnished an impenetrable veil for her thoughts, who glided about her mistress with a stealth almost insolent.

"You will take her to her dressing-room?" Quaile asked.

The woman's mouth moved. He thought it formed the word "yes." He couldn't be sure. He watched Barbara follow her across the stage and from his sight with the dumb faith of a little child.

When he turned back McHugh and Joyce were whispering. In the Englishman's dismayed pallor he read only defeat.

"A doctor!" McHugh cried.

Dolly uncovered her face.

"It isn't too late? Because the cat—"

She broke off. She resumed her shuddering.

"Take hold here, Quaile," McHugh directed. "And, Mike, if you can't find Tommy, go for a doctor yourself. The first one you can nab."

"The police—" Quaile suggested.

"He's alive. We don't want the police."

McHugh stooped and raised Wilkins's feet. Quaile lifted the shoulders. The head rolled from side to side. If it hadn't been for the warmth beneath his hands, for the pronounced fluttering of the coat, stretched tightly across Wilkins' chest, he would have doubted McHugh's announcement that the actor lived.

They carried him to his dressing-room and stretched him on a sofa. Dolly tottered after them and, uninstructed, got water, placed Wilkins' head in her lap, and bathed his temples and cheeks.

"Perhaps he'll pull through," Joyce said from the doorway, "but it's no thanks to you, McHugh. He evidently retained just enough resistance."

Quaile accepted his quiet announcement as a definite condemnation of McHugh's hopes. The manager looked up with a slow unwillingness, but before he could speak a violent controversy reached them from the stage. Quaile recognized Robert Bunce's angry tones above a murmur of protesting voices. McHugh flushed.

"Look out!" Quaile advised. "He's got a strong case against you."

He returned to the stage. The space between the curtain

and the walls of the scenery—small at best—was crowded
with men and women from the audience whose curiosity
had been greater than their fright. Quaile recognized the
three men facing Robert as dramatic critics. The result of
their presence was obvious. The great dailies they rep-
resented would carry beneath scare heads tomorrow sensational stories of the rehearsal. He gathered they had come
for news of Wilkins' condition, and that Robert, looking
after his own and Josiah's interest in the property, was
determined to choke this publicity.

"Don't talk to me about spirits," Quaile heard him cry in
response to a mild inquiry. "McHugh is the only ghost I'm
afraid of in this house."

He turned wrathfully on Quaile.

"The pack of you ought to be handled for staging such a
scare."

Quaile shrugged his shoulders.

"Do we look as if we'd had anything to do with it?"

"Where's that mountebank, McHugh?" Robert demanded. "At least he has authority to drive these scandal mon-
gers from the house. They won't budge for me."

McHugh walked from the wings. His squared jaw
foreboded a tempestuous argument, but when he spoke the
words reached Quaile with an exceptional mildness.

"I'm no angel, but somebody spoke my name."

Robert strode to him.

"I shan't retract the mountebank, McHugh. It's as well
you heard. Will you kindly clear these newspaper men out
of here? Then we'll get down to business."

"Certainly bad business for me to offend the critics,"
McHugh grunted. "I have to pretend to love the vipers.
Boys, stay as long as you want, but I know you want to go
now. You've got all the dope I'll give anybody. Wilkins is
alive, and a doctor's on the way. We have to get quiet."

The critics consulted. They agreed to retreat to the lobby

in return for McHugh's promise to send them the result of the doctor's diagnosis. McHugh aroused Mike sufficiently to clear the stage of all those who had no business there. Then he turned to Robert, who accepted the challenge of his glance.

"Now listen, McHugh. There's no question in my mind that your actor aped the manner of Woodford's death and of Carlton's accident. It's a good story—the best of the lot—but it's brought us to the parting of the ways."

McHugh had resumed a long-abused cigar. It protruded from his mouth at a fighting angle.

"What you mean—the parting of the ways?"

"I mean that you're an ideal showman. Perhaps Carlton died a natural death. That may have suggested the way to fill your pockets. I charge you with my brother's scare this afternoon. You, Mr. Quaile, and Watson were alone in the house with him, and a servant's palm is easily greased. I charge you with arranging this business tonight for the benefit of your audience. It's a good scheme from your point of view. I understand you already have one of the largest advance sales on record. But you've forgotten there's an undesirable tenancy clause in your lease, and Josiah and I have warned you. You'll be off our property bag and baggage tomorrow morning."

McHugh snatched a folded paper from his pocket and shook it in Robert's face.

"I told you not to interfere with what I was doing for you and your brother," he snarled. "I've read this lease a good many times, and I went over it again with my lawyer this afternoon. You get an injunction and I'll get an order vacating it in half an hour. By the time you've proved the nature of my tenancy the show will have gray whiskers, and then you'll find it's clean as soap."

"He's quite right, Mr. Bunce," Quaile said. "McHugh, why don't you let him look at Wilkins?"

"What's the use?" McHugh sneered. "He's too practical."

Robert studied him closely.

"If you're so sincere in your innocence why hesitate to let me examine the actor?"

McHugh turned and stalked toward Wilkins' dressing-room.

"You're on. Come see for yourself."

They filed through the doorway. Dolly still bathed Wilkins' head. Joyce leaned against the table. Constantly Dolly looked at him with a pitiful appeal.

Quaile saw Robert's expression alter as he took in this picture which could not reasonably have been arranged for his benefit. The actor's breathing was audible. There was something about it for Quaile reminiscent of the gasping breaths he had heard from Barbara after the attack of the cat.

Robert tiptoed to the sofa and placed his hand on Wilkins' forehead. In response to the contact the actor's head swayed away from him with a comatose helplessness. The eyelids did not flutter. The relaxed limbs had given no start. Robert glanced up.

"Good heavens!" he breathed. "There's no sham here."

For the first time he appeared to see Joyce.

"What does he say? He's a doctor?"

McHugh shook his head. He explained who Joyce was and why he had brought him to this building. Robert straightened. He went to Joyce and stared at him curiously.

"You don't ask us to take this seriously as—as super-normal?"

"Somebody must," Joyce answered. "I warned Mr. McHugh and he refused to listen to me. The result is before your eyes."

Robert turned to McHugh. The uncertainty of his manner increased.

"Of course," he said, "that's all nonsense, although ordinarily I would have the greatest respect for Mr. Joyce's opinion. Even he can't make me believe this ghastly repetition is due to Woodford—to a man dead forty years. I mean, Mr. McHugh, I regret my temper a moment ago. I don't pretend to understand, but surely you're not to blame."

"Thanks," McHugh replied. "I tried to tell you I was honest this morning."

Joyce spoke earnestly:

"Don't add to his stubbornness, Mr. Bunce. I have studied this house. I have opened my mind to its atmosphere. I have known of such things before, and I tell you unreservedly that the building harbors an evil force beyond human control."

Quaile watched Robert's face scarred more and more deeply by the doubt that had met him on his first entrance, that sooner or later had impressed them all in this theatre. McHugh grasped Joyce's arm with the keenness, the strength of a physical attack.

"You're trying to tell me," he said hoarsely, "that I've got to get out and give it up?"

Joyce turned away.

"You're criminally hard-headed."

"I don't wonder," Robert muttered.

McHugh's voice vibrated with a repressed fury. It seemed to carry enmity for Joyce, a thorough regret that he had ever sought his opinion.

"I'll show you what stubbornness is. I'll have another shot at it."

Quaile had grown less wary of the shadows than of the realities that threatened Barbara. Joyce's announcement had, indeed, been a relief. Now McHugh's persistence might involve her again. Therefore, he joined his protest to Robert's.

"If Wilkins is able to go on," McHugh interrupted, "I'll

bring the show off tomorrow night as I said I would."

"There are limits to any man's courage," Robert said.

Joyce spread his hands.

"It would probably be murder."

"That at least is reasonable," Robert said. "Whatever the cause of this actor's condition it would be a grave risk to expose him to it twice."

McHugh sneered at Joyce.

"Have your cops in the house tomorrow night if you want. All I know is, you can't arrest me for murder until I've killed a man."

Joyce turned away. He made no attempt to conceal his distaste for the other.

"We needn't discuss it. Wilkins himself will keep you from making a fool of yourself. There's no danger of his taking it on again."

The purple signal of the manager's temper faded. A little of the mendicant crept into his manner.

"All I ask is one more chance. I remember what old Mike said the first day. I don't want to go away believing anything like that, either, but after tomorrow night I swear I'll get out and let the theatre rot to pieces."

"As Mr. Joyce says," Robert put in, "it depends on the actor. He won't try it again."

A brisk knock shook the panels of the door. Dolly looked up. She ceased bathing Wilkins' temples. McHugh opened the door on a, tall man in evening clothes with a forceful, intelligent face. He carried a black medicine case.

"Is this Mr. McHugh?" he asked.

The manager nodded.

"What's happened here?" the man went on. "The place is full of hysterics. Nobody outside will tell me anything rational. That man has been hurt?"

"See for yourself," McHugh answered. "It's your opinion I'm after, not mine."

The doctor advanced to Wilkins, stooped above him, drew back one of the tight eyelids, took his pulse.

"Complete coma," he said in a puzzled voice. "I shall make a more thorough examination and I must ask some questions. This lady—will she remain and help me? Can she answer—"

"Sure," McHugh broke in. "She can answer all sorts of questions. Maybe more than you'll want to ask. You're kicking us out, eh?"

"There are too many in this small room," the doctor said.

"Never mind. We'll wait for the word nearby. Come on, boys."

He led Joyce, Robert, and Quaile from the room and closed the door. He brought a chair and stationed himself just outside. Joyce and Robert stood close to him. They commenced to discuss the mystery in undertones. Quaile knew it would be like that—continual and unavailing argument until the physician should appear with the result of his examination. He couldn't face the procession of minutes, dreary, and interminable. What were Barbara's thoughts before their precarious drift? What plans had she made since the conquest of her hysteria? He stepped to the stage and walked rapidly across.

Mike had moved his chair to the alley. It was clear he had been unable to remain longer in the building. He rocked back and forth against the wall, mumbling from time to time in reply to Tommy's clumsy efforts to encourage him. Quaile called to Tommy. The little fellow walked in, white faced and ill at ease.

"Miss Morgan," Quaile said, "was moved upstairs before the rehearsal. Which is her dressing-room?"

"One flight up to the right," Tommy answered, "but she ain't there. Mr. Quaile, has the doctor said anything yet?"

"She's not there!" Quaile echoed. "Surely she hasn't had

time to change."

"Didn't change," Tommy said. "Took it on the run with a long black cloak over her costume. Her maid chased after her, carrying a bag and a bundle. Say, what's going on back there? How is Mr. Wilkins? The doctor—"

But Quaile had turned away. Barbara had left, and her appearance for Tommy had been that of flight. She had taken everything with her. It fixed her intention of not returning. That, however, might be explainable by the natural assumption that McHugh would not have the courage or the ability to force his course any farther. To Quaile even it seemed beyond belief that the manager should dream of persuading Wilkins for a second time to submit to such a risk.

He walked back to the three men still waiting outside the actor's door. The hum of their useless controversy set his nerves on edge. He paced up and down the wings, out of earshot, until the door opened.

The doctor's expression was perplexed. Quaile went closer in time to hear McHugh's gruff inquiry:

"What's the answer?"

"He's coming out of it. It's almost like a trance. He has practically no symptoms, no recollection. That old woman in there—she's superstitious if anything."

McHugh grunted.

"Can't diagnose it, eh?"

The doctor glanced around uneasily.

"Not yet. I'd like to watch the case for a day or two."

"A trance!" Joyce reminded them.

McHugh wouldn't listen.

"I want to know, doc, if I can get the man to my automobile and home?"

The physician ran his fingers through his hair.

"I should say you could, and that's another thing that floors me. I've given him a restorative and he's sitting up—

little more than dazed."

"Then let's take him," McHugh snapped. "It isn't healthy for him here."

The doctor admitted them. Wilkins sat on the sofa, his head buried in his hands. Dolly stood opposite. McHugh entered and threw the actor's coat over his costume and placed his hat on his head. Wilkins didn't stir.

"How you feel?" McHugh asked.

Wilkins' voice was muffled and husky from behind his hands.

"I don't know. I—I feel sick."

But when the doctor and McHugh had lifted him he scarcely swayed. With a lifeless motion he lowered his hands. From out the chalky pallor of his face febrile eyes gleamed.

"Why do you stare at me?" he cried with a childish petulance. "Can't you leave me alone? Oh, my God."

His eyes closed. He clung to the doctor.

Quaile heard Joyce say to Robert:

"A trance! A clairvoyant one?"

McHugh warned the others to silence. With the doctor's help he led Wilkins out of the room, across the stage, and down the alley.

Quaile followed at a distance, uneasy, a little hurt. He felt pointedly excluded. McHugh, Wilkins, and the doctor would drive off alone, in order that he should hear nothing because of his friendship for Barbara.

Joyce and Robert were talking again. Robert, Quaile gathered, was at last defending McHugh's stubbornness, while the Englishman tried to convince him with a recital of what he had felt in the gloom of Woodford's. Such a conversation increased the poignancy of what had happened. Quaile fled from it. He paused in the lobby long enough to satisfy the impatient critics, then walked homeward as slowly as the constant spurring of his recollections would let him. He was nearly unwilling to enter his own rooms. He didn't care to give McHugh the impression he was trying to interfere, or cared to force himself where he wasn't wanted.

The manager and the doctor sat in his study. As he entered McHugh put his finger to his lips.

"Wilkins?" Quaile asked.

"Doc here's given him some dope. Not likely to wake before morning, is he, doc?"

"Certainly he ought not to," the doctor said.

McHugh glanced at Quaile.

"Then leave him in peace until I get here tomorrow. No use threshing over these things. I want his mind fresh for me."

With an effort Quaile choked his exasperation.

"You'll try to urge him on?"

"As loud as money'll talk."

"I shouldn't care to try it," the doctor said. "A strange case from every angle. If physical means were responsible I should look for more physical reaction."

McHugh jumped up.

"We're taking possession of Quaile's hearth and fireside. I've more to do tomorrow than I like to think about. Got to have some sleep, so, if I'm going to run you home first, we'd better get a move on."

Again Quaile was conscious of that cold feeling of exclusion. Immeasurably it increased his worry, for it suggested McHugh's positive belief that the attack of the cat no longer rendered Barbara immune to suspicion.

Nor would the manager yield an inch when he arrived the next morning. Quaile didn't see him at first since he merely called a greeting through the door before entering Wilkins' room. The sound of voices, sustained and unintelligible, was a bitter provocation. Quaile bathed and dressed hurriedly, then waited for McHugh in the study.

When he entered Quaile had to admit the manager carried no discernible unfriendliness for him. His brisk good humor, indeed, was disarming, and his appearance brought a smile of wonder. McHugh was clothed with an unaccustomed and startling precision. His necktie was new, colorful. A white carnation—hitherto unheard-of decoration for him—snuggled in his buttonhole. Yet Quaile's interest was captured by the flushed cheeks, the eyes, sparkling and purposeful, the haste the man's bearing expressed.

"I shall suspect you of magic, McHugh! You don't mean to say you've persuaded Wilkins?"

"Sure thing."

"Then you've told him," Quaile said, "more than you're willing to admit to me, or else the man's courage is inhuman."

McHugh grinned. He fondled his boutonniere.

"You're too suspicious, Quaile."

"I'm not blind. You must have given positive assurances he would be safe tonight."

"On my oath I did nothing of the kind—because I couldn't. He runs his chances as he did last night."

"In that case," Quaile took him up, "maybe you'll tell me what makes you so cheerful?"

"Wouldn't believe me, but I'll give myself away that far."

McHugh bent closer. The satisfaction in his eyes was real.

"It's because I've every reason to feel that tonight's the turning-point. After the performance I guess I'll be able to say for sure whether what's happened is due to Woodford's ghost or flesh and blood. Say, Quaile, after all the uncertainty we've suffered down there, isn't that enough to make a man cheerful?"

Quaile wasn't satisfied. There was more than that, he was confident, behind McHugh's manner.

"Why are you so sure?"

"Ought to've been a cop yourself, Quaile. You ask more questions than I do."

Quaile moved his hand impatiently.

"And I get fewer answers. Dare I ask if you're certain the rest of the company will stick?"

"Heard from 'em all—except Barbara."

Quaile knew that he flushed.

"What about her, McHugh?"

The manager backed out of the room.

"I got to hustle. No time to gossip about her or anybody now. Lots of important people to see this morning. Why else you suppose I dolled myself up this way? Say, keep Wilkins off the subject of the theatre. I've forbidden him to mention it."

"I promise not to pump him, if that's what you mean."

McHugh had gone. The outer door slammed. The barrier remained as forbidding as ever.

CHAPTER XXI

THE OPENING

WHEN later Quaile knocked at Wilkins' door the response was sleepy and grudging. The blinds were drawn and the room was nearly dark. Wilkins lay huddled in a warm nest of bedclothes.

"How you feel?" Quaile asked. "Anything I can do?"

Wilkins' reply was ungracious.

"Nothing but let me sleep. I feel like the devil."

So Quaile closed the door. With nothing else to do, with nothing else to occupy him during the long day, he surrendered himself unreservedly to his misgivings for Barbara. He shut himself in the study and called up her apartment. The voice that replied was certainly not hers. It reached him on a tiresome, level strain. It had a lack of positive qualities equal to the impassivity of the strange maid's appearance. He could picture her at the other end of the line. At the start she made his attempt seem hopeless. He sought for some unique means to impress her, to make her carry his message, but the constraint between them embarrassed him.

"It is very important I should speak to Miss Morgan. Will you ask her?"

"Miss Morgan hasn't arisen," the lifeless voice came back. "It is useless to call up again. She will see or speak to no one today."

"Is she ill?"

"I think not."

"She will be at the theatre tonight?"

It was maddening. The woman's tone did not vary. It expressed no interest.

"I wouldn't venture to say."

The line ceased to hum. The breaking of the connection suggested an unalterable purpose, a studied and vehement impertinence.

His fear for Barbara increased. Just one thing was left that he could do in her behalf. He would find out if she had been discovered at the Bunces', if danger lurked for her in that direction, if any previous acquaintance with the family could account for her presence there.

Watson's greeting was friendly—as of one companion in arms to another.

"It's Mr. Quaile!" he called.

And he pointed in the direction of the library.

"Go right on back if you want to speak to Mr. Josiah."

But when Quaile had reached the twilight of the library his sense of welcome diminished. Josiah, it was evident, did not share Watson's feeling of comradeship, based on yesterday's adventure. The recluse's bloodshot eyes testified to a sleepless night. He made no attempt to hide his ill-humor.

"What you want, Mr. Quaile?" he asked. "People are making too free with my house."

"You've heard no more footsteps, I hope," Quaile said.

Josiah's distrust was tinged with curiosity.

"You didn't come here to ask that. But I haven't, since you're so anxious. I've read the papers, and Robert tells me you and Mr. McHugh are right. I'll have to get rid of that place. Well? What you want? When people come to see me to ask after my comfort they usually want to borrow money.

They don't get it."

Quaile managed a smile.

"I was passing by. I really wanted to know how you were after your scare. I didn't think you'd mind a minute's chat."

But it developed into more than that. It was many minutes before he found the courage to hint at the questions which had brought him, and then they drew no valuable replies. He gathered only that Josiah had no idea of the girl's invasion here. He had never met Barbara Morgan. He had never seen her—never heard of her before this revival.

As Quaile was going Josiah called him back and spoke with a halting restraint.

"So Mr. McHugh's going to try to give that performance tonight after all?"

Quaile marveled at the old man's swift transformation. A determined look had replaced his acerbity. There was a movement, hinting at slyness, about the corners of his mouth. Quaile guessed that behind that wrinkled forehead lay a great deal which the whining voice never loosed. It gave to the next words an added importance.

"I'd like to see what happens to Mr. McHugh."

Quaile left, disappointed in his main quest, but aroused by the alteration in the recluse. It would be wise at his earliest opportunity to speak of that to McHugh. Meantime he took the subway to Wall Street and sought Robert in his luxurious office. But the younger Bunce had little more than his brother to offer.

"I've seen Miss Morgan a few times on the stage," he answered, "and I've heard of her, of course, as an exceptional young actress."

Quaile's excuses for his curiosity were simplified by Robert's desire—that common and natural impetus which Quaile had come to resent—to gossip about the elusive problem of the theatre. Consequently he hurried away, refusing Robert's cordial invitation to lunch with him downtown.

He returned to his rooms where Wilkins still rested. When the actor appeared Quaile had no difficulty following McHugh's wishes. Wilkins was uncommunicative, bristling with guarded information. Yet his bearing suggested that that knowledge was not wholly comforting. While he carried no physical effects from last night's experience he was more a prey to nerves than Quaile. The enforced silence between them on the vital point that filled their minds lengthened the afternoon.

So much had intervened since Dolly's fright over the telephone that Quaile had nearly forgotten his sense of the imminence of those wayward warnings. He knew that the actor was in the study when the attenuated and remote bell sound took him off his guard. He ran in, anxious to spare Wilkins, but he was too late. The actor already had the receiver at his ear, had started back, was listening as one might accept an unquestionable communication from the other world.

"Drop it!" Quaile commanded. "You mustn't listen."

He snatched the receiver from Wilkins' hand and replaced it.

"So that's it!" the actor breathed. "That's what happened the other night!"

Quaile's suspense grasped him. He cursed this evil chance at the last moment.

"Woodford!" Wilkins went on. "That queer ringing! That unnatural voice!"

Quaile spread his hands.

"What did you hear?"

"A straight warning," Wilkins answered, "an unqualified threat of death if I tried it again."

"Magic!" Quaile muttered. "McHugh isn't clever enough—"

Wilkins grasped at the name.

"I must get to him with this. Finish dressing. Let's hurry to the theatre."

And all the way down he gave himself more and more thoroughly to a morose indecision. It occurred to Quaile that after all McHugh's influence would be insufficient to combat this last attack.

Wilkins went to the stage entrance while Quaile elbowed his way into the lobby. Although it was early the crowd there was thick and restless. A cardboard sign above the box-office window informed those without tickets that the house was sold out. Quaile answered to a distasteful enmity for these people. He knew the bait that had caught them. The stories in the newspapers, the rapid gossip of Broadway had filled them with the hope of something sensational, perhaps terrible.

As the doorman let him in, ticket holders, still excluded, pressed forward with a fanatical eagerness. Quaile hastened to the stage where he found McHugh alone. The manager was in evening clothes. He chewed with an unusual absorption at his cold cigar. He answered Quailed inquiry as to Wilkins with an absent-minded air.

"I've talked to him, and he's dressing."

"I wish I knew your power over him."

McHugh studied his cigar.

"I wish," he answered, "it didn't make me feel like a criminal to use my power."

Quaile saw that the former detective was less sure of himself than he had been last night.

"The rest of the company?" he asked.

"All here," McHugh answered, "putting on the frills and paint."

Quaile experienced a vast relief. Then Barbara was not ill, nor had her flight been permanent. She still acknowledged the necessity of meeting his terms.

McHugh had moved to the spot where Carlton and

Wilkins had fallen after the manner of Woodford. He glanced at the single border which was all that burned at this early hour. Quaile wondered what he had in his mind. Then the manager walked to the wings and returned immediately with the candlestick which Carlton had held at the moment of his death, which Wilkins had grasped before his fall last night.

"Perfectly nice candle in it," McHugh mused, "and it's a waste of my good money, because it doesn't once get lighted during the whole play. Put a little fire to it, Quaile."

Quaile obeyed, puzzled by the odd request.

What you want of it, McHugh?"

"Hold it up, so," McHugh directed when the wick was blazing. "And don't do anything else until I pass you the word."

"What's your idea?"

But McHugh left the stage without answering, so Quaile stood as he was, holding the candle aloft while he tried to sound McHugh's purpose.

Tommy entered from the wings.

"Better smother the light, Mr. Quaile," the assistant advised. "There's a fireman outside, and the laws are strict."

McHugh reappeared. He looked at Quaile with a bland surprise.

"What you doing, Quaile. Rehearsing Liberty enlightening the world?"

The manager beyond a doubt desired Tommy's ignorance of his share in the experiment. He blew the candle out, took it from Quaile, and gave it to Tommy to replace.

"I was wondering," Quaile said, accepting the hint, "how it would look lighted in the third act."

McHugh smiled his thanks.

"Nothing doing," he said. "Tommy's got the correct dope on the fire laws."

When Tommy had left McHugh still refused to explain

his odd request or his secretive manner when Tommy had observed Quaile holding the candlestick. He moved here and there about the stage with an apparent lack of purpose. Quaile, to whom he no longer said anything, strolled to the foot of the iron staircase and waited until the company commenced to appear, but again disappointment awaited him. When Barbara descended the maid still guarded her. Nevertheless, Quaile went closer.

"You must give me a moment," he begged.

Barbara turned away.

"It is no use. I can't talk to you yet."

The stolid maid would not move, but Quaile had caught a wistful note of desire in Barbara's reply.

"Then afterward," he said.

But she would not speak to him again, and, discouraged, and foreseeing only evil, he walked through the passage to the auditorium.

The house was already nearly crowded. His senses were caught by the close proximity of many men and women, by their perpetual chatter, by the rattling of programs, by that undertone of individual movement which gives to a multitude an appearance and a sound of unlimited restlessness. Woodford's was alive again, as it had not been alive last night, as it had not lived since its old director's death. And in the warm mingling of perfumes that arose from its audience the singular odor of the scent Woodford had used was finally drowned.

Quaile did not see Joyce, so he entered the lobby where the throng still struggled, some with tickets to enter, others to reach the box office before the standing-room should be exhausted. A procession of automobiles crept along the curb. Policemen worked there. With hoarse shouts they hurried the drivers away.

Quaile's glance rested, fascinated, on one of the cars. It had drawn up. Robert Bunce had descended and waited while from its depth painfully emerged a bent and patriarchal figure. Gray hair strayed from beneath an antiquated top hat. A shawl—recalling a custom many years forgotten—was draped across the shoulders. And after the figure came Watson, carrying a cushion, furnishing the final touch to the picture of an invalid on his first outing.

Between Robert and Watson, and leaning on his cane, Josiah tottered up the steps of Woodford's, once familiar to his youthful tread.

Quaile wondered if this adventure could account wholly for the recluse's determination that morning. As he advanced to meet him the bystanders audibly snickered at the little group. Josiah seemed a trifle dazed. Robert was completely conscious of the attention his brother attracted.

"He would come," he said to Quaile. "He was bound in one way or another the audience should have its money's worth."

Josiah's lips worked.

"Suppose you're trying to say I'm a show in myself. I never was stylish. Can't you get us through, Mr. Quaile? I want to sit down."

Quaile went ahead, clearing a passage. The difficult footsteps of the old man shuffled after him, stirring his memory. He would not think of that.

Josiah paused at the rear of the auditorium, looking around with a quickening interest.

"Place hasn't changed as much as I have."

He leered.

"There's the entrance to the passage back. I used that now and then, carrying flowers and such things, when I was young and generous. Well, God knows, I'll never be either again."

He shined down the aisle, feeling the way with his cane.

"Get me in my seat, Watson. Then you go to the gallery. But don't you fall over the rail. I'm too old to fool with strange servants."

Robert lingered for a moment with Quaile.

"In spite of all these people," he said, "I've a strong feeling I ought to stop this thing."

"You can keep an easy conscience," Quaile answered. "McHugh's a fighter. He'd never let you."

"What's he up to?" Robert asked. "How does Wilkins feel about it? How did McHugh persuade him to go on?"

"Wilkins is pretty sick, but McHugh seems to control him absolutely."

Robert glanced up.

"Here's Joyce. I'll be glad to know what he thinks."

But Quaile didn't wait. He had hoped for Joyce's absence. That would have gone a long way in his mind to justify McHugh's stubbornness. The Englishman's morbid and disapproving expression suggested that he anticipated with confidence a further verification of his supernatural theory.

The minutes had droned away. Every seat was occupied. The crowd in the standing-room was limited only by the fire laws. Quaile, from the chair he had reserved in the rear, waited. Confused with his suspense was a profound dejection. He determined, whatever the evening's issue for McHugh and Wilkins, to force an understanding with Barbara, to tear down once for all the somber and frowning wall circumstances had built between them.

When the curtain had glided up Quaile struggled without success against the emotions that had captured him last night. He tried to urge a lighter humor by watching Josiah, in a theatre after fifteen years of seclusion. But under the half-light the bent figure had assumed a new grimness. The infused eyes were derisive rather than interested. In spite of himself they turned Quaile's glance back to the stage.

The presence of the great audience had aroused the players. They responded to the stimulation of a probable applause; and, as the curtain fell on the first act, it came—wave upon wave of approbation. But during the second act the influence of this new stimulation waned. Morbid expectancy stalked upon the stage again. Slipped cues became frequent. The curiosity of the audience increased.

Quaile went back before the final act, but McHugh wouldn't speak to him. He paced with Wilkins up and down the wings. His cigar hung loosely from between his lips. He appeared to have lost his confidence. His eyes were apprehensive and haggard. Wilkins was even more moved. He turned a white face to Quaile. He started to speak, but the manager hurried him away.

Just before the last call Quaile saw Barbara, ready for her entrance. The maid was no longer with her. He went up and touched her arm timidly.

"You are frightened," he said, "as much as Wilkins. Why? When will this be ended—this waiting without knowing? No matter what happens—you understand? I shall see you afterward."

"I don't know," she whispered.

Lurching a little she walked away from him. The curtain went up, and Quaile returned to his place in the auditorium to face once more that tragic scene with a feeling, caught from McHugh's manner, of utter uselessness and defeat. In a few minutes now

The pitiful courage that had carried Barbara through the earlier part of the piece had failed. Dolly's eyes sought wildly again for the cat. Wilkins, with that same somnambulistic air that had preceded Carlton's death, drifted through his part. Those who had fought for admittance to the performance greeted these signs eagerly. They, too, realized that the vital moment was at hand. Many were bent forward in their chairs as Joyce had sat last night.

Quaile caught a glimpse of the psychist in the rear. He clung to the rail, absorbed, prepared, it was not to be doubted, for the fulfilment of his prophecy.

The almost noiseless tapping of Josiah's cane on the floor reached Quaile. Then Dolly's scream, the prelude hitherto to fatal and inexplicable mysteries, swung him back.

"Marjorie! Look out!"

Wilkins was at the mantel, snatching up the heavy candlestick, while Barbara raised her hands and shrank away from him, gasping:

"Be careful! What are you going to do to me?"

Wilkins turned. The familiar, unfinished line came to Quaile in a strangled voice.

"Pay what debts I can. Kill you if the strength—"

A great cry arose from the audience—spontaneous, unrestrained, suddenly broken off. Quaile sprang upright. He heard a ripping sound. A hand, appearing abnormally red and huge, had crashed through the canvas scenery, had caught Wilkins' shoulder, had thrust him violently toward the center of the stage.

The hand was withdrawn. From the wings a voice, choked and unrecognizable, shrilled. The audience was on its feet, in an uproar. McHugh dashed to the stage. His collar was torn. His hair was disarranged. Above the clamor his voice carried, harsh and vindictive:

"Shut every door. On the job! Don't let a soul leave this house."

CHAPTER XXII

BEYOND THE FOOTLIGHTS

MEN in plain clothes, who had evidently been scattered about the theatre for such an emergency, posted themselves with quiet determination before the lobby entrance and the fire exits. That sense of being trapped alarmed the spectators. They moved toward the doors, arguing with the guards, who, nevertheless, refused to pass anyone.

Quaile hurried back. As he ran for the passage behind the boxes he saw Josiah struggle to his feet, leaning on the back of his chair. The shawl had slipped from his shouldders, and he made unavailing and pitiful efforts with his free hand to get it once more in place. The derision had left his glance.

"Watson! Watson!" he whimpered.

Joyce and Robert, breathing hard, came up, and Quaile went through the passage with them. The curtain was rattling down when they reached the stage. Dolly's eyes no longer sought for the cat. They were turned to Wilkins.

"What is it?" she kept asking. "What is it?"

Wilkins had relaxed. An odd grin twisted his features. He muttered to Dolly.

"God bless McHugh. He's got away with it."

Only Barbara disclosed no relief in the new situation. She looked at the jagged rent in the scenery above the mantel which McHugh's hand had torn. It was like an open wound. Through it Quaile dimly saw figures moving, heard suppressed, incredulous argument.

He ran into the wings. The others followed, but he saw that Barbara's feet dragged.

The sight of men who, he knew, must be plainclothes policemen, confused him at first. He couldn't see, because of them and the members of the crew crowding around, who they held. Then, as Joyce and Robert came up, the group parted, and he fell back before a wrinkled face, scarred by fear. Involuntarily he cried out:

"Mike!"

The property man turned to him, more startled than he had been last night when he had talked of seeing Woodford's ghost.

McHugh stood close by, grinning happily, making ridiculous efforts to rearrange his torn collar.

"It's in his right-hand coat pocket," he was saying. "Good thing you didn't let him grab it out, or there'd have been more ghosts around here than Joyce and his whole darned society could have laid. Easy with it. Don't touch the stopper. Don't press the bulb."

One of the detectives had drawn from Mike's pocket an atomizer of a common, cheap variety.

The end of the spray was closed. The physician who had examined Wilkins last night stepped from the fringe of the crowd and took the contrivance. The detective started to protest.

"That's all right," McHugh said. "You hustle it to headquarters and take the doctor with you. We've got some ideas about that, haven't we, doc? We want 'em proved."

The doctor nodded. He left with one of the detectives who carried the atomizer as if it held something infinitely precious.

"What's it mean, McHugh?" Quaile asked. "Mike—"

Robert stepped closer.

"Yes. What's the old man done? Why is he held?"

McHugh winked.

"Just so he won't break any bones trying to run too fast."

For the first time since entering Woodford's the cloak of its unhealth was light on Quaile's spirit. He could not understand why Barbara showed no similar relief. She leaned against the wall in a strained, expectant attitude. She raised her hands as if in a gesture of appeal to McHugh, but he did not see her. Robert had won his attention and was speaking rapidly.

"It was all a trick, then? But have you any evidence against this man?"

Quaile saw that Joyce had no curiosity.

"Evidence!" McHugh jeered, turning to Mike. "I've so much evidence against you, Mike, that I promise within two months to see you twisting in the electric chair for Carlton's death."

Barbara cried out, but her voice was drowned by Mike's raucous, unformed scream. He controlled the trembling of his lips. The incoherent sound straggled into words, throaty but intelligible.

"You shan't, Mr. McHugh! You haven't the heart! I'll talk. I only did as I was made, and I didn't know—I didn't know. If anybody goes to the chair it ought to be him."

He couldn't point because of the detaining hands, but Quaile and the rest turned, following the direction of his accusing glance. And at first Quaile didn't believe, fancying that Mike groped for any chance, however absurd, to shift attention from himself. For his eyes flashed fear and hatred at Robert Bunce who moved back, shaking his head. But that face, aristocratic and until now always a little sneering, whitened with confession, with surrender to a forbidding and inescapable destiny.

"That's what I was after!" McHugh cried. "Grab that

man!"

But Robert had taken advantage of their momentary amazement. He had slipped some distance toward the rear. At McHugh's shout he turned and ran past Barbara. Flinging his hands above his head in a gesture of despair, he stumbled into the narrow space between the scenery and the house wall.

"Across the stage!" McHugh roared. "Head him off!"

Quaile had already started for the back. As he reached Barbara she touched his arm, not faltering, rather as if to urge him on.

"He mustn't talk," she whispered.

Then he had entered the narrow space, and saw Robert dashing out at the other end. The man held something in his right hand. Quaile shuddered, and stopped, bracing himself for the shock. It came a moment later—above the shouts and the noisy pursuit, one sharp explosion, a cry, then a sudden hush.

He went slowly back to Barbara. She had straightened. She seemed to listen still.

"You heard?" he asked.

She nodded.

"A—a shot."

The color rushed back to her cheeks.

"Probably the final tragedy," Quaile said.

"You mean—Robert Bunce," she breathed.

"Yes. I think when he found the alley guarded—perhaps, though—"

The black-robed maid came from the stage and glided up to them. Barbara's eyes were bright with the question she evidently didn't dare ask. But the maid understood. For the first time Quaile saw her features quicken into positive expression. They exposed a definite satisfaction.

"He is dead," she murmured. "You must come with me now."

"Gone!" Barbara whispered.

Her eyes filled with tears.

"I can't help it. It is terrible, but I am not sorry."

She glanced at Mike whose fear and hatred had been increased by that announcement which had assured him he remained the sole culprit.

"It isn't fair he should have to pay," Barbara said.

A sound of tapping came from the stage.

"Get her away," Quaile warned the maid.

The tapping continued.

"And I will come to you later," he said to Barbara. "I may come now?"

"You have to know," she answered.

She glanced up.

"What is that tapping?"

"Take her to her dressing-room," Quaile directed the maid.

She seemed to comprehend. While the tapping on the stage continued, came moment by moment closer, she led Barbara back of the scenery to the circular staircase.

The tapping sounded just beyond the canvas. The set door shook from a hand on the knob. Mike looked up.

"What you waiting for?" he complained to the detectives. "You've got to lock me up. I don't want to see him."

Nor did Quaile. Watson's voice came.

"But, Mr. Josiah, the people are all in the alley."

The set door opened. A cane waved in the aperture. Josiah appeared and shuffled toward Mike. His left hand gathered the shawl about his shoulders. He had set his ridiculous hat awry upon his unkempt head. If he had heard the shot at all its significance had escaped him. Quaile shrank from reciting the truth. Beneath that harsh and selfish exterior might lurk a real fraternal devotion. He was glad that just then the prisoner occupied Josiah exclusively.

"I remember you," the old man quavered. "We've all grown old since those days. I never realized how old until I came here tonight. You were a fine boy then—Woodford's right bower, weren't you? I recollect. Needn't look away from me. Police got you, eh? It's you that's been playing tricks with my property?"

"Don't, Mr. Josiah," Mike began.

Quaile stepped back, relieved to see McHugh, stalk through the doorway. The manager was visibly shaken by what he had witnessed in the alley. Josiah didn't turn. With an increasing anger he shook his cane at Mike.

"It's you that's finished this house for theatrical purposes! And I liked it. Mr. McHugh would have made it popular again. Now I guess I'll have to sell it after all."

McHugh went to him. He didn't meet his glance.

"It's too late, Bunce," he said in an undertone.

"What you mean?" Josiah whined.

"I mean if you'd agreed to sell a month ago this would never have happened."

The words to Quaile were stimulating. To an extent they suggested the purpose of the illusion of the supernatural, more or less, its clever and mysterious construction. But they meant nothing so illuminating to Josiah. With an amiable smile he offered McHugh his hand.

"Anyway, you were honest, weren't you?"

Gravely McHugh grasped the knotted fingers.

"Why you shaking hands so hard?" Josiah said. "That hurts. I want to know why I shouldn't agree to sell now. Robert's been after me the last two months to sign a deed for this property."

McHugh's voice was husky.

"I mean, your brother won't ask you anymore. He won't trouble you or any of us again."

Josiah withdrew his fingers.

"You're hurting my hand, Mr. McHugh!"

He leaned heavily on his cane. His hands shook.

"Better sit down," McHugh said gruffly.

He brought a chair. Josiah sank into it.

"I'll rest a minute," he whimpered, "before I go back where I belong. I always told Robert he'd get in too deep."

He glanced up as one who seeks justification

"And he always said I was a miserable skinflint who deserved to die poor."

"Stay with him, Watson," McHugh directed.

"If you need me I'll be on the other side of the stage. You cops bring the prisoner along."

As they crossed the stage, in reply to Quaile's questions, the manager muttered:

"I've found out Robert's been spending for years. He'd been eaten alive by war stocks—played 'em the wrong way from start to finish. Borrowed from his firm and doctored the books. Facing jail and everything gone except his share in this property—worth half a million or more for building purposes."

Quaile whistled.

"Yep. Couldn't realize on it without Josiah's signature. I gather he'd just about got that when along I came with the scheme for this revival and spilled the beans."

"I see. Of course he had to get you out—scare you off. I understand. It was his only chance, and the superstitious stories about this place cried out the simple way."

McHugh nodded at Mike.

"And there was his old worshipper, knowing every angle of the building, remembering every quirk of Woodford's habits. It ought to have been the cinch he expected. It would have been with most people, but I've worked like a dog on the case, and I've had to go on tiptoe all the way. If you want I'll tell you about that later."

He stopped in front of the door of Woodford's dressing-room. He beckoned Joyce who stood by the alley entrance.

"I'd like to show Quaile and you some ghosts," he said. "Haven't had a chance to see 'em myself yet."

He turned to Mike.

"They're going to give you a free ride to the lock-up in a minute. You're all the law has to feed on and it has a high old appetite. But there are some things you might tell me that would make me want to help you—for instance, the combination in there."

He indicated the door with its faded gilt star. Mike compressed his lips. McHugh waved his hand at the detectives.

"Sorry, Mike. I've held them off so far, but they've got to come sooner or later. Let him have the wrist watches, boys."

As one of the detectives produced a pair of handcuffs Mike struggled.

"Take it easy, Mike," McHugh advised. "I've held them off to prove to you I'd be disposed to do what I could if you showed the proper spirit. Never mind. I'll find out what I want to know if I tear the inside out of the place."

Mike glanced up. He wet his lips.

"All right, Mr. McHugh. I'll trust you. I'll tell you anything I can. Pull down on the first hook on the left-hand side of the closet."

"Well, that's one thing I want to know, and you can pass me the booby prize on that. As simple as daylight."

"Mr. Woodford never made any great secret of it, sir."

McHugh opened the door.

"You and Joyce go on in, Quaile, and light up while I talk to Mike about some other things before the boys take him away."

Quaile entered and snapped the electric button.

"I don't see yet, Joyce," he said, "exactly how you figure in the affair."

Joyce chuckled.

"Please don't embarrass me."

He was obviously relieved when McHugh walked in and took from his coat a flashlight similar to the one he had bought Quaile. He pressed the control and stepped into the closet. It was an exceptionally large one, formed by a partition running the width of the room. Neither it nor the room offered any probability of a secret compartment.

"You see," McHugh apologized, "we had never used this room before last night. Naturally I'd looked it over, but it seemed to hide nothing. I searched a lot more carefully in the fly galleries and the cellar. Even after Barbara's scare, I couldn't find the way in. Didn't look for any trick so simple. As Mike says, Woodford probably made no great secret of it. When he grew older he wanted a place where he could get away from people and rest entirely undisturbed. Of course Mike knew about it."

He grasped the hook and pulled down. A latch clicked. The entire end of the closet opened outward—to all appearances an ordinary door. Only the snug fit at the angles had veiled its real character.

From the darkness beyond came a stealthy stirring.

McHugh went through, flashing his light on the floor and the walls. Quaile followed. The plan of the hidden room disclosed itself to his first glance. Scarcely more than four feet wide, it ran the length of the dressing-room, and lay between that and the passage. The plaster had fallen from the walls, exposing bricks and lathes. It lay with the long accumulation of dust thickly over the floor and the single piece of furniture. That was a dreary reminder of the room's original purpose—a skeleton of a sofa from about which the upholstery and the wood had decayed. At the foot of this wreck crouched the thing that had stirred. Two tiny, gleaming circles flashed back the light. The lithe body was ready to spring.

"Look out, McHugh!" Quaile cried. "It's the cat!"

McHugh moved to one side as the animal streaked by. It

tore past Quaile and Joyce, through the closet, and into the dressing-room, where it scratched fiercely at the outer door. Quaile answered to an odd repulsion. The cat's anger, its eagerness for escape, were silent save for the fury of its claws.

"Have you noticed?" he asked. "That animal has been caged here for weeks—except when it escaped the night it slipped past us into the alley."

"I've noticed," McHugh answered.

"It's practically wild," Quaile said. "Listen to it! Not a cry, not a sound from its throat."

"It would be a useful ghost of Woodford's cat if it had a voice," McHugh said dryly. "Silent serenades for Mr. Thomas hereafter."

"Pleasant!" Joyce commented.

"I've tried to impress on you," McHugh said, "that Robert played for about the highest stakes there are— respectability and wealth against utter damnation socially and financially. What's a cat or two where half a million's concerned?"

"The ghosts?" Quaile reminded him.

"Sure," McHugh grinned. "Joyce, you shut the closet door."

Joyce obeyed.

"I'm much more comfortable," he said, "with that voiceless animal locked out."

McHugh snapped off the light.

"What's that for?" Quaile asked through the choking darkness.

McHugh's exclamation was annoyed. Then his voice came from close to the floor.

"If I were on the force I'd ask them to transfer me to Canarsie. I've forgotten my alphabet. Of course. It was under the sofa all the time. Bend down here. Maybe you'd better not, Joyce. Might turn you sour on your spook science."

Quaile stooped. He peered beneath the decayed piece of furniture. At once he became aware of light—a pallid, mysterious radiance that carried his mind back to the night of his vigil. The limit of its activity was a narrow circle which quivered with an odd illusion of life.

"Cold, white flame!" McHugh murmured.

His flashlight clicked. The room was bright again. Quaile reached for a small round tin can which rested close to the wall beneath the sofa. But McHugh shook his head. A serious expression had driven the satisfaction from his face.

"Don't bother! That little ghost can't show you any more than it has. It was logic we would find it here. There are things of greater importance for you, Quaile."

He arose and motioned Joyce to leave. He hung back for a moment with Quaile. His tone, for him, was very gentle.

"I hate to speak of it, my boy. But you're not blind. Since we've been in this room I bet you've been thinking what I have."

Quaile glanced away.

"I know what you're driving at."

"Barbara," McHugh said, "evidently knew the combination. She used it last night and opened the door. You've seen how wild Mike's cat is. She must have been scratched locking it up again, and she lied to us about the footsteps to throw us off the track. Maybe she only entered out of curiosity. I don't know about Barbara."

Quaile had no answer. McHugh must be right.

Moreover, the picture of her secreted at the Bunces' was still lively in his mind. Those two incidents furnished staggering proof that she, as well as Mike, had been in Robert's confidence; yet, Quaile was sure, if she had been an accomplice, something more powerful than greed or disposition had been responsible. He would admit nothing until he had seen her. His faith remained even now scarcely shaken, nor had his love ever faltered. Because of this very uncertainty it grasped him stronger than before.

"McHugh," he urged, "no matter what you know, no matter what you think, keep your hands off until I've talked to her. She's promised to tell me. I'm going there now. We've struggled through this thing together. I've tried to do what you wished, and you've let me work in the dark. Now I ask you this. Promise!"

"I know how you feel, Quaile," the manager answered. "Go see her. I don't want to be hard. I'll run up myself as soon as I've taken care of Josiah. Old bird's harder hit than I thought he'd be."

He walked through and opened the outer door. The cat slipped out, as it had done the other night, and was lost in the shadows of the alley.

McHugh returned to Josiah. Quaile followed uncertainly. Dolly had come down and sat now by the old man. She had drawn to his dull eyes a look of interest. It was clear that an ancient acquaintanceship had been renewed, and that in her quiet sympathy he had found some release for his thoughts. Wilkins, flushed and happy, stood nearby. Others of the company and the crew watched the recluse with a curiosity, frank, nearly brutal. But Quaile saw no sign of Barbara, so he spoke to Tommy as he had done last night, and the assistant returned an identical answer. Barbara had left again with a haste suggestive of flight, a cloak thrown over her costume, accompanied by the silent maid. What was there that drew her so quickly home? Quaile knew the answer must lie in that room from which the cry and the sobs had issued.

CHAPTER XXIII

McHUGH IS DISCREET

HE hurried from the theatre and drove to Barbara's apartment. The silent maid answered his ring. Her features were emotionless again. Her movements, as she took his coat and hat, were as before smooth, without individuality. Quaile walked past her into the living room. Barbara waited there by the window. It impressed him that some of the fear had left her face, but her eyes were very sad, her gesture of welcome mechanical. He controlled his eagerness. He held her hand for only a moment. He lost no time in putting her on her guard. He glanced uneasily toward the door to the bedroom.

"In a few minutes," he said, "McHugh is coming here. You need tell me only what is necessary for your protection. Of course, he has guessed you knew of Woodford's secret room. He knows you didn't tell us quite the truth last night. Understand, as far as I am concerned I ask nothing. I trust you as I promised to do."

She stretched out her hands impulsively, but as he tried to clasp them she drew her fingers away. Her voice was wistful.

"I must tell you first. Perhaps then you won't care—"

She shook her head before his incredulous smile.

"I don't know what Mr. McHugh may do, but I have

suffered enough. It's worth it to realize your faith, and last night you were right to make me go on. I was unjust, but I was at my wit's end. You'll understand that in a minute."

She sighed.

"You are looking at the door. You are thinking of the one who screamed."

She walked over and opened the door. Beyond her shoulder the confusion of the room suggested a recent occupancy, but there was none of the paraphernalia of illness, possibly of insanity, which he had expected.

"Whoever it was," he said, "has left?"

She nodded.

"Just now—as soon as she knew Robert Bunce was dead. She didn't dare until then. It was my sister—my elder sister."

He took her hand and led her to the divan. He sat beside her, but he didn't speak at first, for in her averted eyes he read a little of the truth. At last he said gently:

"Then she really was involved in Robert's attempt?"

Barbara indicated the telephone.

"Through that—through those calls."

He recoiled before the seriousness of it.

"How?"

"It was her position that suggested it to him. Listen! It is hard to make her confession. She—she was working for the telephone company, fighting her own fight, and winning it, when he made her help him."

"I can guess," he said softly.

She placed her hand on his arm.

"You mustn't guess too much, for it wasn't really her fault that he could make her do that. It happened six years ago when I was at school abroad. My mother and she lived in the town, so that I didn't know him, didn't see him— until yesterday. There was an elopement—a marriage, but an illegal one. She left him as soon as she found that out.

She wouldn't have my help or anyone's. She got this position and worked year after year until they made her an exchange manager. Don't you see what that meant to him? So he went to her again and threatened her. She saw all she had done crumbling, and at first he said it was not serious—more or less of a joke, as he told Mike. So she made the calls and kept them secret. It was Mike with his perfect knowledge of Woodford's voice who did the talking. It was wrong, but it seemed easier than to give up everything, to face the scandal Robert would have raised in the telephone company. And that far I agreed with her. She never dreamed— Then Mr. Carlton died."

Quaile looked at her with a great pity.

"I see. She had placed herself beyond the law—probably accessory to a murder."

"And she swore," Barbara cried out, "that she would kill herself if I told. The horror of it grew—grew. She came in that night after Dolly had left. She heard what you said to me—all that you said. It seemed to her that she had finished my happiness, too. It swept her off her feet. For a moment she was hysterical, and you see now I had to keep you quiet. But I thought I couldn't stand any more. I went to see Robert the next day. He let me in and made me wait for him, and you found me. Later, when he came back, I could do nothing. He only threatened. He was frightened and reckless himself. He had gone too far. He didn't dare stop. So you can understand how desperate I was last night. If I had told what I knew I believe my sister would have killed herself—her nerves had reached that pitch. If I didn't tell I was almost sure there would be another murder. I thought it all out. There was only one way. I made up my mind to let my own future go, to refuse flatly to play, to make the rehearsal and the performance impossible."

"That was brave," he said.

She turned to him with a wan smile.

"You can grasp now the position in which you put me last night? If I didn't obey you and play, the result would be the same as if I had cried out the truth myself. It was horrible. I was helpless. It seemed to mean death either way. But I chose—one always does—one's flesh and blood. I trusted to providence for Mr. Wilkins, and providence was kind. And she—my maid—said that I did right. She alone through all this time has known everything and has remained faithful. Without her—I don't know. When I was weakest her strength kept me up. You see, when I came into the world—ever since then—"

"No wonder you hated me," he whispered; "yet there is no hatred in your eyes now."

Her flush increased. The ringing of the doorbell angered Quaile. He knew what hand had pushed the button. Yet that had to be faced sooner or later. There was nothing of the spy, however, about McHugh tonight. His voice came to them, high-pitched, apologetic.

"Two is company, but here am I."

Quaile met him at the door. He grasped his arm.

"You were wrong, McHugh. She is only useful to you as a witness, and since you don't need her, surely you won't—"

He broke off. McHugh had pushed past him. He went straight to Barbara.

"Was I right when I said two, Barbara?" he asked.

She pointed to the open bedroom door. McHugh went over and looked in. As he swung around Quaile caught the relief in his face.

"That was the best thing she could have done," the manager said. "It gives us a chance to let sleeping dogs lie. There's about ten times more than enough proof without the telephone calls if what Quaile says is true. And, before you think of me too harshly, remember all I knew was that she was responsible for that trickery and that she lived here with you and that you kept her hidden. You'll have to own up, Barbara, you've been behaving as queer as Dick's hatband. Let me judge for myself. Tell me what you've given Quaile."

She sighed, but she did as he wished. She answered all his questions. At the end McHugh took her hand.

"I guess, after all, you did the best you could, Barbara, and it wasn't very easy. You'll have to try to forgive me."

Quaile saw her lips quiver. He knew she was on the verge of a breakdown. To spare her that, to turn her mind from her own share in the case, he arose and shook McHugh's shoulders, speaking rapidly.

"Maybe you'll open that close mouth of yours now. I'd like to know how you got beyond the spook idea to Mike and Robert."

McHugh took a cigar from his pocket and waved it with an assumption of carelessness.

"Sit down, Quaile. Any good detective—just common sense in fitting the facts together."

But it was clear he was very proud of his success.

"You're modest," Quaile said. "There's a lot I don't pretend to understand of my own experiences—for instance, why my flashlight played such tricks the night I was alone in the theatre."

McHugh's smile was reminiscent.

"Your flashlight! I guess I ought to gild that and wear it as a watch charm, for it's what finally put me on the right track. At first I was like you, Quaile, afraid of the musty, decayed feeling of the place, wondering if there wasn't a lot in the spirit stuff after all. I acknowledge that first afternoon was a shock, for there were only you and Mike and Tommy and me, and, trusting you all as I did, what happened was a poser. It set me to investigating the superstitious stories that have always been told about Woodford's. It was natural enough they should spring up, be-

cause the old place was so gloomy and Woodford's end was
so sensational. But I found there wasn't anything back of
them you could put your finger on. The stock company that
failed there five years ago, I found, tried to stir up business
by giving them a fresh start. But nothing doing. The show
was too rotten, and the scare their leading man had, a
friend of his told me, came from the booze in which he'd
tried to drown his sorrow at losing a good job. But I'd
heard myself that afternoon, and there seemed no answer.
When Carlton died I was scared, children—about ready to
call it spirits and get out. Place was on my nerves like it
gets on everybody else's. Then I noticed that Barbara was
acting queer, as if she might know something. I guess it
was about that time your sister unburdened."

"Yes," she said.

"And along came Dolly," McHugh continued, "with her
talk about the perfume. I began to wonder if a drug hadn't
been used on Carlton, but I didn't see how it could have
been administered, and I couldn't get the motive unless it
was to chase me out of the theatre. That was only an idea,
but it's why I didn't spy there myself, Quaile. If my idea
was right I knew they'd get me sure."

McHugh glanced at his cigar with a yearning doubt.

"Say, my doctor's business isn't what it ought to be. If
you don't throw me out, Barbara, I'll light this torch and
pay the bill."

He struck a match. He stretched himself deeper in his
chair. For some time he smoked contentedly.

"When you told me your flashlight worked before and
after you were alone in the theatre," he said, "but not when
you heard the footsteps, it seemed pretty likely human
fingers had tampered with it. I remembered seeing you go
into the box where you'd left your overcoat and drop it in
the pocket. That was right after you had searched the
house. It would have been simple for a hand to reach in,

take the cylinder, break the connection or remove the battery, then put the light back in your pocket. If that was so, whoever was responsible had done the limping and, after scaring you from the theatre, had put the cylinder in working order again. For the first time I had something that looked real. But I didn't hit on Mike then. He had worked for me off and on for many years. I had come to think of him as about the most dependable man I had ever had. I trusted him to the limit. It wasn't until the next morning when I looked at that spook picture of Woodford in the middle of our group that I got it, and then I could scarcely believe. You see Mike had brought me those pictures from the photographers. He had had time to have that one doctored, and I began to see his share in the game. Everything fitted. That's why I was so staggered that morning. Also why I was so cheerful. I didn't dare let you in on account of Barbara. Besides, I was just getting the first few pieces of the puzzle together. I hadn't come to the real picture."

"Please let's have the pieces," Quaile urged.

When McHugh answered there was a color of shame in his voice.

"I might's well own up I'd made a bad mistake the day before. I'd told Mike I was going to hide you in the theatre. As I say, I trusted him then, and I simply explained wanting a key. But that made it point to him all the surer, for he knew you would be there, and he was the only one who could let himself in the theatre after you'd locked the door. It came to me then that if there was a hiding-place he would know it as well as he did every one of Woodford's peculiarities. I didn't need any more answer to the first afternoon. He had limped like Woodford and had screamed after he had scared Tommy to the alley by putting the lights out. You see, he could always limp like Woodford or do— anything like Woodford."

"But the lights?" Quaile asked.

"A cinch. He had taken the electricians down there and worked with them. It's only when you're on the wrong track or no track at all that things look hard. It was easy for him to cut a wire into that switchboard that would short circuit it, then locate the button anywheres he pleased. He short circuited the border that day just as he played with Barbara's light last night, just as he did with the house lights after Wilkins had fallen. A child who knows anything about wiring can fix those simple stunts. What made it so convincing was, he pretended to be scared to death himself, and there was every reason to us why he should be. Besides, since he was always with us, he could wait for the most startling moment to spring his stuff. You remember that first day I had just been sneering about Woodford, and yesterday he waited until Josiah had got off the same proud and haughty talk. It made the steps doubly convincing. Say, Quaile, you'll have to confess he handed you a flutter the night you were alone. What I got from him tonight is just what I'd figured out. He sneaked in after you, lowered the curtain, got the cat, and carried it to the dress-circle, then limped down, and traced the figure in phosphorus on the passage door. By standing to one side and opening and shutting that he made the figure appear to grow and fade. At first, I couldn't understand about his locking and unlocking the stage entrance after you had run out. That seemed a little too much trouble just to puzzle us, but the phosphorus answers that, too. The stuff is nearly alive, and it lasts for a long time. He had to destroy that evidence and fix your flashlight and he didn't dare risk being disturbed. So he locked the stage entrance and unlocked it again when he had the passage door clean. Then all he had to do was to hide himself with the cat in the secret room while we searched our heads off. When he heard us going he was in too much of a hurry. The cat slipped past him in the dark and got away. You recollect Dolly didn't feel it for several days. Of course, he got that one back or another."

"But the motive?" Quaile said. "That must have troubled you even then. There was nothing in all this to point to Robert."

"Yes, there was," McHugh answered, "and something in the telephone calls, too, although I must say I thought it more likely at first that the trail would lead to Josiah. As far as Mike's concerned, you know he never worked steadily for me. Now a production and then a production. That meant he had some money from another source, and I guessed there would be gossip about it among stagehands and property men of his own generation. There was. Mike had been Robert Bunce's man Friday in the old days and Robert had looked after him more or less—what amounted to a small pension. Then the telephone calls got me on my ear because I couldn't trace them. I found out how that queer ringing was made. You've got one of those light-toned announcers, Quaile, and so has Barbara."

She nodded.

"Anyway," McHugh went on, "by barely making the connection in the exchange and breaking it continually you get that queer sound. So after a few experiments in that direction I had to pass the spirits up there, too. It was easy that Mike had done the talking. I wanted to know who had made the connections and done the ringing. Looked as if it must be somebody in authority who could do it on the sly. So I had the manager of the exchange through which those calls were made followed. She came here."

He glanced at Barbara. His tone was softer.

"And one day she went to Robert Bunce's office, and she left, crying. Then I got the whole game, and I was madder than a hornet, because it had been staring me in the face all the time, as it had you, too, Quaile. That's the trouble with everybody—always let the plain things slip."

"Of course, I see what you mean," Quaile said.

"Sure. There was Josiah owning Woodford's jointly with Robert and clinging to his real estate tooth and claw— famous the town over for it; and here was Robert, a spender and doing business in Wall Street. Queer things have happened there since the beginning of the war."

He grinned sheepishly.

"Some have happened to yours truly, but I know when I've had enough. I found out from my brokers that Robert didn't. He was in pretty deep, but nobody knew how deep until I got his firm to go over the books on the quiet. He needed more than a quarter of a million, and he needed it in a hurry. It sat waiting for him at Woodford's which was a dead loss as a theatre; and, mind you, half of the value of that property was honestly his, but he couldn't realize on it without Josiah's signature to the deed. You know. Josiah would sooner have his hair cut and take a box at the opera than sell his land. The old bird's owned up to me that Robert had found a purchaser and he'd given in finally and agreed to sign when along I came and handed Woodford's another lease of life as a theatre. You bet he changed his mind, because that was one of his hobbies, and refused Robert point-blank. Said he wouldn't sign anything until he found out if I could bring Woodford's back. But waiting, for Robert, was ruin. If he chased me out, on the other hand, and gave the place a final black eye, Josiah would sell, and, by gad, he had to get me out in a hurry. The only way must have hit him square between the eyes, and it ought to have been a sure way with a lot of temperamental artists to deal with. That's why he saw all that publicity got in the papers. But he didn't reckon on my stubbornness and the faith my people have in me. Even so, he might have got away with it if I hadn't smelled a mouse a little too soon. And let me give the devil his due. He was a game sport—like those

fellows that took snuff when they were having their heads
chopped off. After Carlton died, he played his cards to the
limit, for I don't believe he intended that. He had paid
Mike a lot of money and had promised him a couple
thousand more as soon as we had put our tails between our
legs. Old fool tells me he didn't hesitate, for he was glad to
serve Robert who had given him the same dope he did your
sister, Barbara—about a joke on me. After Carlton died
Robert had them both in the hollow of his hand. They
didn't dare break away then because he had involved them
in murder. Say! Can't you get Mike's state of mind? He
didn't have to fake being afraid then. His pale face and
shaky knees came natural as eating to him. So, as soon as
I'd got that far and faced a real explanation, I sent for
Joyce."

"You've a winning way," Quaile laughed. "Joyce was a
little embarrassed about his share tonight. I'd been
wondering what it was."

"Best little come-on a detective ever had," McHugh continued. "I didn't have much legal evidence. I didn't know
how Carlton had been killed. I had to lead them on until I
could catch Mike with the goods. I used Joyce to give the
impression I knew nothing and was still investigating the
spook theory. Maybe you noticed. That first day we
lunched with him he was pretty thoroughly impressed by
the case himself, but when I'd told him what I knew and
what I wanted he was willing enough to help. I instructed
him to pronounce absolutely for the spooks last night after
I'd slipped up on my calculations, and it worked just as I'd
figured. It gave Robert the courage to go ahead. On my own
showing, one more shot and he'd have me out."

"But didn't you have enough evidence then?" Quaile
asked. "Why did you risk Wilkins twice?"

McHugh grunted.

"You're a better playwright than a lawyer, Quaile. I went

on my knees this morning to keep his firm from arresting Robert. I tell you I had to prove who had killed Carlton and what the weapon was. I couldn't even guess about the stuff until after the riot last night. Since Mike had done all the work, I had to put him in a position where squeal on Robert. Of course, I thought I could bring it off last night, but I didn't know quite enough, and I didn't guess how carefully Robert had planned the whole campaign.

"I'd figured, of course, that the attack had come from behind the scenes on the side where Carlton had fallen. That heavy mantel makes an angle in the scenery. I saw Mike slip in there just before the big scene and I was sure I had him. The main trouble was I didn't dare show myself to him. I had to jump him at the very moment he was making the attack. I stepped around when Wilkins hit his line, and I got just one glimpse of Mr. Mike. He had his back to me, so fortunately he didn't see me. He had the right-hand flap of his coat hunched up above his shoulder and pressed against the scenery. His left hand was fumbling inside the mantel. I was just about to jump him when bang! the riot broke. The lights went out. Of course, the beggar had strung his wire along the roof of the cellar. I had the whole thing now and I knew I could bring it off tonight if Wilkins wasn't done for. That staggered me, and I pretty much forgot everything else until I'd run on the stage and found him still living."

"I suspected a drug at the first," Quaile said, "but I couldn't see, and I don't understand now, how it was used. You say Mike held the right-hand flap of his coat against the scenery."

"Yes, so I knew it was in that pocket. You recollect how Wilkins came up here night before last and told us about that time simply dropped out of his life?"

"Naturally. The same drug was responsible?"

"Yes. That started me after the drug hot foot. You saw

how he came out of it last night, strong but dazed, not knowing what had happened, complaining of feeling a little sick. That's the way he acted the other time. Might have been waking from a nap. I questioned Wilkins about the cab driver that brought him up here, and he couldn't describe him, because it was a cold night and the man had his face muffled and his hat low over his eyes. But he remembered the fellow got down from his seat, opened the door, and helped him in. He couldn't recall anything after that until he was turning out of the street your apartment's on, feeling queer. It was easy enough for Mike to have a cab handy there. There's no stand near and Wilkins would be sure to pick it up. Of course, he drove him around until the effect of the stuff wore off. And it nearly worked. If I hadn't been able to go to Wilkins and tell him what we were up against there would have been no revival of 'Coward's Fare.' He'd had enough. He was ready to take the warning and quit. As it was, he was scared enough afterward, but it was a matter of physical courage then, and he knew I'd keep my word and do a lot for him in the profession. Besides, he'd had that shot and hadn't died. I told him what I really thought, that after that experience I didn't believe he'd get any nearer death last night."

"But," Barbara said, "there would have been more effect from the use of a drug."

Quaile nodded.

"Certainly from a drug strong enough to kill one man and put another out twice."

McHugh knocked the ashes from his cigar.

"That's all you know. That's all I knew. I tell you it's the simple thing that floors us all. You remember, Quaile, I took the doctor home from your place last night. He was all worked up over the case. He was stumped by Wilkins' reactions, as he insisted on calling them. When I told him about the affair in the cab and Carlton's death and all I knew and suspected, he got an idea. You see, it's his business to have ideas about drugs. He took me into his library and went through a lot of murderous books. Say, I never knew there was so much learning in the world. Finally he put his fingers together and said it might be hydrocyanic acid. He doped out a theory that the analysis has verified."

"That's dangerous and powerful stuff, isn't it?" Quaile asked.

"So powerful," McHugh answered, "that as much as you could put on a pin head would knock a man over like a fifteen-inch shell."

Quaile sprang up excitedly.

"I begin to see. It wasn't swallowed."

"Of course, it wasn't swallowed," McHugh said.

Quaile struggled with his memory.

"It reminds me. When I was a freshman in college I tried to get a stopper out of a bottle. I've forgotten what it was labelled. The chemistry professor grabbed my hand and warned me never to uncork that bottle without proper precautions. I laughed and said I didn't intend to drink it. He laughed, too, a little uncomfortably, and said I didn't need to. One smell would be enough. I wanted to know if he meant it would have killed me. He looked away and said it was a weak solution and would probably have knocked me down. He asked me if I'd ever been hit with a sledge hammer when I wasn't looking. I said not even when I was looking. It didn't make much impression. There was too much else to think about."

"Sounds like the same stuff," McHugh grunted, "and I was figuring on something like those old Italian dukes used. You know. They'd shake hands with a dear friend or give him a hard look, and the next time he'd blow his nose or manicure his nails he'd fade away. I was looking for some subtle work like that. This is a common poison. I've heard of suicides by it, only they swallow it when they do that. That was the little joker. It does its job just as well if you smell it.

"Anyway, the doc nearly killed me with a dose of big words out of his books. Somehow or other I've managed to remember them. The book says the stuff is a highly volatile liquid which gives rise to vertigo if inhaled in minute quantities. It's one of the most rapid and deadly poisons known, if not the worst."

"Hasn't it an odor?" Quaile asked.

McHugh laughed.

"Sure. The doc and I hit on that, but, as the book told us, it is very volatile. I expect you're going to ask me what that means. What I get is that it means the smell evaporates rapidly in any open space—"

He looked up.

"Like a stage, for instance. Besides, it seems it can be modified by alcohol. But this is the real point. The doc hit the ceiling when I told him about the perfume you and Dolly had been sniffing about the stage. He dug in the books again and told me about a thing called oil of benzldehyde. It's full of hydrocyanic acid. When the acid is removed the oil is sold as the basis of a perfume, and it used to be a popular one. He found a lot of instances of poisoning from this perfume and proved that they were all due to traces of acid remaining in the oil. That settled the whole business. All they had to do was to put a tiny quantity of that deadly acid in the perfume—what they figured would put a man out, sprayed as Mike did it, directly in Carlton's and Wilkins' nostrils when they stood by the mantel lifting the candlestick. Talk about your sledgehammer. That was it—applied to the base of the brain. The only good thing to be said for the acid is that its effects pass off very quickly, provided it doesn't instantly kill. I'd never have forgiven myself if Wilkins had got an overdose last night. As I say, I don't believe they intended to kill Carlton. He was probably in worse shape physically than we thought, or else they gave him a little too much, or else he breathed it deeper.

"So I knew exactly what to expect tonight. I was sure that Mike had the atomizer in his pocket, and without taking it out had lifted the nozzle to a hole in the scenery, but I couldn't find that hole until I had you hold the candle flame directly in front of the mantel. Then I found it. He had pasted brown paper across so that you had to get light close up to it to tell the difference from the canvas. After the third act had commenced, when I knew it would be too late for him to investigate, I went down to the cellar and dished his wire for him. He wasn't going to cover himself with darkness tonight. Of course, I had to wait again until the last minute, but I knew the light would last, and I didn't see how he could destroy the evidence. So as soon as Wilkins started that line, I grabbed mine. But of course, he had his coat up to the scenery and I knew the spray was in the hole. I couldn't take chances of his pressing the bulb, so I shoved Wilkins away. Didn't want him to go through that experience again."

Quaile's laugh was a trifle resentful.

"You're clever. I guessed you had told Wilkins all you knew."

McHugh arose. He glanced at Barbara.

"If I didn't trust you more, young man, it was because of this young lady. I knew if you were any good at all your first instinct would be to protect her. I guessed you'd come to her with all you knew."

"So I would have," Quaile confessed. "So I did."

McHugh grunted. He took Barbara's Hand. His voice trailed into a sigh.

"I'll dance at your wedding, my dear; and I suppose that means you are leaving the stage."

"You'll do more than that," Quaile said. "As an extra

humiliation you'll be best man. It will remind you that, although you're a great detective, you do make mistakes."

McHugh grinned.

"Anyway, that won't prevent my kissing the bride."

He grasped her shoulders. He touched his lips to her forehead. There was something pathetically paternal about the caress. Quaile suspected moisture in the narrow eyes. McHugh tried to carry it off.

"Have you asked that maid of yours yet, Barbara? Maybe she won't let you have him."

She flushed, turning to Quaile.

"If Mr. McHugh is right—about us—I mean, you'd better overcome your dislike for her."

McHugh slipped out. The door clicked behind him. They faced each other alone in this room as they had done the other night. Only now her cheeks showed no pallor, and, if she shrank away, it was with a different fear. When he followed, her struggle possessed an unconscious witchery.

"If McHugh is right!" he jeered.

"I guess he's right," she whispered. "He is always right."

There was no longer any point in struggling. The room was very quiet.

Bruin Asylum

Make Your Reservations Today!

The Witching Night
    C. S. Cody – Booking Now
A Garden Lost in Time
    Jonathan Aycliffe – Booking Now
I Am Your Brother
    G. S. Marlowe – Booking Now
Dr. Mabuse
    Norbert Jacques – Booking Now
Walpole's Fantastic Tales, Volume I
    Hugh Walpole – Booking Now
The Magician & Other Strange Stories
    W. Somerset Maugham – Booking Now
The Bat Woman
    Cromwell Gibbons – Booking now
The Undying Monster
    Jessie Douglas Kerruish – Booking now
The Unholy Three
    Tod Robbins – Booking now

BRUIN CRIMEWORKS

Visit the scene of the crime

David Dodge

-*DEATH AND TAXES*
-*TO CATCH A THIEF*
-*THE LONG ESCAPE*
-*CARAMBOLA*

Fredric Brown

-*KNOCK THREE-ONE-TWO*
-*MISS DARKNESS*
New **Fredric Brown**
        Double Novels:
-*Vol. I: THE FAR CRY &*
THE SCREAMING MIMI
-*Vol. II: NIGHT OF THE*
JABBERWOCK &
THE DEEP END

Wadsworth Camp
-*HOUSE OF FEAR*

Bruno Fischer

-*HOUSE OF FLESH*

Edward Anderson
-*FEELS LIKE RAIN*

C. St. John Sprigg
-*PASS THE BODY*
- *THE CORPSE WITH THE*
SUNBURNED FACE

James Hadley Chase

-*NO ORCHIDS FOR MISS BLANDISH*
-*FLESH OF THE ORCHID*

Elliott Chaze

-*BLACK WINGS HAS MY ANGEL*

Paul Bailey
-*DELIVER ME FROM EVA*

Printed in Great Britain
by Amazon

58185368R00170